EA

ells Toll

__ɔ1

Also by M. J. Williams

On the Road to Death's Door

On The Road To Where the Bells Toll

M. J. Williams

On The Road To Where the Bells Toll
Copyright© 2014 Mary Joy Johnson & Margaret M. Williams

Cover Credit: The cover art for *On The Road To Where the Bells Toll* was created by Joshua Williams © 2014. Photo by Peggy Williams.

This is a work of fiction. All characters and events portrayed in these pages are entirely fictional; any resemblance to actual persons, living or dead, is purely coincidental and not intended by the author.

ISBN-10: 1505286859
ISBN-13: 978-1505286854

ACKNOWLEDGEMENTS

Many thanks to all our readers who encouraged us to take Emily and Stan on a new adventure.

To Christine DeSmet, Dave Thome, Jean Joque, Ann Wood, and our editor, Erin Williams Hart, thank you for slogging through our early drafts and taking the time to give us much valuable feedback.

Special appreciation goes out to police officer Michael Mawhinney of Madison, Wisconsin for sharing his knowledge of police work. Any divergence from actual law enforcement procedures in this book is the sole responsibility of the authors. And a shout out to Rob Velella, literary historian and National Park Ranger, who provided an insightful tour of the Longfellow House in Cambridge, Massachusetts.

And what would we do without all those YouTube videos sharing tours of the Old North Church, the USS Constitution, and other Boston historic sites which enhanced our in-person research? If you notice a room that doesn't exist or a location that's out of place in this book, please know that we took advantage of literary license to serve our plot.

Finally, we are ever grateful to our cover artist, Joshua Williams. And to our families for their love and support.

In loving memory of
Emily and Genevieve
avid readers,
lovers of a good mystery both

CHAPTER 1

FOURTH of July fireworks always set Emily Remington's nerves on edge. The heart-pounding booms, cascades of flaming lights, and the acrid smell of smoke all brought her back to the horror of that one night, decades ago.

She shut her eyes momentarily against the pop-pop-popping flashes of the bottle rockets and took a deep breath. *It'll be okay*, she told herself. *This is a different time. A different place.* She was on vacation.

She opened her eyes and allowed herself to enjoy the sight of her family sprawled out on the blanket, nine-year-old twins Annabel and Allyn snuggled on either side of their Grandpa Stan like pixie bookends. Thirteen-year-old Wynter leaning placidly against son-in-law Philip's legs, ignoring the bombs bursting in air as she thumbed furious texts into her phone. And daughter Megan, transfixed by the melting colors in the sky layered one on top of the other.

Nope. This was a good night. No murder. No mayhem. No dead bodies. Nothing like the night that building exploded on campus. Just good old-fashioned Fourth of July family time.

The celebration on the Boston Esplanade ended in the

usual mind-numbing, heart-thumping white-out of a hundred fireworks all going off at the same time. The crowd around them erupted in a roar of approval, clapping, shouting, whistling.

"I love it! I love it! I love it!" Allyn shouted, she and her twin deserting Stan to jump up and dance.

"Good show, huh?" Megan said to her mother.

"My ears are still ringing." Emily stood and stretched.

"We might as well stay put for a while," Philip said, rolling over onto his back. "It'll take a while for this crowd to disperse, and I'd rather sit here and enjoy the evening than fight for space on the T."

A hush had settled over the park as families gathered their belongings, folded blankets, searched in the dark for lost flip-flops.

"I'm not in any rush." Stan grabbed for Annabel then Allyn and began a tickle fight.

Emily didn't often agree with her son-in-law's take on things, but surveying the dispersing crowd, she was relieved; this was the first Fourth of July in a long time that she wasn't responsible for crowd control. She was happy and content to sit back and relax in the balmy night air.

Disentangling himself from the girls on the blanket, Stan struggled to his feet and reached into the cooler for a bottle of water. "Anyone else?"

"I'll have one, Dad. Thanks." Megan held out her hand.

"Mumsy, may I have another tonic?" Wynter asked.

"Mumsy?" Emily asked.

"It's a phase. I hope. Dad, can you grab a can of soda for Wynter?"

Allyn and Annabel, realizing their older sister had beaten them to the forbidden pleasure, bounded to the cooler.

"I got the last root beer!" Allyn waved the can in her sister's face, and then shrieked when Annabel grabbed it and dodged away.

"Mom! She knows I hate grape. And that's all that's left."

Allyn lunged for her sister, now standing ten feet away and taunting her. Annabel side-stepped. Allyn flew past, stumbled and spun, trying to stop herself.

"Allyn!" Megan cried out. But it was too late.

The little girl tumbled over a nearby beach chair taking its occupant down with her. Allyn immediately jumped up, her hands over her mouth in remorse. But Emily was at the woman's side in an instant, mumbling apologies for her granddaughter. She bent over to extend a hand, but sensed something was wrong. Deadly wrong. The woman stared up at her with vacant eyes. Emily reached down to feel for a pulse then recoiled at the cold flesh.

"What is it?" Stan asked, moving toward her. "Is she okay?"

"I think you and Megan should leave now and take the kids home. Philip, call 911."

"Did I hurt her?" Allyn asked.

Emily wrapped Allyn in her arms. "Honey, you go with Grandpa to help your Mom with the blanket."

"Why? What's wrong with her?"

"Come on, sweetheart. Grandma will take care of it." Stan took the girl's hand and walked her over to her mother. "Let's pack up," he said to his daughter. "Annabel, grab that cooler and drag it over here, okay?"

While Philip spoke tersely into his cell phone, the others gathered up their things. Emily took the small blanket from under the dead woman's picnic basket and draped it loosely over the body to keep the curious passers-by from stopping and gawking. But she hadn't noticed Wynter, who was hovering over her shoulder.

"Grandma." The slender teenager stood with her arms wrapped tightly around herself, as if she were deadly cold. "That's the lady Grandpa and I went to see yesterday."

CHAPTER 2

"DAMN the drivers in this town! They're all crazy!"

Two days earlier Emily had opened her eyes with a jerk at the sound of Stan's harangue. She rubbed her eyes in sleepy confusion then braced herself as the RV lurched to stop.

"Where are we?" She rolled her head to loosen the stiff muscles in her neck.

"Good question. Cambridge Avenue maybe?"

"Cambridge Avenue? Isn't that—"

"Boston. Yes. And don't start in on—"

"How the hell did we end up in Boston?" She eyed the tow mirror to assure herself the VW Bug was still trailing along behind. "I thought we were going to take 495." She fumbled in the door pocket and brought up a handful of maps.

"I dunno. You were sleeping. I missed my exit, so I took the next one." He checked the side mirror, then tapped the accelerator. "And here we are."

Emily considered the traffic jostling for position along six lanes of road. "So, what were you doing back on the freeway? Daydreaming again?"

"Meditating. Can you readjust the GPS?"

"I can find it faster the old-fashioned way." She snapped open the state map but tossed it aside in favor of the Boston city map, which crackled as she spread it over her lap. "Give me a cross street name." She peered at sign posts flashing by.

"That's Soldier's Field Road ahead. Or I can cross the river."

"No. Take a right."

Emily strained against the seatbelt as Stan made a hard right and narrowly avoided a Prius that decided at the last minute to swerve left in front of them. Amid a chorus of angry horns, he straightened the RV out and they headed down Soldiers Field Road following the course of the river.

"Did you know the Charles River was named by Captain John Smith?"

"Maybe he can figure out the GPS for you," she snapped.

"In honor of King Charles the First of England."

A honking horn caught Emily's attention. The driver in the car next to them was gesticulating wildly. "Something's weird," she said.

"What's weird is that you refuse to live in the twenty-first century." He picked up the GPS and shook it like one those magic eight balls as if it had the answer.

"There aren't any trucks on this road. Or buses," she mused.

"Maybe I should take a look at that map." He thrust the GPS at her before she could refuse again. "I can pull over."

"Where? There's no parking anywhere."

A familiar trill—"Für Elise"—sounded. Fumbling for her aging flip phone, she grabbed unsuccessfully for the map and the GPS sliding onto the floor between her legs.

"Damn! Hello? Megan. Hi, Honey."

"Mom, how close are you?"

"That's what we're trying to figure out."

"What do you mean? Did Dad miss an exit again? Where exactly are you?"

Emily glanced at her husband whose expression was stony. "Um, dunno. I thought we were on Soldiers Field Road, but now it says Storrow Drive."

"You're *in* Boston?!?! Mom, you were supposed to get off at 495. The campground is up near Lexington."

"I know, honey. We got cut off by a semi before your dad could get into the lane." She nodded in acknowledgement as Stan mouthed *thank you*, then wriggled in her seat, wiping beads of sweat from her forehead and lip. She reached for one of the still folded maps and began to fan herself. "Damn hot flashes," she murmured under her breath.

"Put me on speakerphone!" Megan demanded.

"Hold on, honey." Emily fumbled with the phone looking for the right button. "Okay. We're on."

"Dad? Can you hear me?"

"I hear you, Meggsie."

"Dad! Listen carefully. You're not allowed on Storrow Drive. It's a parkway. No trucks, buses or RV's allowed on Storrow Drive."

"Yeah, well it's a little late for that piece of news, honey."

"You've got your GPS, right?" Megan asked.

"Um…" Emily looked down between her legs.

"Okay, Dad, listen. There are bridges, low bridges. You've got to get off Storrow."

"Stan!" Emily yelled. "That bridge up ahead only has a twelve-foot clearance."

Stan slammed on the brakes to slow their rig to a crawl. He checked his side mirror, then edged to the middle of the road, straddling the line.

"If you stay in the middle, I think we can clear it," Emily said.

"Dad! What are you doing?"

Car horns echoed off the walls of the overpass as Stan inched the RV through the short tunnel, sticking to the center line and taking up space in both lanes. As they finally emerged from the underpass, Emily gave Stan a silent high five.

"Dad, the next bridge is the Longfellow. It only has an eleven-foot clearance."

"Oh, shit."

"We have to get off this road," Emily said.

"Any suggestions as to how?"

"Pull over."

"Where?"

"Here. In the right lane. Everyone else can go around you."

"Mom? Dad? What are you doing?"

"Hang on a minute, Megan."

Stan braked to a stop. "Now what?"

Honking cars whizzed around the RV. Emily grabbed Stan's phone from the cup holder and punched in 911. When the dispatcher answered, she said, "We have an out-of-state RV that needs a squad for a turn-around assist on Storrow Drive. It's eastbound between the Harvard Bridge and the Longfellow Bridge. This is retired Michigan police officer Emily Remington. The vehicle has stopped in the right lane and will remain stationary until the assist arrives."

She paused, listening for a moment, then said, "Thank you."

Stan's knuckles on the steering wheel were white in contrast to the rising red in his face. Moments later they heard the wailing of a police siren. She focused on the side mirror, watching as a squad car positioned itself to let those vehicles stuck immediately behind them pull around and be on their way, but blocking all other traffic to give the RV room to maneuver. The officer didn't bother to get out of his car, but rolled down the window and waved for Stan to drive the Winnie across the lanes, over the boulevard divide and into the opposing lanes of traffic.

Stan grunted and shifted the RV, moving it forward and back in a clumsy twelve-point turn. Emily bit her tongue seeing his face redden even more at the long lines of cars piling up impatiently behind the angled squad. People stepped out of their vehicles to snap cell phone pics of the renegade RV and its companion VW Bug straddling the lanes.

"What's going on?!" Megan's frantic voice broke the silence.

Emily quickly shut the speakerphone off. "I'll call you back in a couple of minutes," she said, then shut the phone off completely.

She gritted her teeth as Stan bumped the rig up and over a curb. She could hear the cups and glasses in the cupboards behind them rattle violently. Stan seemed to hesitate a moment while cars in the westbound lane whizzed past. But then, he eased the rig forward. Emily braced herself and held her breath watching the oncoming cars in the nearest lane slam to a stop. Cars in the far lane zipped around them, narrowly avoiding the wildly jerking RV as it bumped down off the curb, tugging the little car behind. A moment later Stan had all ten wheels on the pavement and they were in their lane heading safely west. The squad car pulled away, letting the eastbound traffic flow again.

Emily breathed out for the first time in what seemed to be one of the longest moments of her life. She resisted the temptation to switch the air conditioning knob to high and direct the vents to blast her face with cold air, even though her hot flash had ramped up to high gear.

Stan slowed the RV and positioned it again down the center of the road to creep under the Cambridge Street Bridge one last time. His face was about as deep red as she had ever seen it, and his jaw was clenched so tight she wondered if he'd be able to move it to eat or speak again. But once they were out from under the bridge and heading back toward the ramp to the freeway, he rolled his shoulders, shaking away the tension.

"Well, that was fun," he said, cracking his jaw.

Emily grimaced, but a moment later broke into a grin, and then laughed. She stretched her arms above her head to get rid of her own tension then bent down to pick up the wayward map and the GPS. Finally, she flipped open her phone to call Megan back.

"Hey, Em?" Stan pointed at the dashboard. "What does this blinking light mean?"

"Red or yellow?" Emily snapped the phone closed.

"Red." Stan rubbed at the bald spot on the top of his head. "Engine light?"

"Better pull over again."

He scanned the vicinity and found an empty parking lot near an abandoned fast food restaurant. *At least we're not in the middle of the road.* He shut the engine off.

"I'm beginning to wonder if we'll ever see those girls," Emily complained.

She grabbed a socket wrench from the glove box and hopped out to open the hood. Stan followed, glad that he'd married someone who liked tinkering with mechanical stuff. That sure wasn't his forte. He peered over her shoulder. "Anything?"

"Nothing looks amiss," she answered, poking at wires and hoses, checking the oil, air filter and transmission fluid. "What do you think? If we do the aquarium one day, then maybe the children's museum? And I'd love to take a whale-watching tour with the girls." She eyeballed the coolant and the batteries.

"How about just sitting around the pool enjoying them? We don't have to be on the go the entire time we're with them."

She poked at the condenser. "Like you're going to be sitting around the pool for two weeks? You'll be off interviewing people and doing whatever it is you do when you're researching a book." Then the radiator. "How about the Freedom Trail Tour?" She slammed the engine cover closed and yanked the screw bolts tight.

"So, yeah? The Freedom Trail. We've been planning that

since we started talking about this trip."

"Uh huh." She stalked around the side of the motorcoach.

Stan looked at her, perplexed. "Maybe it just needs to sit a few minutes." He was a big proponent of the wait and see method of solving problems.

"Maybe." She kicked at a tire.

Stan wondered what tires had to do with the engine warning light. He shook his head as Emily walked around the rig, running her hand over the metal sidewalls, like a doctor examining a sick patient. Flipping open the fuel tank lid, she checked the gas cap.

Her brows furrowed. "Did you tighten this cap when we fueled up last time?"

"Of course I did."

She gave it an audible twist then gave him an "I told you so" look before slamming the tiny door shut.

"Maybe it jiggled loose when we bounced over those curbs back there. Is something bothering you?"

"Start it up and let's see if this makes a difference. "

"Emily?"

"Sometimes the engine sensors misread the pressure when the cap isn't tight enough."

"I'll take your word for it." He climbed into the RV, settled into the driver's seat and inserted the key. The engine revved, then purred. The engine light glowed red, but just as he was about to tell Emily that her diagnosis was wrong, the light flickered and went out.

"I'll be damned."

Emily shrugged her shoulders. She climbed into her seat and snapped the belt snug across her chest. But to her surprise, Stan shut the motor back off.

"I thought we wanted to get to the campground and set up before dinner?"

"Talk to me."

"About…?"

"About this pissy attitude." Stan crossed his arms like he

wasn't planning to go anywhere anytime soon.

"I dunno. This is our vacation, and you're planning to spend it researching a book."

"Is this about me and the book? Or about something else?"

Emily sat silent for a long moment. Then, "I feel... driftless."

"Driftless?"

"Since we retired. I don't know. Being a cop was what I did. Now I don't have anything to do."

"Then find something to do!"

Now they both sat in stony silence. Finally he turned to her.

"Look Em, I can't create purpose for you. And it's fine that you want to do stuff with the girls. But you can't use them to define your retirement. You'll figure it out. You always do. You just have to be patient with yourself."

She nodded and accepted his proffered hand, and then the kiss he leaned over to give her. Finally he reached for his seatbelt.

"Damn!"

"What now?" he asked.

"Hot flash." She fanned herself with a folded map.

He shook his head and cranked the air conditioning up for her. "Let's hit the road."

CHAPTER 3

"WELCOME to Colonial Pines Campground!"

The large wooden sign greeted them at the entrance to a drive lined with billowing American flags. Stan parked the RV under a stand of towering pines next to a small, Lincoln Log-style building and went in to pay and get their site assignment. Emily stayed in the RV to reconnect with Megan.

The young woman behind the counter squinted out the window at their vehicle. "You should have plenty of room to park your dinghy," she said. "Our sites are pretty big."

"Dinghy?" Stan was puzzled.

"Your toad. A newbie, eh? Your car. The one you're towing."

"Oh, yeah. My dinghy."

"Your first trip?"

"Second."

She nodded. "How'd the first one go?"

"Not as well as you would have liked." Stan shrugged, pushing away the memory of their ill-fated trip to Wisconsin's Door County nine months earlier and the murder of his good friend Father Victor Virchow. Handing over his credit card, he signed the registration form. "Have a nice day."

"Have a nice stay," the woman echoed.

Back in the RV he revved the motor and steered the rig slowly along the narrow winding camp road, relishing the relative quiet of the forest. Leaving behind the traffic noise of the freeway settled him into a quiet sense of peace. He slid the side window open to take in the scent of pine and the dank, musty smell of damp earth. Even this early in the day, tendrils of wood smoke wafted up from occasional camp fires, the scent making its way into the RV. Was that skunk in the air? He hoped this campground didn't have skunk problems.

"Hey! What's that?" Emily pointed to a bit of red fur slinking behind a shiny aluminum Airstream camper and disappearing into a stand of jack pine.

"Dunno. A cat?"

"Awfully big for a cat. Did you see its tail? Here we go. This one's ours."

Stan tapped the brakes, rolling to a stop in front of an empty campsite situated between a trio of mountain tents and a pop-up camper. He breathed a sigh of relief when he saw it was a pull-through. He didn't much like backing the Winnie up in confined spaces. *Particularly with a toad in tow*. He chuckled inwardly.

"Unhook the dinghy and park it over there in the shade," he directed Emily.

"Dinghy?"

"Yeah, you know. The toad-in-tow."

"The toad in…?" Chuckling, she fished her car keys out of her pocket then raised her hand in mock salute. "Aye aye, captain."

Once the car was parked, they worked together to stabilize the motorhome. Stan tapped open the newly-downloaded Stanley leveling app on his phone. Studying the virtual bubble sliding back and forth, he signaled Emily to crank the stabilizer jacks up and down, up and down.

"You're obsessing, you know that?" Emily chided.

"Don't want the donuts rolling off the counters," Stan teased.

"It's fine. It's level. Go take care of the water hookup. I'll do the electricity."

Pocketing his phone, he lumbered around to the back of the rig and yanked out the water hose, hooking it up to the campsite spigot and then to the RV. Inside, he proudly turned on the tap in the kitchen sink while Emily activated the living room slide-out. The water in the pipes gurgled and spat. Then stopped. Puzzled, he cranked the handle even more. Nothing happened. Then a squirt of water hit him in the face. Before he could react, the water jetted out, spraying him and the counter and everything within reach.

"Oh shit! Oh shit! Oh shit!" Reaching through the torrent of spraying water, he fumbled for the faucet handle.

"Whoa! What'd you do?" Emily ran to help him.

"I can't get it to stop!"

She dove between his legs and yanked open the cabinet under the sink, water raining down on her head. Leaving Stan to fight with the faucet, she grabbed a large pot and up-ended it over the spraying faucet, redirecting the water down into the sink.

Finally Stan was able to crank the handle and the spray fizzled out.

"Whew!" He grabbed a drenched towel from the countertop to wipe his face.

Emily dropped the pot into the sink and giggled.

"What?"

"You look like a drowned rat."

"Thanks."

She snorted.

He snapped her with the wet towel.

"Ouch!" She reached for the spray nozzle, laughing.

"Oh, no you don't!" Stan grabbed her wrist and wrestled her away from the sink, laughing even harder.

"You folks need help in there?"

An aging Hulk Hogan stood in the doorway. A handlebar mustache draped down either side of weathered, blistered lips; wiry hairs curled out from the top of his muscle shirt. His beefy arms sported tattoos. What was left of his graying hair was tied back into a greasy pony tail. Stan unconsciously reached up and rubbed his own bald spot.

"I'm guessin' you could use a few more towels?"

"If you've got any. Thank you!" Emily said.

"Looks like you forgot to put your regulator on the water hose. I'm Lyle."

"Regulator?" Stan shook Lyle's outstretched hand. "Stan. My wife Emily here."

Lyle wiped his now-wet hand on his shorts. He smelled of Old Spice and baby powder. "Pressure regulator. This campground is notorious for over-pressurizing their water. Could just as easily have blown up the water line. Then you'd be in a real pickle."

"A pressure regulator, huh?" Emily asked. "Where do we get one of those?"

"There's an RV supply store coupla miles east of here. But don't get one of the cheapies. You'll regret it. Let me go get some bath towels and help you clean this mess up."

Once the water had been mopped up, they thanked their Good Samaritan for his help.

"Stay for a beer?" Stan offered.

Lyle shook his head. "Gotta move on. The wife's waiting. But I'll take you up on it later." He strode off down the road.

Stan waved and closed the door. "Think I'm ready for a cold one myself right about now. How about you?"

Emily shook her head. "Let's get that awning down before your head starts to fry."

"You call Megan back yet?" Stan asked, reaching with the pole cane to slide the awning down.

"Her line was busy when I tried to call back. I'll try again." Emily pushed the metal arm up and locked it into place then reached for her phone. "Megan? Sorry about not getting back to you sooner. But we're at the campground and all settled in." She paused, listening. "No, your dad got us turned around. It wasn't a big deal." She winked at Stan who was dragging chaise lawn chairs out from one of the undercarriage storage compartments. "Yes, of course he has his golf clubs with him." Pause. "Really? I'll tell him. So, we'll meet you at the ticket kiosk in the morning, okay?" Pause. "Love you. See you then." She hung up.

"What's up?" Stan asked.

"Seems Philip is hoping to golf with you while we're here."

"Really?"

"I think it's a prerequisite for him tolerating our visit."

"I guess if I had to I could tolerate a little golf. To mitigate relations with the son-in-law."

"Hold on with those. I want to spread the rug down first." She popped open one of the other storage compartments and tugged at a rolled up Persian carpet. When Stan caught his breath, she hesitated. "Are you okay with us using this?"

"Yeah, sure. Why not?" Stan said, but his jaw tightened at the sight of it. "It's not the same rug we found his body in anyway." He nudged her aside and yanked the rug out, noting the vague musty smell emanating from it.

"What do you have on the itinerary for tomorrow?"

"The Freedom Trail Tour." She looked at him askance. "Unless you'd rather sit by the pool all day?"

"Nope. I'm good with the tour." Together they positioned the rolled up rug under the awning. "I am hoping to get to the Longfellow House in the afternoon, though. I need to talk with that archivist for my research." He paused. "If you don't mind, that is."

"That's fine." She kicked at the end of the carpet, positioning it an inch in the other direction. "This okay?"

Stan set his foot on the carpet roll to push, but suddenly froze.

Emily touched his arm. "It's okay. I'll do it. You go get us those beers."

With a nod he went into the RV. He grabbed two bottles of Sam Adams from the fridge and popped the caps off. Through the window, he saw his wife nudge the carpet roll with her foot. Immediately he was taken back to the dark waters of Lake Michigan, the fog, being taken hostage at gunpoint. He took several deep breaths, pushing back the panic he thought he'd let go of after that first trip with their RV. He was surprised to find himself fighting back tears. He reached for his handkerchief and blew his nose. *It's just a silly carpet.* Like the one they found the dead body of his friend in. He took a long swig from one of the beer bottles. *Maybe I'll get us one of those indoor/outdoor rugs to replace it. The practical kind that are supposed to look like grass.* He carried the bottles out to where Emily was admiring her work.

"Damn, but I like that pattern," she commented.

He forced a smile.

"Afternoon!"

Stan swiveled around to see a couple standing at the edge of the campsite, as if waiting to be invited onto their property.

"Good afternoon to you!" he answered.

"Nice rug," the woman said, her wide-brimmed straw hat shading her freckled face. She tugged at a strapless sundress and tottered on strappy heels. Stan wondered how she could walk over the gravel and grass.

"Thank you."

"What're you gonna do when it rains?" The husband chuckled and elbowed his wife. His orange Hawaiian shirt matched the fabric of his wife's dress. He tipped his own straw hat which sported a band of the bright orange material. "Must be newbies." He waved and they walked on.

Handing Emily her beer, Stan noticed she seemed a bit crestfallen.

"Aw, what do they know?" he said, sidestepping the rug.

"When you think about it, it isn't very practical. What if it rains?"

"Save it for home. We could look for one of those indoor/outdoor kind."

"The ugly green ones?"

"Doesn't have to be green."

"Until we find something better, let's think of this one as sort of a memorial. To Vic."

"We'll drink a toast in his honor." He held his bottle up and they clinked, before taking long draughts. Solemnly he shook his bottle, allowing the beer to fizzle upward. He dipped his fingers into the foam and sprinkled it onto the carpet, then waved his hand in blessing. "In nomine Patris et filii…"

"A bit sacrilegious, don't you think?"

"…et spiritus sancti. Yeah, what the hell. Vic wasn't exactly a model priest anyway." He held his bottle aloft. "To Vic."

"To Vic."

With a satisfied nod, he lowered himself into the lawn chair. Halfway down he realized he was in trouble and despite his best efforts, splashed his beer as he landed on the chair with an "oof!" After wiping his wet hand on his shorts, he opened a much thumbed compilation of the papers of George Washington. Next to him Emily flipped open her romance novel. But she set it down moments later.

"I think I just read the same paragraph four times," she complained.

"Want me to test you on it?" Stan mumbled without taking his eyes off his own book.

Emily threw her reading glasses onto the picnic table and walked over to check the coupling on the septic system.

"Worried I didn't do it right?" Stan asked, still refusing to look up.

"Nope. No. It's fine. Want to go for a walk?" Now she was hovering over him.

Finally, he set the book down. "Awe, Em. This is the only

time I'll have to get this reading done before the kids come. You go on."

"Okay. I'm gone. Have fun." She grabbed her sunglasses and a baseball cap and stalked off down the camp road.

"Got your phone with you?"

She patted her pocket and waved him off dismissively.

Peering over his reading glasses, he watched her walk away, her strawberry blonde hair bouncing with each step. He smiled. Then he picked up his beer and took a long, satisfying swig. Peace and quiet at last. This was what a vacation should be.

CHAPTER 4

GOT your phone with you? Emily gritted her teeth. That was her line. At least until he'd gotten the new smart phone a couple of months ago.

She turned right onto the rustic, wooded camp road and willed herself to slow down and take some deep breaths. Before long she found herself strolling past a cluster of tiny teardrop campers, their owners sitting in lawn chairs chatting, playing cards, staring at small TV sets. A young couple several sites down struggled with an old canvas tent with heavy wooden poles that didn't want to cooperate.

A large black lab sat in the shade, tongue hanging out, observing the couple's every move. *Smart dog.* Emily realized she was getting warm. Without warning, the dog lunged, barking ferociously, startling Emily into backing up. But then she realized it wasn't her the dog was barking at; it was a small flock of wild turkeys, three tall scrawny hens and a plump tom who fanned his plumage warily before strutting off.

Emily wandered on down the road, stopping moments later in front of a huge red and white motorcoach that looked like a cross between a 1940s bus and an old elongated, overgrown hippy camper, but sleeker. A woman was draping wet towels from a rope strung between two trees.

"Hey, there! That's some rig you've got."

"Why thank you. We like it." She wiped beads of sweat from the back of her neck. "It's a vintage 1946 Flxible. Aren't many of them around anymore."

"I'd guess not. Is this spelled correctly?" Emily pointed at the winged logo mounted under the windshield.

"Craziest thing. But yes. My name's Marion. We're from Ohio. My husband Tyrell is out skeet shooting."

"Emily. I just left mine under the awning on the chaise lounge." She shook Marion's outstretched hand. "I like the art deco look. Did you do the conversion work yourselves?"

"My husband did most of it. I was the interior designer on the project. Would you like to look inside?"

"Sure."

Emily followed Marion up the steps of the coach, blinking in astonishment at the interior. The floor was laid with black and white checkered tile. Bright red curtains fluttered in the open window. And the chrome appliances in the soda fountain kitchen made it feel like she'd stepped into the 1950s. A tableside jukebox sat above a chrome-edged dining table with red dairy bar chairs. Shiny 45 rpm records and autographed black and white photos of 1950s musicians lined the walls.

"Does that work?" Emily pointed to a vintage television set with stubby antennas perched on a corner shelf.

"The bunny ears are just for effect. It's hooked up to a satellite dish up top."

"I've never seen anything quite like this." Emily hesitated a moment before blurting out, "So…what do you do all day?"

Marion laughed. "It's a full-time job just cleanin' up after Tyrell. And ooh! That man can pack away a meal like Yogi Bear at a church picnic. I'm lucky I get time to watch my soaps."

"Really? Sounds like…fun. I better keep going."

"Wouldn't want your husband to worry about you. You take care now."

"Nice meeting you, Marion. Thanks for the tour."

Emily took her leave and continued down the winding blacktop road. Once she was out of sight of the Flxible, she paused long enough to tap out a text to Stan: "Check towels. If dry, fold and put away."

A moment later her phone dinged. "You betcha," flashed on the screen.

Noisy kids splashed and whooped in the pool on the far side of a chain link fence. Emily stopped, enjoying their antics as they swooshed down the corkscrew waterslide and danced under the sprinklers. *The girls are going to love this*, she thought. For the second time in five minutes she found herself tapping keys on her phone: "Tell girls bring swimsuits." She sent the message off to Megan.

Moving on, she waved at a woman driving a bright, neon pink, over-the-cab style camper, apparently just arriving at the park. *Fuchsia.* Emily grimaced. *Is that the right word?* She hoped the woman wasn't planning to park in the empty spot next to theirs with that god awful paint job. And was that a cat sitting on the dashboard?

She noticed a well-used RV—one even older than hers and Stan's—with people milling around tables piled with knickknacks, ceramic figurines, pots and pans, old CDs. A traveling yard sale! The man tending the cash box looked like Barney Fife's twin brother. Now there's a man with a plan. Emily loved yard sales.

She scanned the tables of items, quickly by-passing the colored glass bottles. She remembered sweeping up shards the first time they took their RV on the road. *What was I thinking?* She couldn't imagine what had made her decide that Avon perfume decanters were the perfect collectible for a home that stops and starts, bounces and sways. Stan had called her bottles tacky. But Emily had insisted on using them to spruce up the décor and add a touch of color to the RV.

The bottles had crashed to the floor as soon as they came to the first stop sign. *Not tacky, just stupid.*

A box of old books drew her attention. She scanned the spines but didn't see anything she thought would interest Stan. Next to it was a box of Wysocki jigsaw puzzles. She picked one up and ran her fingers across the harbor scene, three-masted ships in the foreground, a scattering of colorful boxy, clapboard buildings, horse-drawn carriages and the ubiquitous American flag front and center. It brought back memories of snowy winter evenings, her father leaning over the dining room table, a beer in his hand, grousing at the cat knocking pieces to the floor. She chose two puzzles, took them over to Barney Fife and handed him the money. The stub of a well-chewed cigar, smoldering in a tuna can, made her wrinkle her nose in disgust.

"Thossse are sssome might fine picture puzzssles," he said, whistling through the gaps in his teeth and fingering his red suspenders. "Nicssse way to passs the time." He popped the cigar back between his lips.

Emily coughed and waved the smoke away from her eyes. That's when she spotted another carton of books lying on the table near the cash box.

"Are these for sssale….sale?" Emily asked, picking up two small leather-bound volumes.

"Everything here is for sssale, misss. Thossse'll cossst ya another two bucksss."

"I'll take them." Emily fished more money out of her pocket. She couldn't wait to see Stan's reaction to her little find.

She hurried back to the RV to discover Stan, slumped in his chair, legs stretched out in front of him, book on his lap, snoring softly. And right there next door was the pink camper, brighter than a neon sign on Broadway. Emily winced, shaded her eyes. The stack of folded towels on her own picnic table made her smile. Stan jerked awake when she tapped him on the head.

"Whoa! What's that over there?" He had just caught sight of their neighbor.

"No accounting for other people's taste," Emily said with a smirk. She held out her find.

"Whatchya got?"

"Found a couple of books I thought you might like."

"Whoa, Emily!" He sat up. "Where'd you find these? A first edition Hawthorne—*The Red Badge of Courage*."

"A yard sale."

"Yard sale? Thought you were just out for a walk." He wrinkled his nose. "You have a secret assignation with a cigar-smoking Casanova while you were gone?"

"More of a busssinesss proposssition."

Stan raised an eyebrow.

"What did these cost you?"

"Two bucks for the pair."

"Somebody didn't know what they had." He flipped the other book over. "Henry Wadsworth Longfellow. Emily, this is so cool. His is the house I've been telling you about. The one in Cambridge."

"Oh, yeah. Can't wait." As usual, her sarcasm went right over his head.

"*In the Harbor*. Huh. This one will be fun to explore."

"Really, Stan? It's a book of poems. You don't *explore* poetry."

" 'We shall not cease from exploration, and the end of all our exploring will be to arrive where we started...' "

"Now you're just making shit up."

"T. S. Elliot."

"Uh huh."

"Hey, but thanks for thinking about me, Em."

She beamed with pleasure as he caressed the leather binding, then opened the book and sniffed the pages. Not like the way you smell a flower. Rather, he inhaled deeply, like you would with a snifter of brandy.

"What are you...?"

"The gentleman who previously owned this book liked to smoke cigars," he said, eyes closed, savoring the aroma.

"Really?"

"*Hoyo De Monterrey Double Corona*, to be specific. One of Cuba's most exquisite exports."

"No way you know that. You're telling me you can still smell the cigar smoke on that old book and you're able to discern the exact brand?" Emily was more than a little incredulous.

Stan's eyes twinkled as he held up a thin slip of paper neatly folded once down the center. "He left the receipt from Churchill's Lounge in the book."

Emily punched him in the shoulder. "Let me see." She took the receipt from him, ignoring his chuckles. "Looks like it's from five years ago," she mused, examining both sides before handing it back. "Guess he liked a good smoke while reading his poetry."

"An expensive smoke. Well, what do you know?" he held the book out to her, opened to the title page.

"Is that a signature?"

"You might have just given me a signed first edition."

"Could it be worth something?"

"I would assume so. I'll ask when I meet with that archivist at the Longfellow House tomorrow."

Emily patted him on the shoulder and headed toward the RV, clutching her puzzles.

"Hey! What other loot did you find?" He tucked the receipt back into the book.

"Just something for me to play with," she hedged.

"Like what?"

"Couple of puzzles."

"Jigsaw puzzles?"

She didn't stop.

"Emily!"

"I know. I know. Not terribly practical."

"Yah think? Where are you going to set them up? And

what if you don't finish them before we hit the road again?"

Emily gestured helplessly toward the picnic table. "You said I should find something to do."

"I meant like finding a part time job. When we get home."

"What kind of a job? A door greeter at Walmart?"

"You know what I mean. What about volunteering?"

"You have to have a passion to volunteer. I have no passions." She grabbed one of Stan's new books and started fanning herself. "Damn, these hot flashes."

"So find a passion. C'mon, Em. What do you want me to say? You've never been bored in your whole life. What's going on now?"

"I don't know."

Stan threw his hands in the air as Emily stomped off into the RV. She slammed the door behind her, but not before she heard him say, "What the hell do you want? Another murder to solve?"

After a dinner of salmon on the grill—with a mango salsa that Stan made from scratch with fresh fruit and vegetables— and a bottle of pinot grigio to share, Emily seemed more like her usual self. Stan maneuvered his lawn chair as close to hers as he could to put his arm around her. Together they gazed up at the swath of stars that arched across the night sky. The breeze was warm and carried just a hint of pine and something else Stan tried to identify. Was that blueberries? He breathed deeply, savoring the night air that tantalized the way a good bottle of wine does.

"Sorry about the tantrum earlier," Emily said.

"No problem."

"The thing is I really wasn't planning on retiring."

"I know. But look on the bright side. If you hadn't hurt your back chasing that naked guy through the mayor's backyard, we wouldn't be sitting here now looking forward to spending the Fourth of July with the girls."

Emily sighed. "Maybe I should have stayed with the department."

"And worked the desk for the last years of your career? Or dispatch? Em, that's not you."

"No, you're right. I just need time to figure it out."

"Maybe when we get back you should check up at NMU about teaching a course or two. You've certainly got the credentials."

"Me? A teacher? Maybe I'll get me one of those Walmart applications."

He pointed up just in time for her to see a shooting star streak across the sky.

"It's a sign," he said.

"Yeah…" She leaned over and nuzzled his cheek. Whispering into his ear she said, "I'll become an astronaut when I grow up." Then she swatted his arm.

They sat in companionable silence for a few moments, listening to the hushed murmurs of campers cleaning up after their dinners, setting up their fires, settling in to their favorite TV shows. Stan wondered why so many people would choose TV over the outdoors, when nature provided its own entertainment if you just bothered to pay attention. He nudged Emily and pointed to a raccoon scuttling toward a nearby trash can.

"What time are we meeting the girls tomorrow?"

"Around ten. We'll do the Freedom Trail in the morning, then after lunch the girls and I will find something to do so you can make your appointment at the Longfellow House."

"You don't want to go with me? You know that house was George Washington's headquarters during the Revolutionary War?"

"So you've said. I think we'll pass."

"Even if I wasn't doing research, I couldn't come all the way to Boston and not see it."

"Heavens no!" She tousled her hair the way she tended to do when she was being snarky. Stan doubted she even knew she did it. But even more, he doubted she knew how sexy he found the gesture to be.

"Hey, I know something you can focus on in your retirement." He leaned over and murmured into her ear, letting his voice drop to a low growl. "Right here. Right now." Emily's lips took on a lascivious curve. "And what would that be?"

"Why don't we go inside and I'll explain it to you." He fingered the strap of her tank top. "Give you a little demonstration, if you like." He nuzzled her neck.

"But it's so lovely out here. Under the stars." She stroked his thigh.

"You want me to demonstrate right here?" His voice was a husky whisper. "For all the other campers to see?" He brushed his fingers lightly across her breast.

"Umm…no. You're right. Let's go inside. The stars will be here tomorrow night."

Stan took her hand and led her up into the RV.

CHAPTER 5

"HUZZAH!"

The man in the waistcoat, breeches and tri-cornered hat raised his fists in a triumphant gesture. "Huzzah!"

"Why's he doing that?" nine-year-old Annabel asked.

"To be dorky," commented Wynter, sniffing in disgust as only a thirteen-year-old could.

"He's a re-enactor," countered Annabel's twin, Allyn. "We learned about them on our spring field trip. They pretend to be someone from the Revolution, about forty years ago before they had cell phones and stuff."

"I know about re-enactors!" Annabel shrugged off her yellow hoodie and held it out, not knowing what to do with it. "I just want to know why he's being so dorky. I'm hot."

"Here, honey, I'll take it." Emily stuffed the sweatshirt into her backpack.

"Annabel, that's my hoodie! I wanted to wear it." Allyn pushed at her sister.

"Come on, girls. It's too hot for sweatshirts anyway." Emily peeled off her cotton overshirt and stuffed that into the backpack as well.

Earlier that morning Emily and Stan had left their VW bug at the Alewife Station park-and-ride lot where they caught the Red Line into the city to meet their daughter Megan and their grandchildren. By the time they'd stepped off the train near Boston Common, the sun had chased away the morning chill and the day promised to be warm and muggy.

"There they are!" Emily had pointed to a silver SUV pulling up to the curb. A Lexus, she noted. The hazard flashers came on and Megan and the girls spilled out.

"Grandpa! Grandma!" the twins called, racing over to throw their arms around their grandparents.

When did they get so tall? Emily wondered. "Wynter." She smiled and took a step toward her eldest granddaughter, who was hanging back by the car.

"Mom. Dad. Sorry we're late. It's so good to see you." Megan gave each of them a warm hug. "Wynter, get your nose out of that phone and come give your Grandma and Grandpa a hug."

The thirteen-year-old heaved an exaggerated sigh and wrinkled her nose at her mother before wrapping effusive arms around each of them then she quickly pulled away and hovered at the edge of the group.

"I hate to rush you," Emily said. "But the tour starts in just a couple of minutes."

"Go! Go! I'm parked illegally anyway. I'll see you tonight. Have fun, girls! Be good for Grandma and Grandpa. No souvenirs. And Mom, try to limit the sweets, okay? All right, gotta go. Have fun! Say hi to Ben Franklin for me if you see him!" With a wave and a whirl, Megan jumped back behind the wheel of her car, tooted her horn and steered into traffic.

"Let's go find the start of the Freedom Trail," Stan said eagerly.

"Huzzah!"

This time it was Stan, getting into the spirit of the Revolution by mimicking the posture of their tour guide.

Emily doubted that she and the girls would enjoy this venture as much as he, as steamy as it was. Twice already she'd had to put herself between the bickering twins. Wynter twirled her damp hair around her finger and began sucking on the end of her pony tail. Emily cringed. She was about to chastise the girl, but chose to shrug it off for the moment. Not worth antagonizing her.

"A fine looking family you have with you, Sire. From whence do you hail?"

Sire? Emily groaned inwardly. But Stan had already perked up at the question and answered in kind.

"We've traveled from the former New France, many a day's ride from here."

"Grandpa, we live in America," Allyn said.

"He's talking about a long time ago," her twin countered. "Aren't you, Grandpa?"

"I certainly am." Stan puffed himself up into his lecture mode. "Michigan was part of the Northwest Territory that the British wrested away from the French about the time of the American Revolution."

Emily opened her mouth to cut his oration short, but the guide beat her to it, checking his pocket watch and motioning for the tour group to come closer.

"Hear ye! Hear Ye!" His booming voice carried easily above the noise of the nearby traffic. "Gather ye round, and I'll tell ye tales of the secret—and not so secret—goings on wherein the great people of this colony of Massachusetts have begun to rebel against the edicts of that tyrant, His Majesty King George. But before we commence on our short journey together, I must inquire—are there any among you who are loyal subjects of the Crown?"

Two people, a young couple, raised their hands.

"And might I inquire from whence you hail?"

"Liverpool," the man said proudly. "And we love our Queen!"

"Queen?" The guide seemed outrageously puzzled. "Ah,

no matter. For I speak for my fellow colonists when I declare we have no quarrel with the fine people of England, only the policies of their Crown. So you, Sire, and your fair lady are thusly welcome to join this gathering this fine morning." He doffed his hat and bowed solemnly in their direction.

"And now…" He addressed the whole group again. "I must in due course introduce myself. Ye may call me Caleb Wintergreen. I am but a humble shoemaker by trade. Though I daresay my loyal customers will attest that I make the finest boots and shoes for gentlemen in all the colony."

He brandished his hat toward his feet, shod in buckled shoes, for all to see.

"Notice they are made of the finest leather to be found in the new world. My silver buckles were fashioned by that great patriot himself, Paul Revere!"

Emily and the girls leaned in to see the shoes for themselves.

"Dare ye not confuse me with the cobbler down the street. For his trade is only to repair the shoes that a cordwainer…" he paused dramatically and gave a solemn bow, "…such as yours truly, hath fashioned. Ho there! You!" His shout startled them. "The pair of you!"

He pointed at two young men who had sauntered up to listen in. "Have you gentlemen paid your fare for this tour? Observe that my guests are wearing an insignia which evidences payment for the privilege of listening to my tales of this fair city. Purchase a token if you would like to join us. Otherwise, move along." He waved his hat as if at a flock of birds. "Move along now!" And the interlopers retreated.

With a flourish, he plopped his hat back on his head and beckoned for his flock to follow. They filed past a small duck pond and up a hill to where the shoemaker stood and waited by a large tree for stragglers to catch up.

Emily frowned as Wynter lagged behind, head down, thumbs flicking over the keys of her phone. "Wynter, honey, put it away. It's rude. And dangerous."

"Dangerous?"

"You're distracted when you walk."

Wynter rolled her eyes and stuffed the offending phone into her pocket. Emily focused her attention back on the tour guide who was pointing to a bronze plaque embedded into the sidewalk.

"What's he saying?" Emily whispered to her husband, and then immediately regretted her question as Stan launched into an elaborate, if hushed, explanation of the ancient elm that had once stood at this spot, and from which the Sons of Liberty had hung in effigy supporters of the detested Stamp Act. She found it ironic that he could be so long-winded about something that was no longer there. "Oh, wait, there he goes," she interrupted. "We'd better catch up."

She herded the girls down the street and around the corner, following their guide into a fenced-in graveyard snugged up against an old church.

"Em! Paul Revere is buried here somewhere!" Stan eagerly studied the map at the entrance.

"I know where it is, Grandpa." Annabel latched onto his hand.

While Stan happily followed the twins toward the rear of the cemetery, Emily wandered about keeping one eye on Wynter and studying the weathered slate tombstones, challenging herself to find the oldest one. So far, she'd found one engraving dated 1672.

"Gather ye! Gather ye!" Their friendly shoemaker waved them all toward a tall marble monument. Emily could just make out that he was saying something about the Boston Massacre and a young boy who was the sixth, unrecognized victim. A persistent pinging distracted her. It stopped when Wynter turned her back and sneaked her phone from her pocket, thumbed hurried messages, then slipped it quickly out of sight again. Emily sighed. By then, Stan and the twins had rejoined them, and the tour guide was on the move again.

"Grandma, I'm hungry." Now Annabel was tugging on

Emily's arm.

"We'll get lunch when the tour is over," she assured her.

"How much longer is it going to last?" Allyn whined. "I'm hot and my feet hurt."

"That's because we're walking in the footsteps of history!" Stan said, taking her hand. "How often does one get to do this?"

"Every year," Wynter said, popping her gum.

"Daddy says if he goes on this tour one more time…" Allyn started.

"He's gonna barf," Annabel finished.

Stan looked crestfallen. Emily bit her lip to keep from laughing out loud. "Girls, let Grandpa have his fun."

After traipsing past several famous churches and meeting houses and through Quincy Market, Emily could see that the girls were getting slower and whinier. Stan, on the other hand, was revving up, chatting with the guide between stops, both men a full ten paces ahead of the rest of the group. As they approached the steps of Faneuil Hall, a plaintive voice called out.

"Grandpa…!"

"Stan!" Emily shouted, when he didn't respond to the sound of Annabel's voice. This caused both Stan and the guide to stop and survey the bedraggled tour group.

To Emily's relief, the shoemaker put a hand on Stan's arm to stay his running commentary and waited for the group to gather around him. The guide then beckoned Annabel to come closer and, kneeling down beside her, he pointed up at the cupola crowning the building.

"Can you see what that is?" he asked.

"Looks like a grasshopper." Annabel craned her neck. "Why is there a grasshopper up there?"

"It's a weather vane," her grandfather jumped in.

"I'm hungry," Wynter complained. "Can we get ice cream?"

"Honey, we'll get something to eat when the tour is over."

Emily shushed her.

"That grasshopper was used as a shibboleth," the guide said. "During the Revolutionary War."

"What's a shibetlo?" Allyn asked.

"A *shibboleth* is a secret word," Stan answered, taking up the story. "When the colonials suspected that someone was a spy, they would ask them a question to see if they were truly from Boston."

"What would they ask?" Allyn held her breath.

"What sits atop Faneuil Hall? Of course."

"A grasshopper!" Annabel shouted.

"Good girl! Now we know you're not a spy."

"What happened if they got it wrong?" she wanted to know.

"They'd shoot 'em," Wynter said, sticking her finger into her sister's rib. Annabel shrieked.

"Really? Grandpa?"

"Not on the spot. They'd have to try them first," Stan reassured her.

"Then they'd hang them." Wynter wrapped a pretend rope around her neck and let her tongue loll out.

"Ewwwww!" the twins said in unison.

"Wynter, stop!" Annabel complained.

"Or they'd run a bayonet through them." She lunged at the girls, a pretend bayonet in hand. "And then shoot them and hang them."

The girls screamed and ran, pushing through the crowd.

"Now look what you've done," Emily accused Stan.

"What? I was just giving a bit of history."

"Allyn! Annabel! Get back here now." Emily sensed the irritation of the other tourists as the girls pushed their way back to her. "Wynter, enough with the killing stuff."

Wynter scowled, switched on her phone and again turned her back to her grandmother.

The guide urged his charges toward a large, busy intersection. "This way, my good people! This way!" He waited for a break in the traffic, then raised his hand and stepped boldly into the street like a school crossing guard. The group dashed across, eyeing the oncoming cars nervously. Emily grabbed each of the twins by hand, hurrying them along right behind Stan. When they got to the opposite curb, she checked to make sure Wynter had kept up. But Wynter was still on the far side of the street thumbing her phone, oblivious to the cars whizzing by and the fact that her family had left her behind. Without looking up, the girl stepped off the curb.

"Stop!" Emily screamed.

A taxi roared by and Wynter jumped back. She looked up at the car in surprise, then at her panicked grandmother. Rolling her eyes, she shrugged her shoulders. When the traffic finally skidded to a stop and the walk signal started beeping, she stepped back into the street and crossed.

"Give me the phone," commanded Emily.

Wynter, surprised at her grandmother's stern voice, handed over the offending device. Emily slipped it into the zippered pocket of her backpack, while Wynter stalked off after Stan and the twins, leaving Emily to trail behind.

Emily found a small shady spot to sit on the low wall near the entrance to the Paul Revere house. Taking a long sip from her water bottle, she realized that she hadn't really taken in any of the details of the historic home. The guide had said something about it being the oldest building in downtown Boston. And she vaguely remembered fire places in every room. But her attention had been wholly devoted to keeping her granddaughters from bickering and bothering the other tourists. Stan had seemed relieved when she offered to take them out into the courtyard to wait for him, so he could take his time studying the placards and displays.

For her part, Emily was feeling hot and crabby and needed a few moments of respite to cool off. The twins pranced and galloped around the bench in the center of the courtyard. From what she could hear of their excited conversation, they were deeply into a game of 'let's pretend we're riding horseback.' From the corner of her eye, she could see Wynter sitting cross-legged on the brick walk, hiding behind a hedge and sulking.

Emily sighed. What was it that had gotten her so out of sorts these last few days? First at the campground and now this. She always thought of herself as a cheerful, easygoing woman. She felt ashamed of her crankiness with the kids. She had so been looking forward to spending time with them and now she was just frustrated. *They're just being kids*, she mused. *They feel comfortable enough with us to be themselves. And that's a good thing. Now they've probably pegged me as the mean witch in the tower.*

She became aware of the tension in her jaw and forced herself to smile. Rolling her shoulders and stretching her neck muscles, she vowed to make this a much more pleasant experience for all of them. No more unrealistic expectations. She should have realized the kids had done this Freedom Trail before. From now on, she'd let them take the lead, even if it meant hours at the campground pool.

"Hey, kiddos!" Her reverie was interrupted by Stan emerging from the house, corralling the galloping girls who whinnied to a stop. "Whoa! What are you? Pony princesses?"

"No, Grandpa! We're midnight riders," Allyn said. "She's Paul Revere and I'm Sybil Ludington."

"Sybil Who?"

"Geez, Gramps. I thought you were a history teacher. You don't know who Sybil Ludington is?"

Annabel piped up, "She rode farther than Paul Revere. She warned the soldiers about the British just like he did."

"Except she lived in Connecticut and she was only sixteen," Wynter said, preening.

"Hmm...never heard about her. I guess I have some homework to do."

Emily chuckled. "That's what you get for spending all

your time hunched over biographies of dead old white men."

"If there's one thing I've learned, there's more to history than what the textbooks teach us. Thank you for that," Stan said sincerely, giving the twins a hug. "So, shall we all gallop off to the Old North Church?"

"Yes!" the twins shouted, circling him with their imaginary horses.

"Do we have to?" Wynter asked. Her feet were firmly planted where she stood.

"It's the last stop on the tour." Stan looked to Emily, obviously hoping for backup.

She shrugged. He gazed wistfully in the direction of the cordwainer, who was leading his weary group up the narrow street and around the corner. Off in the distance the clanging of church bells beckoned. But Wynter had dug in her heels, arms crossed. The expression on her face that said she wasn't going any further.

To Emily's surprise he patted his belly. "You know what? I'm hungry. We can always come back another time."

He was hiding his disappointment Emily knew, but she was relieved that he understood there would be rebellion in the ranks if they pushed the girls any further. And she was even more relieved when he suggested a lunch of pizza and ice cream. She didn't realize how famished she was herself.

With a satisfied belch, Stan set the tip on the table.

"Grandpa, you burped!" Allyn said.

"No! Did I?" He checked his phone for the time and said to Emily, "We'd better get going if I'm going to make that appointment at the Longfellow House."

"I wanna go on the swan boats!" Allyn bounced in her seat.

"Swan boats? Oh, now…" He frowned and checked his phone again.

"Please, Grandma. Please, please, please!" Annabel danced

around the table.

"I think that's a wonderful idea," Emily said. "Grandpa doesn't need all us girls hanging on his arm while he does his research."

"Swan boats are for babies," Wynter spoke up. "I'd rather go with Gramps."

"I'm okay with that," Stan said to Emily. "What do you think?"

Now Emily was conflicted. She wanted to make amends with her granddaughter, but forcing her to stay behind with her and the little girls was likely not the way to do it.

"I guess Wynter is old enough to make up her own mind how to spend the rest of the day." She dug for the phone in her backpack and handed it to her granddaughter. "I think you'll need this. Grandpa gets lost easily."

The teenager sat up straighter in her chair and blinked at her grandmother in surprise.

CHAPTER 6

STAN stood his ground, studying the grimy oversized wall map, as a crowd of commuters bumped and jostled their way past him in their hurry to catch the next train.

"This way, Gramps."

"Do we want inbound or outbound?"

"Outbound. Hurry, there's a train coming!"

"Okay. Okay." Stan hustled to follow his granddaughter. "I guess if we get on the wrong train, we can always get off again and turn around."

"We won't get on the wrong train, Gramps. Trust me. I've been riding the T my whole life."

Wynter jumped deftly onto the train. Stan squeezed in to keep from being pinched by the doors sliding shut behind him. As the train jerked forward, he followed the girl through the car, dancing around a couple nuzzling in the aisle to a set of empty seats. A trio of raucous, laughing teenage boys shouldered their way past the same couple, and lurched for the handholds next to Stan and Wynter. She swiped at an image on her cell phone, studiously ignoring them.

Stan peered up at the Red Line map on the wall over their seats.

"We get off at Harvard Square."

"Uh huh."

"That's one, two, three, four stops."

"Uh huh." She popped her earbuds in.

"You don't mind walking when we get off? It's about five blocks."

"Unh, unh."

Stan sighed. Well, that conversation was over. He glared at the boys who were ogling his granddaughter, and they spun away suddenly silent. At the next stop, Wynter followed them with her eyes, watching them shove and tumble over each other, laughing, pushing to get off the subway car. She arched across her grandfather to get a longer look. The train jerked into motion and she settled back into her seat, eyes on her phone again.

The train picked up speed, jostling them as it rounded a corner and lunged into the dark tunnel. Stan was startled to catch the reflection of an older pudgy man sitting next to his beautiful teenage granddaughter. His shoulders sagged. Then he became aware that Wynter was looking at the same reflection. Large black letters—*Kendall Station*—displaced the image. Wynter slipped the buds out of her ears.

"Hey, Gramps, wanna see something cool? Let's get off here."

The train squealed to a halt and the doors opened.

"This isn't our stop."

"We can get right back on. C'mon."

She was already up and out the door.

"Wynter! Wait." Stan had no choice but to follow as she stepped off onto the platform.

"This way, Gramps!"

He ignored the sudden ache in his Achilles tendon and

hopped off, hurrying to keep up with her. A dozen yards away she stopped. The train rolled away with a whoosh and a roar. Wynter grabbed for a large lever on the wall and started pulling on it slowly and rhythmically.

"What are you doing?"

"Watch!"

He heard it before he saw it. His eyes widened as sixteen large chimes, tubular bells of different lengths hanging between the tracks, began to vibrate. Wynter cranked back and forth on the lever. Large mallets between each tube swung back and forth striking the chimes, creating a mesmerizing medley of musical notes. *A minor chord.* But he had no clue which one.

"Cool, huh?" she said.

"Very cool."

"Wanna try it?"

"Sure." Stan grabbed the lever and jerked it toward him. But nothing happened.

"You have to do it like this." Wynter squeezed in between her grandfather and the lever and put her hands over his. She guided his movements, helping him pull the lever to get the rhythm. The musical tones reverberated over the platform, haunting and beautiful. They rang them over and over, until the next train roared in, drowning out the chimes.

"That's ours!" Wynter yelled.

And Stan found himself chasing after her again. After settling himself into the seat beside her, Stan gazed at his granddaughter in wonder. "I think you just made my day."

To his surprise Wynter grinned and leaned in next to him. She held her phone in front of the two of them and snapped a picture.

A moment later his phone dinged. It was a message from Wynter. The photo of them she'd just taken. He leaned over to say thank you, but she had already popped the earbuds back into her ears.

Stan's heart quickened even as his steps on the cobbled sidewalk slowed. He savored the moment, delighting in the gnarled trees, the old church, the two-hundred-year old houses preserved as living testaments to a time when the country was young. If he could afford to retire anywhere, this is where he would choose to live out the rest of his days, in the lap of history.

As he and Wynter strolled the few blocks from Harvard Square, he imagined the Founding Fathers walking the neighborhood that had long since grown up around the gallant old house at 105 Brattle Street. Henry Wadsworth Longfellow's house. But more than that, General George Washington's headquarters during the Revolutionary War. That was Stan's target.

"Is something wrong, Gramps?" Wynter, several paces ahead of him, looked back.

"Just checking out the neighborhood. Ever wonder what it must have been like to live here two hundred years ago?"

"No."

"In the days before cars and buses and electric wires?"

They stopped at the corner, waiting for traffic to pass and the light to change.

"I bet there was a lot of horse poop in the road."

Moments later they stood in front of the yellow, three-story Georgian house. A classic white picket fence surrounded the manicured lawn.

Stan pointed to a sign: Headquarters of General George Washington 1775-1776, Home of Henry Wadsworth Longfellow 1837-1882.

"Longfellow lived here a lot longer than Washington did," Wynter observed. "The house is over two hundred years old."

"It was built in 1759."

"Two hundred and fifty-five years old."

Stan did the math in his own head. "You're right." *The kid's pretty quick at math.* He never knew that about her. Seems there was a lot he didn't know about this child of his child.

"You know what he was famous for, don't you?" he prodded.

"Duh! He was a poet. Paul Revere's Ride. Song of Hiawatha. Everyone knows that."

"Not as many people as you would think."

She shrugged.

"Let's go inside."

They followed the path around to the back of the house. Wynter darted over to a massive tree that Stan judged to be more than a hundred years old. She threw her arms out as if to hug the trunk.

"Gramps! It would take ten people to hug this tree!"

He chuckled in delight as the inner child in this surly teenager danced joyfully around the tree.

A large veranda skirted most of the backside of the house, overlooking a small but elegant garden. Wynter's face lit up. She threw her shoulders back, nose in the air, and stepped onto the meditation path.

"Butler, I'll have a cup of tea with my morning walk." She meandered along the low hedges, pausing to sniff at flowers. She pirouetted, and curtsied toward her grandfather. "Will you join me, Jeeves?" Suddenly she froze, her face reddening.

Stan saw a young man, wearing khakis, a button-down shirt, and a National Park Ranger's hat, emerge from the carriage house. *Why is Wynter now so intent on studying that rose bush?*

"If you're looking for the visitor center, it's in the back of the house. You can get tour tickets there," the young ranger said.

"Actually, I have an appointment with Belle Carter, your archivist."

"You must be Stan Remington. Ranger Carter got called into an unexpected meeting." At Stan's look of disappointment he hastened to say, "She suggested you join my two o'clock tour. She should be able to meet you when we're done."

Stan brightened. "What do you think, Wynter?"

Wynter ducked her head in a half nod, then skirted behind her grandfather and followed the two men into the house where several people waited for the tour to begin.

"Gramps, why is that guy wearing a Smoky Bear hat?" Wynter whispered.

"He's a Park Ranger. This house is part of the National Park System."

"Doesn't look like a park to me."

"Not a place where you would go camping, if that's what you mean."

"What's the point if you can't go camping?"

"The point is--"

"Hey, folks!" The young park ranger had gathered the group together. "I'm Eric. I'm a summer intern with the National Park Service, and I'll be your guide this afternoon."

He couldn't have been more than twenty, Stan guessed. A local college student most likely. His dark brown hair curling out from under the hat needed to be cut. He offered his hand to each of them in turn, asking their names and where they were from.

Jim and Rosalyn Addison, from Haverhill "up north," introduced themselves next. The couple, in their late thirties, shook hands with Eric and nodded at Stan and the others.

"I am Nakamura. Kiyoshi Nakamura. I am visiting from Osaka, Japan and lecturing this summer at Boston College." Mr. Nakamura bowed deeply, but quickly straightened and held out his hand to Eric and then to each of the others, causing a flurry of bowing and handshaking, much to Stan's amusement.

"Stanford Remington, from Michigan. And this is my granddaughter, Wynter. She's a Bostonian."

"Brookline, Gramps. Not Boston."

Jim Addison laughed and winked at her, causing her to

blush.

"Nice to meet you all." Eric pushed back the brim of his hat. "I'll be senior at Northeastern in the fall, majoring in history with an emphasis on research and archiving."

"My grandfather is a historian," Wynter blurted out. "He's writing a book. About George Washington."

Stan stared at her, surprised she even knew that.

"He already wrote one about shipwrecks." Wynter preened.

"Really? Awesome. "

What Stan found to be awesome was his granddaughter bragging him up.

"Okay, folks, let's start the tour, shall we?" Eric said. "It's a pretty cool place and I've got lots to tell you, not only about Henry Wadsworth Longfellow who lived in the house for forty-five years, but also about General George Washington who used it as his Revolutionary War headquarters."

They followed the young park ranger down a hallway and past the centuries-old kitchen where they stopped, trying to wrap their minds around how long ago it was that people cooked in this room, what it was they used to cook, and how it felt to work over the large cast-iron wood-burning stove on hot days like today.

"Stay on the runner," he advised, leading them toward the homey, if formal, dining room. "And please don't touch the walls. This is the original wall paper from Longfellow's day."

Stan studied the period floral wall paper, itching to touch it. He noticed Wynter, whose fingers lingered just millimeters from the deep golden print. Quickly she stuffed her hands in her shorts pockets. Stan suppressed a grin and strode after their guide.

They rounded a corner and stepped into the front parlor. This room, Eric told them, had been shared by Fannie Longfellow and Martha Washington--though nearly a half century apart--as their personal domain, a salon to receive the many guests who came to call.

"It is said that when Martha Washington arrived in the winter of 1776, she invited women in to participate in sewing circles in this very room. They mended clothing for the soldiers and made bandages for use in the hospital that had been temporarily erected across the street."

Eric's voice had taken on the quality of a storyteller. Wynter appeared to be hanging on to his every word. Stan sighed happily. He had lots of stories of his own about the Washington family and their role in determining the early fate of the country. He imagined spending time with Wynter regaling her with vignettes of early American history.

The tour group sauntered from room to room, but it was Longfellow's corner den that drew the most comments.

"Amazing!" Jim Addison exclaimed. "I could live here."

"Kind of a man-cave," Wynter blurted out, before realizing she'd even spoken. Blushing, she put a hand over her mouth and took a step back so that her grandfather stood between the park ranger and herself.

"It is a man-cave," Stan agreed. He took a deep breath. He swore he could still smell the leather and cigar smoke from the members of the weekly Dante Club—local literati who met to critique Longfellow's translation of Dante's dark allegory, *The Divine Comedy*.

"How could a poet afford a house like this?" Jim Addison asked.

"Didn't he teach at Harvard?" his wife suggested.

"Still…"

"As it turns out Longfellow was paid rather handsomely for his work," Eric informed the group. "One of his poems went for three thousand dollars! To *The New York Ledger*. And that was back in the mid-nineteenth century."

"You might think of him as the Stephen King of his day," Stan added. "Wildly popular, but debatable as to whether his talent was truly high literature or simply storytelling that appealed to the masses."

As they were leaving the library, Eric told them how

Longfellow's second wife, Fanny, had tragically caught the sleeve of her summer dress on fire holding it too near a candle, and how the next morning she died of her burns.

"Mr. Remington, there she is." Eric cut his story short and waved to a woman just emerging from an office followed by an elegantly dressed, portly man brandishing a gold-knobbed cane. "Ranger Carter, your two o'clock is here. Stan Remington and his granddaughter, Wynter."

"Hello. Welcome to Longfellow House. I am so sorry about the delay," Ranger Carter greeted them. "This is Judge Duncan Calderwood, a member of our Board of Directors."

"I hope you're enjoying your tour," the judge said, reaching out to shake hands as Eric introduced the rest of the tour group.

"Yes, Ranger Eric was very informative," Stan said. Then he shook the woman's hand. "I appreciate your taking the time to meet with me."

In contrast to the judge's three-piece vested summer suit, Ranger Belle Carter—Stan guessed her to be in her mid-fifties—wore a khaki park service uniform similar to Eric's, but decidedly more feminine.

"So where's your Smoky Bear hat?" Jim Addison teased.

Belle pointed through the door to a cluttered desk. And sure enough, there on top of a pile of books and papers sat a large brimmed park ranger's hat.

"I don't typically wear it in the house," the woman said, laughing. "But yes, all National Park Rangers have them."

"I'll leave you in Ranger Carter's hands," Eric said.

Stan slid his wallet out of his pocket and handed the young man his business card. "Give me a buzz once you graduate. I'd love to hear where you land."

At which Mr. Nakamura quickly bowed and ceremoniously presented his card to Eric as well, bowing again.

"Thanks!" Eric said, awkwardly returning the bow.

"Sorry, I don't carry business cards," Jim Addison said.

"Me either," his wife added.

"I guess I don't either." Wynter blushed.

"My card's good for the two of us," Stan said, winking at her, at which Wynter blushed even more deeply.

While the others took their leave and followed Eric out, Stan unzipped his backpack to produce the small book Emily had found at the camp yard sale.

"I'm here to pick your brain about George Washington, but first I wonder if you'd take a look a Longfellow book I came across the other day. A signed, first edition it seems." He handed the book to the woman. "Probably too good to be true, huh?"

Ranger Carter checked spine first, then opened the cover with a delicate thumb and checked the fly leaf and title page. "It's definitely a first edition."

Stan studied her expression closely as she examined the signature under the main title. A jaded smirk curled the corners of her lips and he wasn't entirely surprised when she said, "But, I'm sorry. This isn't an authentic Henry Wadsworth Longfellow signature."

"You're sure?"

"For one, *In the Harbor* was published four months after his death." She smiled with sympathy. "I'm afraid someone faked the dead poet's autograph. It's a pretty good imitation, though. What do you think, Judge Calderwood?"

The portly man coughed politely. "Yes, well, a bit obvious, to my eye. If you could find out who did it, sometimes there's a market for the work of a particularly good forger."

"You're kidding," Wynter said. "People will pay money for a fake?"

"If it's done by certain notable artisans, yes," the judge replied.

Ranger Carter laughed. "Certainly not as much as if it was the original signature. But you'd be amazed at what people collect." She flipped through the pages. "You do have a good condition first edition, however. Slightly marred by the fake autograph. But it still could be worth holding onto." Her smile froze and her brows furrowed just the slightest bit. "Where did you say you came across this book?"

"My wife found it at a garage sale up in the Lexington area. It was in a box of old books. She bought it for a buck."

The archivist nodded, chewed her lip. She stole a querulous glance at the judge whose face was stony. But just as quickly she closed the book and handed it back to Stan. "I hope you enjoy owning it. Despite the fake signature, it's a lovely collection of poetry written by one of America's great poets at the end of his life. But it wasn't Longfellow you wanted to see me about, was it? How can I help you with your research on Washington?"

Stan tucked the Longfellow book back into his backpack. "I'm interested in the influence of his years during the French and Indian war on his leadership during the Revolution. I was hoping you could steer me in the direction of some of his correspondence from his time here in Boston."

"You've come to the right person," the judge said magnanimously and patted the ranger on the shoulder. "Belle is the expert on everything having to do with Washington's stay here. But with that I need to take my leave." He bowed slightly and swiveled, lifting his cane to step out with a flourish as Ranger Carter motioned Stan and Wynter into her office.

A short while later, they walked back out into the bright sunshine, Stan having gotten the names of some people in the Boston area who could answer his myriad questions about General George Washington.

"Thanks for your patience in there," Stan said.

"What?" Wynter popped the earbuds out of her ears.

Stan squeezed her shoulders.

"Grandpa, are you disappointed?" she asked. "That the autograph is a fake?"

"A little. But we have a great story to tell now, you and I, don't we?"

Wynter put her arm around her grandfather's waist, and they walked down the sidewalk toward the street. "Yes we do."

CHAPTER 7

"GRANDMA, that's the lady Grandpa and I went to see yesterday."

Emily noticed her granddaughter was shivering even though the night was warm and humid. A smoky haze from the spent fireworks lingered in the air.

She drew the blanket further over the dead woman's face and rose to embrace the girl, but Wynter stepped back and ran to her father. Emily let the quietest of sighs escape her lips. Philip immediately put his arm around his daughter and walked her over to where Stan and Megan hustled the little ones to pick up their picnic things. Emily couldn't hear what Wynter said, but she could tell by the look on Stan's face and the way he braced his shoulders that he was shocked by the girl's news.

She squatted and reached for a large leather handbag lying haphazard next to the toppled chair. Riffling through the woman's belongings she found her driver's license and strained in the dim light to make out the name.

"Belle…"

"Carter." Stan was standing over her now. "You'd better let me see."

Emily lifted the blanket from the woman's face. Stan

blanched and nodded.

"Yeah, she's the one I had the appointment with yesterday."

Emily tugged the blanket back up. "Seems odd that she was alone. Did you see anybody with her?"

"I never saw her to begin with. There were a ton of families around."

Chagrined, Emily wanted to kick herself for being too much on vacation. A good cop, even a retired one, always paid attention to the crowd, looking for any unusual behavior, any unusual activity. A woman sitting by herself might not mean anything, but when she turns up dead, you have to wonder.

"Maybe I should stay here with you instead of Philip," Stan offered.

Emily stood up and faced him. "It's likely she died of natural causes. A heart attack or an aneurism. It doesn't really matter that you met her yesterday. I'll deal with the police. If they need to know, you can be sure they'll contact us asking for more information."

Stan shuddered. "Thanks."

She nodded. Out of the corner of her eye she saw Allyn sidle over to get another look at the body lying on the grass. Emily quickly intercepted her, dropped to one knee, and grasped the little girl by the shoulders.

"Allyn, honey, I want you to understand something." She spoke in a quiet, but firm voice. Allyn's wide eyes drifted toward the form under the blanket. "No, look at me for a moment." Emily waited until Allyn was looking directly into her eyes. "I want you to know that nothing, I repeat, nothing you did hurt this woman. She was… she was sick and asleep long before you ran into her."

"Is she dead?"

Emily knew better than to gloss over the facts, as tough as it might be for the girl. "I'm afraid that's what it looks like, sweetie."

"Cool!" Allyn straightened up and preened at her twin who was now staring at her with admiration.

"Allyn! Get over here," Philip ordered. Allyn turned and ran to her parents, Stan following close on her heels. When he, Megan and the girls had left for the T, Philip came back to where Emily stood guard over the body. Already they could hear the wail of a distant ambulance siren growing louder.

"What do you think happened?"

"Hard to say," she told him. "Could have been something as simple as a heart attack." But her gut told her situations like this were never simple. She supposed she should have told Stan to stay. But after his experience of being under suspicion for the death of Father Vic—one of his best friends—she felt better not involving him.

"Natural death?"

"Most likely." There was nothing on the woman's body to indicate foul play. But Emily had been a police officer long enough to know not to make assumptions.

She was glad of Philip's company as they waited together for the police and medical examiner to arrive. When the officer in charge asked if she knew the woman, she shook her head and answered truthfully, no. "I did check her wallet," she said. "The name on the driver's license is Belle Carter."

It was well past midnight when the ME's van finally drove away with the woman's body. Philip used an app on his mobile phone to summon a taxi. Giving the driver his address in Brookline, he climbed into the back seat after Emily. Fortunately they didn't have far to go; she wouldn't have relished the long commute out to pick up her car and then to the campground.

All three girls were in bed by the time Emily and Philip walked in the front door. Megan and Stan were full of questions as the four of them sat around the kitchen island with drinks in hand. But Emily had questions of her own.

The next morning, Emily sat bleary-eyed over her third cup of coffee in her daughter's newly renovated colonial kitchen. Megan and Philip had left for work an hour before. Stan and the girls were still upstairs in bed, the events after the fireworks having postponed for a second night their plans to camp with the girls.

When she and Philip had finally gotten to the house last night, Stan and Megan pressed them for details. Then Emily questioned Stan about his visit to the Longfellow House, trying to ascertain whether they should be worried about the woman's death. "Did she seem ill? Was she worried or agitated? Did you notice anything that seemed strange about her?" Stan shook his head. She was a pleasant woman who seemed competent and knowledgeable, he told her. In fact, she'd been helpful and gave him some good leads for his research. But still he was worried about what the police were thinking.

Emily reassured him, and Megan and Philip, too, that people die of natural causes all the time, and it was just an unfortunate coincidence that they happened to be there with the kids at the time. However, part of her didn't believe in coincidences, and she'd tossed and turned all night, unable to sleep. She arched her back and realized she was aching in spots that didn't usually ache. Was it from the restless night or from the long drive from Michigan earlier in the week?

Either way, she knew she needed to get some exercise to work out the kinks. She'd be happy when they were finally out at the campground where they would have room to roam and a pool to swim in. But when it came right down to it, what she really wanted was time alone to clear her head.

Upstairs she checked on her charges, making sure they didn't sleep their day away. The twins were just stirring. "Morning, Sunbeams!" The girls rolled over and burrowed deeper into their blankets. Wynter, in her own room, never moved. The sound of the shower running drew her to the guest bedroom.

She poked her head into the adjoining bathroom. "Nice butt," she said.

"Hey! A little privacy here." But Stan's voice told her he was secretly pleased at the attention.

"I'm going out for a walk. You okay with the girls?"

"No problem." He shut off the water and Emily handed him a large fluffy towel. "Is there any coffee made?"

"About half a pot. Megan said to feel free to rummage through the fridge for eggs or whatever you like."

"Okay. Have a good walk."

"Oh, and she said the password for the Wi-Fi is on the fridge."

"Sweet."

Emily loved walking through Megan's Brookline neighborhood. Granted the homes on Aspinwall Hill were bigger than anything Emily could have ever hoped to own, but it was fun looking. The Barnett house was a three story brick colonial with twin dormers on the attic level. Emily couldn't imagine what Philip's income was that he could afford this kind of home in this particular neighborhood. Sure, Megan contributed to their income stream, but as a librarian, her salary was like pin money compared to her husband's as a CFO for a large architectural firm. Not that it mattered. Megan seemed happy and the girls were happy and obviously well loved, and that was Emily's bottom line.

Trailing the circular sidewalk up to the little park at the top of the hill, she enjoyed peeking between houses to catch a view of the city of Boston below. She found herself at the foot of a series of steep steps. A miniature street sign labeled it "Addington Path." A shortcut to the summit. Lucky for her the twins had slept in. If they were along she'd have been forced to accept the challenge of the climb.

Those two girls had more energy than anybody she knew on earth. The image of their chase ending with Allyn knocking over that woman in her chair was stuck in her head, particularly the look on the girl's face when the woman first fell over. She wondered if she needed to have another talk with Allyn and her sisters to help them process what had happened. And while it seemed to be purely chance that Stan and Wynter had met the woman the day before, Emily was concerned about what she might be thinking.

She stopped in confusion. She'd followed the sidewalk around and around, but now she was disoriented. Not recognizing the houses on this block, she read the street sign: Rawson Road. She was still in the neighborhood; that was a good thing. Remembering that Rawson eventually looped back around to the other end of Winthrop Road, she started out again. It didn't really matter which direction she walked, she would end up where she began one way or the other. Five minutes later she was back at the brick colonial.

When she walked into the kitchen, all three girls were eating scrambled eggs and bacon with their grandfather.

"Good morning!" She hugged each of the girls and gave Stan a peck on the cheek.

"Eww!!! Grandma!" Allyn made a face of disgust.

"It's okay. They're married," Annabel explained.

Wynter just grinned and poked her grandfather in the arm with her elbow. Her earbuds were already in her ears and her phone lay on the counter next to her eggy plate.

"Grandma, when are we going to go camping?" Allyn asked.

"We'll go as soon as everyone's had their breakfast. Could I try some of those?" Emily grabbed a fork and spooned eggs off the plate that Annabel offered.

Once they'd eaten, the three girls raced to be the first up the stairs to get their backpacks while Stan helped Emily load the dishwasher.

"You okay?" he asked.

"I'm fine," Emily answered. "Could take a nap already. How about you?"

"I'm ready to get back to my vacation." He leaned over and kissed her on the cheek. "*Our* vacation."

CHAPTER 8

TWO hours later Emily dozed on a poolside chair, her Kindle on her lap, while Stan and the girls happily splashed in the campground pool.

"Grandma, look at me!"

Emily jerked awake in time to see Annabel holding her nose and jumping feet first into the roiling water. Without warning, Stan cannon balled into the water alongside the little girl. All three kids shrieked and laughed, paddling as hard as they could to get out of range of the tsunami he created.

"Shark attack!" he shouted and he dove to grab at their feet. More screams, more laughter.

A tall figure striding alongside the pool caught her attention. The lanky African-American woman seemed out of place poolside in her gray pant suit. *Police officer?* Emily's brow furrowed. *Detective.*

"Hello. Are you Emily Remington?"

Emily shaded her eyes and tilted her head up at the woman now looming over her.

"I'm Detective Ellison. Dayanna Ellison. From the BPD." She showed her identification. "May I sit down?"

"Yes. Of course."

The detective perched on the edge of a cushioned chaise lounge, her long gabardine-clad legs stretched out in front of her.

"I understand you found the woman who died last night on the Esplanade. I've been assigned to the case."

"It's a case now? Have they confirmed her identification?"

"Belle Carter. Yes. She's a local. Likely a heart attack, but anytime there's an undetermined manner of death we have to look into it."

"Of course." Emily nodded.

"I'm most concerned about your granddaughters. Finding a dead body can be a very traumatic situation."

Emily immediately envisioned Allyn peering curiously at the shrouded figure on the ground. Just then a series of shrieks caught their attention.

Both women watched as Stan and the girls engaged in a ferocious splash fight.

"Yeah. I'm not thinking they are terribly traumatized at the moment," Emily said.

Detective Ellison smiled. "Looks like they're engaged in a therapy session as we speak."

"What else do you know about the woman? Does she have family?" Emily asked.

"Two sons. Grown. Both in their thirties. She was single, apparently."

"This must be very difficult for them."

"Actually they seem grateful that someone cared enough to notify the authorities. Whitman Carter, the younger son, asked me to give you his card. He would like to thank you in person." She handed a business card to Emily. "When I told him I couldn't give out your contact information, he said he understood, but still hoped to talk to you. It's up to you."

"Thank you. I'll think about it."

"Here's my card as well. If you or the kids' parents have any concerns, be sure to give me a call."

"Thanks. I'll pass it on to my daughter."

After the policewoman had left, Emily threw off her beach cover-up and slid into the water to burn off some energy and join in the play. The cool sting of the water made her skin tingle, and she dove under to get her hair wet. When she came up for air, rubbing the chlorinated water out of her eyes, she found she'd been surrounded by Stan and the girls, positioned to douse her with one giant, coordinated splash. She yelped with laughter and spun in a circle splashing back as furiously as she could.

When it was time to get out of the pool, she directed the girls toward the changing room showers. "You'll have to rinse off here at the pool. Our hot water heater is way too small to shower five people."

"We could all shower together," Allyn suggested.

"Have you seen their shower?" Wynter asked. "I'm surprised Gramps can fit in it."

"Hey!" Stan protested. He snapped his towel at Wynter. She shrieked and ran toward the pool's showers.

Emily grabbed a towel and snapped it at Stan. "You'd better go squeeze yourself into our shower. You smell like a chlorine factory."

"Here they come!" Annabel waved at the silver Lexus rounding the corner and gliding into a spot next to the VW bug. She ran to greet her parents as if she hadn't seen them in ages.

Stan waved from his position on the chaise lounge. "You're just in time for dinner," he called out.

"Quite the neighborhood you got here," Philip commented, nodding toward the RV in the next site. "Could do with a little less luminosity, wouldn't you say?"

Just then Emily emerged from the RV. "Allyn and Wynter are watching TV. Swimming tired them out. I've got brats boiling in beer, and we found local corn on the cob."

"Bratwurst! Ah, the Wisconsin delicacy," Philip said. "Hey! Nice rig—for a used one. How many miles on her?"

"Less than ten thousand," Emily said. "Aunt Dottie never went very far. She liked to park in one spot and stay for a couple of weeks. C'mon, I'll give you the grand tour."

Groaning his way off the lawn chair, Stan followed them into the motor home. Megan and Philip politely ooh-ed and ah-ed over the kitchenette, the living area where the girls were sprawled in front of the TV, the tiny bathroom with its even tinier shower stall and the bedroom that didn't leave much room beyond the queen size bed.

Stan took two bottles of beer from the fridge and held them out. "Meggsie? Philip?"

"The brats are ready to go on the grill whenever you are." Emily turned off the burner under the pan. "Everyone grab something to carry out and we'll dine under the pine trees. Annabel, you're in charge of the ketchup and mustard. Wynter! Buns and chips. Allyn, plates and forks. Megan, can you slice that tomato and bring it out?"

Philip and the girls, their arms loaded with condiments, followed Emily outside.

"Oh, my God, look at the size of this thing!" Megan sliced into the ruby red, softball-sized tomato.

"I think the family has another historian-in-the-making," Stan said proudly to his daughter, grabbing a pair of tongs to pluck the brats from the beer bath and pile them onto a plate.

"Who?"

"Wynter. She volunteered to go with me to the Longfellow house the other day."

"Wynter? Really? Interested in history? Are you sure, Dad? She's always been more into math and science…and sports."

"Maybe new worlds are opening to her. You should have seen how intently she listened to everything our guide said. See, I even got a picture of them when she wasn't looking."

He tapped on his smart phone a couple of times to bring up a photo of Wynter gazing intently as the young college student gesticulated.

"Ah! Yes. And…how old was your guide?"

"I don't know. Twenty maybe? He's a student at Northeastern. A history major. Wynter even told him about the book I wrote."

Megan's eyes sparkled with amusement. "Oh, yeah. I can see Wynter developing a new interest. Definitely." She chuckled, carrying the tomato slices out to the picnic table.

Stan studied the photo, baffled, then tucked the phone away. He shook his head and hefted the plate of brats to follow her outside.

After the picnic, when Wynter had gone back into the RV to text friends in private and the twins had found a couple of badminton rackets, Emily handed Megan a small card. "A detective from the BPD stopped by this morning to check on the girls. Her name is on the card. Ellison, I think. Dayanna Ellison."

"What did she want with the girls?" Megan studied the card with a frown, then passed it to Philip.

"She said she was just checking on their welfare. She was worried they may have suffered some trauma from finding that dead woman in the park."

"And did they act like they were traumatized?" Stan shook his head. "Swimming and having fun in the pool?"

"That's the whole point. She could see that they seemed okay." Emily shrugged. "But she wanted you to be able to get ahold of her in case you have any questions or concerns," she said to Megan and Philip.

Philip nodded his appreciation and tucked the card into his shirt pocket.

"Hey, Philip. Give me a hand with the tent." Stan swung his leg over the picnic table bench and pushed himself to his feet.

"Tent?"

"I promised the girls a real camping experience."

"Ah. Yeah, sure."

While Emily and Megan cleared the table, Stan and Philip dumped the contents of a battered old rucksack on the ground. They surveyed the jumble of poles, stakes, and canvas from several angles.

"Got any instructions to go with this?" Philip asked.

"Don't need instructions. Done it lots of times." Stan knelt to organize the poles by length and began to assemble the frame while Philip popped open another beer for each of them.

He kicked at the pile on the ground. "How old is this thing, anyway?"

"Older than you, by the looks of it." Megan grinned, swiping at the picnic table with a wet rag.

"Your mom and I took you camping when you were little. Do you remember? We used this tent." Stan struggled to stretch the canvas out on a bare spot of ground. "Hand me a couple of those stakes." He reached for a hammer. Together he and Philip got the four corners staked out. Then they started fitting the poles into the tent's grommets.

"Hey, girls! Get over here. We need your help," Philip shouted. "Megan, grab the rope on this corner."

Stan and Philip guided the poles into position, trying to outshout one another as they commanded their tent team. Finally the tent was up, if a bit wobbly.

"Looks like the mice have made a meal of it in this corner." Philip stuck his finger through a small ragged hole in the tent roof.

"Don't make it any bigger! I'll patch it up when we get home." Stan stood back to admire their work and catch his breath.

"Have to throw it out when we get home," Emily said, walking by with an arm-load of firewood.

"You do know that today's nylon tents have poles that snap in place?" Philip jabbed at the tent again. "And are rain-proof?"

"This tent will do just fine." Stan tested a wobbly corner.

Suddenly the poles tilted and the tent began to collapse. "Oh, shit!"

Philip and Megan ran to catch the tent just before it toppled over.

"I think maybe you forgot a couple of steps," Emily laughed.

Fifteen minutes later a serviceable-looking tent sat nestled under a tall oak tree, its flaps tied back. The twins immediately claimed it as their castle.

"Grandpa, this is so cool!" Annabel poked her head out from between the flaps.

"Can we sleep in it tonight?" Allyn asked.

"As long you don't bother the bears," Philip winked at Emily.

"Bears!!!" the twins shrieked.

"I'm not sleeping in that thing," Wynter announced, flopping into a lawn chair.

"Philip! Look what you've done," Megan admonished.

"There aren't any bears here," Emily assured the girls.

"I'm just sayin'." Wynter crossed her arms.

"Let's start the campfire. We can discuss who sleeps where after we make s'mores." Stan brought out a half dozen marshmallow sticks.

"S'mores! I love s'mores!" the twins chorused, rushing out of the tent.

"What about you, Wynter? Think you can handle a s'more?" Emily asked, waving a marshmallow under the girl's nose.

Wynter shrugged. "I guess." She grabbed the marshmallow and popped it into her mouth.

"I hear bears like s'mores," Philip teased.

The twins squealed again.

"Nice, son. Nice. Way to scare your own kids." Stan slapped his son-in-law upside the back of his head as he walked by to grab another beer.

"I'm not afraid of bears, Grandpa. I'll sleep in the tent,"

Allyn declared, loading her stick with marshmallows.

"Me, too. I love sleeping in tents."

"Gramps, show them the book," Wynter slid a gooey burnt marshmallow off her stick and nibbled off the blackened sugar.

"What book is that?" Philip grabbed for Annabel's stick in time to save the marshmallow from dropping into the fire.

"Grandpa's got an original fake!" Wynter's eyes crinkled with delight. But in the next instant she shuddered. "It was that lady who died that told us about it." She told them about the visit to the Longfellow House while Stan went inside to get the book from his backpack. "She was really nice. Even when she had to tell Gramps that someone faked Longfellow's signature into the book. But you're not going to believe this…if we can find out who did it, the book might still be worth money. People actually collect forgeries from famous forgers just like they do the real thing. Isn't that crazy?"

"What's a forgery?" asked Allyn.

"When someone signs someone else's name, pretending the real person did it," Megan explained to her daughter.

"It's illegal," Philip said. "So why would anyone pay money for the fake one?"

"There have been a number of famous forgers throughout history," Stan explained. "Their work is so good, they make a name for themselves."

"But how does anyone know the real thing from the fake, if they're that good?" Megan passed the book to Philip who examined it before passing it on the little girls to take a look at with a "careful, honey, don't let it get too near the fire."

"That's the thing," Stan said. "Experts have learned to spot a forger's unique take on the handwriting of a notable figure. Sometimes the forgery is more than just a name. It can be an entire letter or a single page from an 'original'…" Here he made air quotes with his fingers. "…manuscript. There have been some very clever and famous hoaxes that whole books have been written about. There was one guy, Joseph Cosey. In the nineteen-thirties he went into business forging documents of some of America's most famous presidents—Washington, Lincoln, Jefferson, Teddy Roosevelt. The guy was so good, there are still some documents today that historians aren't sure if they are real or fakes done by him."

"How do you know all this stuff?" Philip asked.

Emily laughed. "Stan and Google are best friends."

Stan continued with his story. "He went to prison a couple of times, but still managed to make a living at it. Today people collect his work when it's been identified, and pay a pretty penny for it, too."

"That's just bizarre." Megan unwrapped a Hershey bar and slipped a chunk into her mouth. "Mmm...so good."

When the book finally came back around to Stan he flipped through the pages. "Here's something you'll find interesting, Philip. It's a receipt from Churchill's Lounge." He frowned, paging back and forth. "Did anyone see the slip of paper that was in here?" He looked at the circle of faces around the fire. Everyone shook their heads.

"Maybe the witch stole it." Annabel squashed her marshmallow and a chocolate square with two pieces of graham cracker and licked her lips.

"What witch?" Megan asked.

"The one in the pink camper with all the cats."

"Someone took their cats camping?" her mother said.

"Why would a witch steal a cigar store receipt?" Wynter asked.

"Maybe she needed it for a special potion. Or a magic spell." Allyn waved her hands in the air, casting her own spell over the flames of the fire.

"Or maybe I lost it on the train on the way home," Stan said.

Allyn shrugged and bit into her own gooey s'more.

"It's likely in the bottom of your backpack," Emily suggested. "Megan, what time did you want to meet your dad in the morning?"

"The change ringers start their practice at eleven. We should be there a few minutes early to meet Roger. You think you can find your way to the Old North Church by yourself?" she asked Stan, yawning.

"I've got the GPS on my phone. I'll be fine."

She nodded at her dad and patted Philip on the arm. "We'd better hit the road. It's getting late and I can barely keep my eyes open."

The moon was just poking its head above the trees when Stan got up to stoke the fire. The heat hit him in the face as the embers flared into flames, sending sparks skyward. "Did I tell you the one about the ghost ship?" He saw the little girls slumped over in their camp chairs.

"I think that's one for tomorrow night," Emily said.

The girls had loved sitting up late around the campfire listening to their grandfather tell ghost stories, but even Stan could see that he'd worn them out. The twins sleepily took turns brushing their teeth in the RV's tiny bathroom, then crawled into the tent and snuggled into their sleeping bags.

"Grandpa, there aren't really any bears here, are there?" Annabel asked.

"No, dear. No bears. Go to sleep. I'll see you in the morning."

Stan zipped the tent closed against late roaming mosquitos. He and Emily and Wynter sat out under the stars, watching the fire burn itself out.

"So, what's it going to be, Wynter?" Emily asked. "The RV or the tent?"

Wynter sighed dramatically. "Someone has to protect the little girls. What if bears *do* come around?" She winked at her grandfather in conspiracy and took herself off to the tent.

In the RV Stan stretched out on the bed until Emily had finished up in the bathroom, then he curled his body around hers and spooned her. Her soft snoring lulled him to sleep.

A scream ripped Stan from his dream. He sat bolt upright.

CHAPTER 9

STAN sprang out of bed and raced toward the door, Emily on his heels. The three girls tumbled through the door, pillows in hand and flashlights waving wildly, and threw themselves at their grandparents.

"There's something out there!" Allyn wailed.

"It's a bear!" Annabel cried.

"It's not a bear," Wynter insisted. The beam from her flashlight hit Stan square in the eyes and he flinched, ducking away. "But there *is* something. I'm *not* going back out there."

"Grandma, can I sleep in your bed?" Allyn asked.

"Me, too!" Annabel cried.

Emily looked at Stan.

"Okay…okay. I'll sleep in the tent. The girls can sleep in here with you."

As Emily settled Annabel and Allyn into the big bed, he pulled out the dinette hide-a-bed for Wynter to sleep on. "Give me your flashlight," he said to the girl, then stomped out of the RV.

Groaning, he bent to crawl into the tent. His knees creaked. Clearly they were not made for this anymore. The flashlight beam bounced erratically off the canvas walls as he settled himself onto one of the too-short sleeping bags. Good thing it was a warm night and he didn't need it to sleep in it.

"Aw, shit." He rolled to avoid the lump in the ground that pressed against his shoulder. His back muscles cramped in protest. Finally, after more readjusting he fell fitfully asleep…only to be jarred awake by a flash that lit up the inside of the tent and a loud boom that rumbled on and on. Another flash and Stan threw his arm over his eyes. Then came the patter of rain, which quickly escalated into a torrent. A drop of water splashed on his chin. He opened one eye. With the next flash of lightning he could see water dripping from the mouse hole. Grumbling, he rolled to the far side of the tent, hoping the storm wouldn't last long. But now the water began to pool on the floor of the tent.

Stan grabbed his pillow, unzipped the flap, and crawled out. Lightning lit up the sky again as, pillow in arm, he dashed for the RV. *Damn!* The door was locked. *Why did they do that?* He stood under the awning in his t-shirt and boxers, holding his wet pillow. He banged on the bedroom window until Emily finally poked her head out the front door.

"What are you doing out here in the rain?" she asked.

"Checking to make sure the fire is out," he snarled, pushing past her.

A beam of sunlight hit Stan smack in the face. It took him a moment to figure out where he was—lying on the passenger seat of the RV which was pushed all the way into a reclining position. Someone—must have been Emily—had covered him with a blanket. He groaned. His back hurt worse than ever. And that damned sun! Where were the storm clouds when you needed them?

He climbed off the seat and stumbled back toward the bathroom. Wynter was still snoring softy on the dinette bed. In the bedroom, the twins sprawled across the queen size bed. Where was Emily? *Oh! that smells good. Coffee.* A movement out the window caught his eye. There she was, already under the awning, coffee cup in hand, greeting the growing parade of fellow campers on their way to the public bathrooms. Arching his sore back, Stan relished squeezing into his own private bathroom, tiny as it was.

A short while later he emerged from the RV with his cup of coffee, a roll of duct tape in the other hand.

"Well, look what the sunshine brought out," Emily teased. "What's that for?"

Stan set his hot mug down on the corner of the picnic table. "Patch those holes in the tent. Not sleeping in the co-pilot's chair again tonight." He unzipped the flap of the tent and tied it back. "Who knows, maybe I can convince the girls to try it again if I sleep in there with them."

"The twins maybe. Wynter…not likely. I think she's already made up her mind she's going to be a full-timer when she grows up."

"Likes RV life that much, huh?"

"Today she does. We'll see what tomorrow brings."

Grunting he crawled into the tent and around a small puddle on the floor. He bit a notch into a small stretch of the tape, then ripped the piece off. Thankfully the canvas had already dried in the morning sun. He stuck the tape up across the small hole and smoothed it tight. He patched three more similar holes before he was done.

A few moments later, sitting with his coffee, he saw two sleepy-eyed girls emerge from the RV.

"Good morning, sweet ones," Emily said.

"Morning, Grandma. Hi, Grandpa," Allyn said.

Annabel just waved sleepily.

"Think you could eat some pancakes?"

Both girls nodded and settled into lawn chairs near their grandparents.

"Wynter's still sleeping," Allyn announced.

"Teenagers have a different internal clock than the rest of us," Stan said.

"What's an internal clock?"

"It's what gets you up in the morning when the sun doesn't do the trick."

"Do I have an internal alarm clock?"

"You're up, aren't you?"

Allyn nodded.

Stan patted her on the shoulder then went into the RV to make the pancakes. By the time he had them ready, Wynter had finally stumbled off the hide-a-bed in a morning stupor.

"Good morning, Sunshine," he addressed his granddaughter.

Wynter grunted and plodded back toward the bathroom.

Outside Stan set the platter of pancakes on the picnic table. Wynter joined them a few minutes later, still in her pajamas.

"Can we swim again today?" Annabel poured enough syrup onto her plate to drown an ant farm.

"That's what you're here for, isn't it?" Stan checked his phone for the time. "But you'll have to do it with Grandma. I'm meeting your mother in the city to see the change ringing at the Old North Church today." He stood up to take his empty plate into the RV.

Allyn blurted out, "Hey! Where are my goggles?"

"I don't know, honey," Emily answered, gathering the rest of the dishes. "Where did you leave them?"

"Right here on the picnic table."

"Are you sure? Maybe they're in the RV. Oh, Stan, don't forget your camera."

"I set them out here before we went to bed in the tent." Allyn balled her fists at her hips and glared at the others. "And my towel's gone!"

Stan's gaze followed her pointed finger to the clothesline he'd strung from a straggly pine to the back of the RV. The girls had hung their swimsuits and towels out the night before to dry before the storm came and doused them again.

"Maybe the wind blew it," he said. "Sorry, but I've got to get a move on if I'm going to catch the train. Emily, where did you say the camera is?"

"It didn't blow anyone else's towel." Allyn stomped her foot.

"Check the closet in the bedroom."

"Maybe someone stole it," Wynter suggested.

"And your goggles," Annabel added.

Allyn pouted. "How am I going to swim?" she demanded.

Stan shrugged at Emily and stepped up into the RV. He was sorry to leave her with this problem, but he had no interest in solving any more mysteries.

Emily dozed on the chaise lounge in the shade of the awning and swatted at the occasional mosquito buzzing across her face. She could hear the thwump of the badminton rackets as the twins hit the shuttlecock. The day had become hot and muggy, and that refreshing feeling of having been in the pool all morning was wearing off. Allyn had been somewhat placated by a new pair of swim goggles and a towel purchased from the camp store.

"Cut it out!"

She opened one eye to see Wynter sitting at the picnic table, thumbing her phone and glaring at her sisters. The birdie had apparently just hit her on the head and she held it in her hand.

"Give it back," Allyn shouted.

Wynter tossed the shuttlecock over her shoulder, causing Allyn to scramble to fetch it. A few moments later the birdie flew back over the picnic table, this time bonking Emily's head. She groaned. Just then her phone trilled.

"Sorry, Grandma." Annabel picked up the shuttlecock and headed back out to the road, sticking her tongue out at Wynter on the way.

"Hello?" Emily rubbed her head as she spoke into the phone. "Hello...?" She held the phone away from her for a moment and squinted at the small screen to see who was calling. "Stan? Are you there? Hello?" No one answered, but she could hear Stan in his lecture voice. And other odd sounds, like footfalls on a wooden floor, or maybe stairs. She stared at the phone again, in confusion. "Stan! Are you there?" she shouted. When he didn't answer, she gave up and flipped the phone closed. Must be pocket dialing, she thought. She looked up just in time to duck another wayward birdie.

The next time the shuttlecock hit Wynter on the head, the teenager jumped up from the bench and started toward the younger girls. They screeched and ran around to the side of the RV. Wynter gave up and stalked into the vehicle, slamming the door behind her. The twins began a game of batting the birdie over the top of the RV. But most of the time it landed on the roof, and the girls scrambled in delight up the back ladder to retrieve it.

Emily dozed again, but something woke her up. It wasn't a noise. In fact, it was the absence of noise. The twins were quiet. Too quiet. Emily sat up and glanced around. Where were they? A giggle floated down from above. She shaded her eyes to see the girls lying on their stomachs on the top of the RV. Annabel was peering through Stan's binoculars. Emily swiveled to see what they were spying on. The pink camper truck. A plump little woman with frizzled hair—a god-awful shade of red—and dressed in a brightly colored Jamaican-style sundress stepped out the door carrying a small plastic garbage bag that bulged and sagged at the bottom. A swarm of cats scurried behind her.

A flurry of whispers from the top of the RV caught Emily's attention. "There she is!" "It's the witch!" "What's in the bag?" "Dead cats!" "My swim goggles."

Oh for goodness sake! "Get down here, you two," Emily ordered.

"Hi, there!" came a fluttery voice from the next site.

Emily saw the woman smiling and waving at her. She gave a little wave back, then decided to do the polite thing and go over and meet her neighbor.

By now the girls had scrambled down the ladder and Emily signaled for them to follow her.

"Hello. I'm Emily Remington."

"Kitty litter." The plump little woman shifted the bag from her right to her left to shake Emily's outstretched hand. "In the bag. Not my name! Oh, dear. I hope you didn't think… Alvina Pendergast is my name. But everyone calls me Vinie. I'm on my way to the dumpster."

Emily laughed. "And these are my granddaughters. Annabel and Allyn."

She turned, but the girls, standing behind her, shifted with her, trying to avoid direct contact with "the witch." Emily grimaced. "Girls, say hello."

"Hi," they mumbled.

"Oh, dearies, look who came to visit," Vinie cooed at the cats swarming around her legs. "I told you someone would come by to sample the cookies we baked this morning."

Their eyes wide, the twins shoved and pushed trying to hide behind each other. Emily flushed, her face reddening under her light brown freckles.

"Children are such delights. Come along, dearies." Vinie headed down the road to the camp dumpster, four cats following, their tails held high. A fifth cat jumped up onto the picnic table, licked its bottom and pointedly ignored Emily.

"I told you she's a witch!" Allyn said in a loud whisper.

"Allyn!" Emily chastised.

"Who else would travel with so many cats?" Annabel defended her sister.

"She's not a witch, and it's unkind of you to say so." Emily scooped up the long-abandoned shuttlecock and tossed it to Annabel. "Where are the rackets?"

"I'm tired of that game," Allyn pouted. "And Annabel cheats anyway."

"I do not."

"Do too."

"Do not."

"Okay. Stop! How about some lemonade?" Before the girls could answer, Emily's phone began to trill. She flipped it open. "Hello? Hello…? Stan? Are you there?" But all she could hear was a clamor of bells clanging in the background." Emily rolled her eyes. She shut the ringer off in disgust, and said to the girls. "So how about that lemonade?"

Annabel nodded. Allyn shrugged, peering down the road searching for the woman in the rainbow dress. "I bet she stole my stuff," she said under her breath.

CHAPTER 10

STAN inhaled deeply and breathed in the aroma of old wood and varnish. He could smell the very history of the place. Walking up the center aisle of the Old North Church, he ran his hand along the whitewashed wood of the boxed pews. In front of the sanctuary, he surveyed the altar and the raised pulpit from which sermons had been delivered for almost three hundred years.

He gazed in delight at the same radiant scene that Paul Revere had gazed upon at the dawn of American history—towering brass pipes of the organ, pillars gleaming in streams of sunlight from arched windows, the old wooden clock hanging on the gallery wall above the center aisle. He compared the time on his phone with that of the old timepiece. The idea that this very clock had been keeping time since the days of the American Revolution tickled his fancy.

"I know what you're grinning about." It was Megan coming in the front door. "You can't believe you're looking at the same clock Paul Revere set his watch by." She kissed him on the cheek.

Stan stuck his cell phone into his back pocket and gave it an unconscious pat. "Hey, if we hurry, we can get in on a tour of the crypt. We're a little early for the change ringing anyway, right?"

"Sure. Whatever you like. Let's go get tickets."

Five minutes later they joined a small group of people tromping down a flight of worn wooden stairs, bowed in the middle from centuries of footfalls.

"I understand a funerary archaeologist from the Peabody Museum over at Harvard did some work down here not too long ago," Stan commented to the crowd in general.

"A *funerary* archaeologist?" Megan questioned.

"That's someone who specializes in burial rituals and customs," their guide said after identifying herself as Ellen Merriweather. She was a fiftyish woman whose stylish bob had already gone completely silver grey. Trim and athletic looking, wearing khaki capris, a beaded peasant top, and cross-trainers, she more easily navigated the creaky old steps than Stan did. "In the case of our crypt, that was a most appropriate sort of researcher. She learned that there have been over a thousand bodies buried down here. Watch your head, folks, this first beam is rather low."

"A thousand bodies?" Megan shuddered.

"They would be mostly bones now," Stan ducked to avoid the beam.

Entering the main tunnel with the small group, he breathed in the cold, dank air. The roughly mortared brick walls were littered with recessed name plates which indicated the final resting places of people who'd lived and died long ago. He noted a sense of timelessness. Other than the ductwork, it was the original ceiling. Holes in the brickwork had not been touched. He ducked again to avoid the low hanging boiler pipes. The constant creaking and groaning of footsteps above their heads provided an eerie backdrop to their exploration.

"Samuel Nicholson, Captain Continental Line, Revolutionary war 1743 to 1811," he read aloud from a polished plaque.

"Some of these crypts look newer," a young woman said,

"like they've been more recently plastered over."

"They have been," Ellen said. "The original tomb doors were made of wood. Over the years they've rotted away. Apparently the bones were literally spilling into the tunnel corridors at one point."

Megan clutched Stan's arm, startling him. He was amused to see her shuffling her feet as if to avoid ghostly debris. He touched her hand.

"It was all swept up long ago," he reassured her.

"Workers in the early 1900's," continued their guide, "put the bones back into the tombs and sealed them with concrete."

"Oh, Dad. Look! Here's one from 1742! Ann Ruggles. " Megan ran her fingers along a dusty, faded nameplate.

"Oh, please don't touch," Ellen chastised.

"Must have been pretty important to be buried here under this church," a man at the back of the group said.

"Surprisingly, no," Ellen responded. "People buried in the Old North Church came from all walks of life. Of course, if you were rich and prominent, you got a better location."

"Better location, but still not a better view," Stan commented.

"But less likely to be found lying in the halls a century later." Ellen pointed at a brass plaque. "Take a look at this one."

"Strangers Tomb—1813," Megan read.

"Each of the tombs down here contains anywhere from thirty to fifty bodies," Ellen informed them. "A surprising number were infants. And of course there are many Revolutionary War veterans. It wasn't uncommon for someone of standing to purchase a tomb and then invite his friends or old army buddies to be buried along with him and his family."

"Oh, man. It's one thing being tight with your family and friends..." Megan began.

"And another to spend all eternity walled in with them,"

Stan finished her sentence.

Ellen chuckled and motioned the group toward the next plaque. Before long—all too soon in Stan's view—the tour was over and they climbed back up the winding stairs to the foyer.

"Thank you so much," Stan shook Ellen's hand. "That was one of the most unique tours I've taken."

"And one of the creepiest." Megan shuddered again. She checked her watch. "Roger should be here by now. We were supposed to meet in the foyer."

"I wonder if he forgot and is already up in the bell tower?" Stan suggested

"Let's go up and see. I think we've been around enough dead bodies for one day."

"Will you girls just sit down for two minutes?" Emily pleaded.

The twins had been shrieking and arguing non-stop for the past hour and a half. If they ran in and out of the RV one more time, she was going to lose it. And now her head was throbbing in the heat. She could only imagine what the neighbors thought. She'd give anything if she could have taken them back to the pool, but it had closed temporarily because of problems with the drain cover.

"Grandma! Annabel tried to kick me."

"Did not!"

"Did too!"

"Stop!" Emily stood between the two girls, who danced around her trying to ankle kick each other. "How about a game of Crazy Eights?"

"Yeah!"

The girls pushed and vied with one another to be the one to sit next to their grandmother at the picnic table. Once she'd settled who would sit where, she tried to entice Wynter, who decided she was too cool to play with the younger ones.

After she poured them all glasses of lemonade, Emily shuffled and dealt the cards. Finally! The two little girls sat quietly, studying their cards and making plays. Emily relaxed, enjoying the game. But, fifteen minutes later Allyn accused Annabel of cheating, and the game ended in scattered cards and tears.

"And that's why I won't play cards with them." Wynter, in the chaise lounge in the shade of an old maple tree, popped her bubble gum without taking her eyes from her phone.

Emily sent both girls to sit at opposite ends of the campsite, but she knew that short reprieve wasn't going to last. She had to do something. And soon. Her own nerves were on edge and she considered taking a good brisk walk—alone. But she didn't dare leave the girls without supervision.

She stood in the shade of the awning and stretched, flexing her back muscles. In the forced silence of their campsite, Emily could hear the buzzing whine of summer cicadas—more evidence of the building heat. Bending over, she reached down to touch her toes. The tendons in her back ached from underuse and too much sitting in the passenger seat of the RV. What she would give for a session with Dana Kim, her Tae kwon do instructor. Wait. She stopped in the middle of a thigh stretch. That's what these girls needed. Something active but disciplined. She wondered if they would go for it.

"Allyn! Annabel! Get over here!" she yelled. The twins came running, happy to be freed from their time out. "Wynter! You, too." The teenager looked up from the chaise lounge.

"We're starting a physical fitness project," Emily announced. Wynter rolled her eyes and pointedly ignored her grandmother. "Okay, then." Emily said to the twins. "A very special physical fitness project. Have you ever heard of Tae kwon do?"

"My friend Jeremy takes it. He has a yellow belt," Annabel said.

"Yellow is good. But you start by first earning a white belt. How would you like to work toward earning a white belt?"

"Really?" Allyn jumped up and down with excitement. "How do we do it?"

"You stand here with your two feet together, like this." Emily positioned them under the awning and demonstrated the stance. "Put your hands together like this, and bow to your *sabumnin*."

"What's a *sabumnin*?" Annabel asked.

"I am a *sabumnin*. Your teacher." Emily bowed toward the girls. They clapped their hands together and bowed back. "Now we stretch, to loosen our muscles." She reached up, and the girls followed her lead, reaching their arms skyward.

One after another, hands stretched upward grabbing thickly twined ropes. Firmly, deliberately the ringers pulled them downward. Over their heads the giant bells, unseen high in the steeple tower, pealed and reverberated in a cadenced clamor. The deep rhythmic clanging resonated throughout Stan's entire body.

Mesmerized, he leaned against the wall of the ringing room in the Old North Church and observed the circle of change ringers reaching, tugging, letting the ropes slip back through their hands, then reaching, tugging, ringing again…and again…and again… How could someone so small as the woman in purple, standing on a wooden box, manage those huge bells so seemingly effortlessly? And how did each of the ringers know when to pull on the red and black woolen sallies wound around the ropes to keep the pattern going? He had heard the bells from outdoors the day he and Emily took the girls on the Freedom Tour. But this…this was a visceral experience he'd never imagined.

He put his arm around Megan and gave her shoulder a squeeze. "Thank you," he mouthed. His daughter smiled back at him, but a slight frown creased her forehead.

"Okay, people. Stop! Stop! Stop!" A tall gangly man waved his hand to get the attention of the ringers. "Miranda, *feel* the rhythm. Don't look at the ropes." He spoke to an elderly woman, who sheepishly apologized for her lapse of concentration.

He then turned to the half dozen people, Stan and Megan included, most of them sitting on benches along the walls of the ringing chamber and introduced himself as Obadiah Garde, the Ringing Master and Master of the Steeple. Megan smirked at Stan and raised her eyebrows at the nomenclature. Stan gave her a look that said, *don't be snooty*.

Stan estimated the Ringing Master was well over six feet tall. Overly thin, but sinewy, Garde wore his graying hair tied back into a pony tail, a throwback to the hippy days of the 1960's. In contrast, his eyebrows were so perfectly shaped that Stan wondered if the man plucked them. His gray slacks were precisely pressed and his white dress shirt lacked only the requisite tie. The man's sleeves were carefully rolled to just below his elbows, so that Stan could see the muscles in his forearms ripple as he grasped his bell rope. More of a caress. Even after five full minutes of non-stop reaching, tugging, reaching, tugging in the hot, stuffy upper room, Garde had barely broken a sweat.

"Where's Roger?" Miranda asked.

Garde's jaw tightened. "Late again, one would assume. Luckily Brandon here has rung before and agreed to step in." He nodded toward a young man in cut-off jeans and Boston University t-shirt. "Okay people, let's try it again,"

"Look to!" the short woman in purple called out as she yanked on the tail end of her rope, then grabbed for the sally. "Treble's going...she's gone!" One by one the others grabbed their ropes and picked up the rhythm, the bells ringing again in a cascade of sound.

Megan leaned toward Stan, puzzled, and shouted into his ear, "Rhea said he would meet us here to give us a tour of the steeple afterward. I can't imagine why he's late."

Stan shrugged his shoulders. "Sounds like promptness isn't his strong suit," he shouted back, his voice almost lost in the clamor of the bells.

"Four after two!" Garde called out. The sequence of the tones shifted subtly as the ringers changed the order of the bells, keeping up a steady, if occasionally uneven rhythm. "Five after three." The tolling struck an unexpectedly somber chord in Stan's heart and he blinked to hold back tears.

Emily was relieved; she had finally managed to harness the unbridled energy of her twin granddaughters and get the much needed workout she'd been craving without even realizing it.

"Tae kwon do—any martial arts—is about focus, energy, and attitude," she explained. "You've proven you have the required energy. What we need to work on is the focus and attitude."

"When do we learn to kick?" Allyn twirled her arms and ran in place, copying her grandmother's fluid moves.

"We'll get to that. Be patient, young grasshopper." Emily said. "We start with a warm-up, stretching to limber up our muscles."

"Grasshopper? That's Grandpa's secret word!" Annabel exclaimed.

"Now let's do some jumping jacks."

"I'm good at jumping jacks!" Allyn launched into a clumsy, hopscotchy bounce, arms flailing. But before long, she found her rhythm and her arms and legs began to move in sync.

"Looks like you girls found a nice shady spot for a workout!" The voice came from a young woman strolling with her friend past the campsite.

"We're learning Tae kwon do!" Allyn bragged.

"Really?" The two women stopped. "I have a green belt, and Amy here has just started to earn her white belt. I'm Tara.

Do you think we could join you? I'm aching to get my body moving and the pool's closed."

"Be my guest!" Emily indicated that they should take a spot under the awning. "The more the merrier." As she guided the small troupe through their workout, Emily counted the beats, the metallic humming of the cicadas providing accompaniment.

The last of the reverberations left a humming in Stan's ears as the change ringers stepped away from their bells to end their practice session. The small crowd of observers thanked Obadiah Garde and the other ringers, then started down the creaky old stairs.

"I'm so disappointed Roger didn't show up," Megan said to Obadiah. "Dad came out all the way from Michigan. He's a historian. Roger was going to give him a tour of the bells and the steeple."

"Of course. Yes. I can see that would be rather irksome." The bell master wound the tail end of his rope into a loose knot. "I suppose *I* could show you around. Would you like to try one of the bells for yourself first?"

"You mean, try pulling the rope?" Stan gazed up to where the ropes disappeared into their own individual collared holes in the ceiling.

"Sure, try this one," he motioned Stan over to one of the ropes. It's the Treble D. A midweight bell. You," he indicated Megan, "can try, too, if you like."

"Awesome! I've always wanted to do this." Megan eagerly took her place at a rope next to Stan's. The Treble C, Garde told her. Father and daughter grinned at one another at this unexpected opportunity.

Garde positioned himself in front of the two novices. "So! You start by holding onto the tail end of your rope. Hold on firmly now." He reached both arms out, one hand on the striped sally wound around Stan's rope, the other on Megan's.

First he gave Stan's sally a great heave, and the bell above them began its swing. The rope rose high, Stan's hands and arms rising with it. Once the rope reached its peak, Obadiah's hand slid down to just above where Stan held it, and he gave what seemed like a gentle tug. Stan suspected the motion carried far more force than it appeared to. A moment later the bell rang out. Swiftly Obadiah grasped the sally as it came within reach, then he tugged again. To Stan's amazement, with his other hand Obadiah reached for Megan's rope and sally to get her bell going—the man had the arm span of a condor. Soon the bells were clanging.

"Okay, now," Obadiah said to Stan, "Keep the tail end in one hand, and grab for the sally with both hands and pull. Don't let go of that tail end!"

Stan heaved the sally down, surprised at the effort it took.

"Don't look up."

"Why can't I look up?" Stan asked.

Just then a small bit of plaster and dust trickled down from the ceiling and hit him in the eye. Stan blinked, let go of the sally to the wipe the debris from his face. The rope bobbed wildly before Stan could catch it again.

"That's why," Obadiah said sonorously.

Soon Stan and Megan were handling their ropes independently, and their bells rang in opposition to each other. Stan was delighted to be allowed to ring one of the very bells that Paul Revere had rung so many years ago. He wondered if the neighbors even noticed this impromptu ringing session right after the scheduled practice.

"That's good, that's good!" Obadiah motioned for them to stop. As the bells came to rest, Stan and Megan both found themselves rubbing their arms and rolling their shoulder muscles. How did the regular ringers do this for an entire practice session?

"Now that you've got a feel for it, would you like to go further up into the tower and see the bells for yourself? It's a bit of a climb, I must warn you."

Megan grinned at her dad. "I'm guessing wild horses couldn't keep him out of that steeple."

"Then it's onward and upward." Obadiah led them to a set of exposed steps at the far end of the ringing room.

"Am I correct that these are the oldest bells in North America?" Stan asked.

"The oldest and perhaps the sweetest sounding. They were cast in Gloucester, England in 1744." Obadiah took on the same professorial tone that Megan had heard Stan use many times before. "They were hung the following year. In fact, they have tolled the death of every U.S. president since George Washington died in 1799. Here's something you'll be interested in. He pointed to a framed document on the wall. The date on the document was 1750. "It's a charter, creating the ringers' guild."

"Megan! Look at this signature, the second one down!" Stan's heart fluttered.

"Paul Revere?"

"He was fifteen when he signed that," Obadiah informed them. "The church supposedly spent so much on the bells and transporting and installing them they couldn't afford to hire ringers, so Mr. Revere organized a group to solve the problem."

"Well, I'll be. This isn't an original, is it?"

"Heavens no," Obadiah laughed. "That's kept at the Massachusetts Historical Society, my good man."

As he led the way up the creaky steps—two flights that were appreciably steeper and darker than those leading up to the ringing chamber—Obadiah explained that the largest of the bells, the tenor, weighed three quarters of a ton. The lightest, the treble, only 500 pounds.

"I can't even wrap my mind around those sizes," Megan said as they rounded the corner and approached yet another flight of stairs that took them to the giant bells hanging on their fly wheels in the shadows of the platform. "Whew! Did something die up here?" She put a finger under her nose.

"Likely a bat." Stan had noticed the faint fetid odor as well but chose to ignore it.

"Bats have always been a problem up here," Obadiah waved his hand dismissively. "They're a nuisance."

Bats in the belfry, Stan mused.

After admiring the huge bells, they continued up yet another set of increasingly steeper, almost ladder-like steps, these obviously more recently constructed than the ones below.

"Are you doing okay?" Obadiah asked.

Stan had stopped half-way up to catch his breath.

"Fine. I'm fine." He waved them on. But when their backs were turned he grabbed for his handkerchief and swiped it across his brow. Glancing back at the bells in their casings, he hoped there was no one downstairs who might decide to avail themselves of an impromptu ringing session. He grasped the sides of the steps, sucked in a deep breath, and started up again behind his daughter and the bell master.

"This portion of the steeple is not the original," Obadiah told them at the next landing. "The original steeple was destroyed in a storm in 1804. A new one was designed by Charles Bullfinch. But a hundred and fifty years later that one was destroyed by Hurricane Carol. That was 1954. They were able to salvage the original weathervane, however, and that sits atop the current steeple."

Two more flights through the gloom of the dimly lit steeple, then on the last set of steps—had they climbed eight flights from the ground? Stan wondered, pausing yet again to catch his breath—they could feel wind playing through the slatted walls, and there was daylight again. At the top, they found themselves in a small, but bright room with four arched windows, one on each wall.

"Oh, my gosh, Dad! Look at that view!" Megan exclaimed.

Stan followed her gaze out over the expanse of Boston, the harbor, the Charles River with its iconic bridge. For a moment they stood together in speechless silence.

Then Megan pointed up, "Are these the real ones?"

Two dusty lanterns hung above the window.

"You mean the one-if-by-land, two-if-by-sea lanterns?" Obadiah shook his head. "No. These are replicas we keep for tourists."

"That was Longfellow's version," Stan cut in.

"Version? You mean…it didn't happen that way?" Megan asked.

"Your father is correct. Unlike in the famous Longfellow poem, the British weren't marching on Boston as people generally think," Obadiah said.

"What *were* they doing?"

Stan reached out and touched the cool glass of the north-facing window. "They were searching for weapons."

"Weapons? As in…?"

"Guns, ammunition," Obadiah filled in. "Over in Salem and up in the back country of New Hampshire. Of course, it wasn't called New Hampshire then."

Stan picked up the story, echoing their guide's professorial tone. "The Royal Government knew a rebellion was in the offing. They had sent troops to confiscate weapons that the resistance had stashed away in their barns and under haystacks. Revere and his buddies—the Sons of Liberty—had been out riding, warning the locals ahead of the British troops. Did a pretty good job of thwarting the redcoats. General Gage, the commander, was determined to—"

"Oh man! Look at that giant sailboat coming into the harbor!"

Both men leaned to see what she was pointing at. Garde eyed his watch.

"I'm sorry, but we'll have to go now. I have to close up the ringing chamber. I hope you enjoyed the little tour."

Stan nodded. "Almost as good as the crypt." At Garde's horrified look he quickly amended, "Kidding! Just kidding. This has been phenomenal! Thank you."

The threesome backed down the topmost flight of steep

steps, then down the next two flights to the bells platform.

"That's odd…" Obadiah stepped around one of the giant bell wheels.

Stan and Megan followed his gaze. Something dangled from a thick beam in the shadow of the bells. Something large. It was difficult to make it out because of the play of light and shadows, but it appeared to be about the size of a—

"My god!" the bell master breathed out in a ragged rasp.

Megan gasped at the exact same instant, put her hands to her mouth and fought the urge to scream.

CHAPTER 11

"THAT was an awesome workout!" Tara said, reaching for the glass of iced tea Emily had offered. "Thank you so much for letting us join you. Any chance you'll do it again tomorrow?" The three adults sat at the picnic table.

"Stop on by. If we're here, I'm happy to lead another session. What do you think girls?"

The twins clapped and shouted their agreement.

"I love Tae kwon do!" Allyn took her stance and kicked out.

"Nope," Emily chastised her. "Only during practice sessions. If I see either of you using moves just to show off…"

"…you won't ask mommy and daddy if we can join a Tae kwon do school," Annabel finished her sentence.

"They won't let you anyway," Wynter said snidely from her lounge under the maple tree.

"Will too," Allyn countered.

"Will not."

"Let's wait and see." Emily interrupted the argument before it could gain ground. "Are you RVing? Or tent camping?" she asked her guests.

"Tent. We came up on my Harley."

"Harley? I used to ride one. Gave it up when my back went out. Where are you from?"

"Just north of Philly," Amy replied. "Tara is a speech therapist and I'm a teacher. That's why we have the summer off. Our site is just down around that corner." She pointed down the road.

"I'm so glad you stopped by," Emily said as they got up to leave. "Like I said, stop in again tomorrow." Then she checked the time. "Wynter, have you heard anything from your mother or Grandpa?"

"I texted Mumsy twice. She's not texting back." Wynter set up a pout at the slight from her mother.

"Hmm…all I get are pocket dialed voice mails." Emily checked her own phone.

"Gramps butt dials you? Gross."

"Not *gross. Just annoying. When he's distracted, your grandfather doesn't pay much attention to details like his phone."

"Yeah, I've seen that look on his face."

Emily nodded. "Like he's in seventh heaven."

"Dear god in heaven!"

Stan fought the urge to gag, his brain refusing to make sense of the figure dangling in front of them. A morbid chill ran down his spine, and he instinctively and protectively reached out to Megan just as she thrust herself, sobbing, into his arms.

"Who…?" he asked Obadiah in a hushed voice.

But the older man sagged in horrified shock against a nearby support post, unable to speak.

"Roger," Megan managed to say between sobs. "It's…it's Roger."

"I think I'm going to be sick." Obadiah Garde swayed precariously.

Stan took a deep breath, one arm still around Megan, her

shoulders heaving. He fingered the keyboard of his cell phone awkwardly with his other hand, to press 911.

"Hello. Yes. There's been a…there's a…a body. Dead. I think. Must be. He's…please, send someone. Quickly. The Old North Church. Up in the bell tower. Stan. Stanford Remington. No. I'm quite sure he's dead. Yes, please hurry." He tightened his arm around his now shivering daughter. "They're coming," he said to her and Obadiah. "The police."

"I have to go," the man said. "I'm going to—" he began to gag.

"Megan, honey. Take Mr. Garde downstairs. Okay?"

"And leave you alone? With…?"

"I'll be okay. I'm calling your mother." He punched buttons as he spoke. Put the phone back up to his ear, only to hear it kick in to her voice mail. "Damn."

"Your mother?" Obadiah covered his mouth with his handkerchief.

"It's okay," Megan assured him. "She's a police officer. Was. She's used to…she knows what to do."

By now Garde was beginning to hyperventilate.

"Take him downstairs. Show the police where to come. And wait for your mother. Go. Now." He punched more numbers into the phone.

Megan nodded and took the discombobulated bell master by the elbow and gently pushed him toward the stairs. "Let's go. The police will be here soon."

Already Stan could hear the siren in the distance.

"Wynter, let me talk to your grandmother," Stan said into the phone. "Emily. Thank God. Something horrible has happened. We're at the Old North Church. Up in the bell tower. We found Roger. He's…he's…Emily, he's dead!"

Emily stepped out of the taxi and into the throng of sight-seers and locals crowding the newly established perimeter in front of the nearly three-hundred-year old church. Yellow crime scene tape stretched across the wrought iron fence in front of the church and fluttered in the slight breeze. Three different news teams vied for position, their on-air reporters gesticulating for the cameras to make sure the Old North Church was directly behind them.

Emily had put in a call to Philip at his office, and he had agreed to leave work early and go out to the campground. Wynter assured her grandmother that she could handle the twins until her father got there. Philip made Emily promise that she would call him again as soon as she knew what was going on. Then she found Tara and Amy, and Tara agreed to take her to the train station on the Harley. From there she took a cab into the city.

Now she surveyed the half-dozen police officers positioned to keep the curious out and any suspects in. Five of them were men of various ages; one was a woman in her mid-thirties. Emily walked past the woman and approached the officer she judged to be the youngest of the set.

"Can you help me?" she asked. "It's my husband in there."

"Your husband?"

"They told me to see a Detective...," Emily bluffed. "Sorry, I don't remember the name."

"Ellison?"

A lucky coincidence, Emily thought. "Yes. That's what they said. Detective Dayanna Ellison."

"Just a moment." He leaned his head and spoke into his shoulder radio. "I've got the vic's wife here. You want I should tell her to wait? Got that. Ten four." But before he could relay the order to Emily, she had already ducked under the yellow tape and was hurrying toward the red doors.

"Ma'am!"

Emily didn't stop. She dashed into the building before the officer could react.

Inside the whitewashed foyer, she stopped to get her bearings. An empty gurney stood sentinel in the small entryway. A bump and a thump from the stairwell caused her to turn just as a short, chunky man stepped awkwardly backward down the stairs, holding up one end of a zippered white plastic bag the length of a man—a dead man. A second man, tall and slender, held up the other end with clenched fists. He lumbered even more awkwardly than his cohort as he fumbled to negotiate the last of the steps and the corner just before the foyer. Emily wondered how it was that the taller of the two had gotten the short end of the job, as it were.

Together, with grunts of relief they hefted the body bag onto the gurney. Once the bag had been secured with straps, the tall man arched his back to work the kinks out and catch his breath. "Son of a—"

"Gentlemen?"

Emily swiveled toward the female voice. Detective Ellison pushed through the set of double doors from the sanctuary of the church. The police woman stopped cold when she saw Emily.

"Who let you in?"

"I understand it was my husband who found the body. And my daughter."

The short, chunky guy ignored Emily and spoke to the detective. "Do you want one last look before we take him out to the van?"

The detective gave Emily a chagrined look, but nodded at the men. Short 'n Chunky reached over and unzipped the body bag to about shoulder length. Emily supposed the detective had already been up in the bell tower and had had a good look at the body and the scene before letting anyone move it. She wished she had arrived in time to go up also, though she doubted she'd have been allowed anywhere near the actual spot where Roger's body was found. She also knew that the detective wasn't about to let the body bag leave the premises without first confirming the body inside was indeed the body found in the bell tower.

Emily stepped closer. "May I?"

Detective Ellison drew in a breath, ready to rebuke her, but at the last moment shrugged. "Why not?"

Emily sensed the woman's eyes on her as she viewed the puffy, discolored face of the dead man.

"I understand you had a connection with the victim." Ellison said.

"My daughter did. He was the husband of a co-worker of hers. I'd never met him."

Detective Ellison waited. Emily knew that most people would have naturally expanded on their statement. She could have said that Stan and Megan had an appointment to meet this man here at the church. But she knew that Stan and Megan would have already explained that. And she wasn't about to give this woman the satisfaction of seeing her act like a neophyte at a crime scene.

She also knew the two men were eager to see her blanch or maybe turn away in horror at the sight of the body. But Emily had seen too many dead bodies in her years on the Upper Michigan police force to find this one any more disturbing than any others.

"Oh, detective," Short 'n Chunky said, "We found this in his pocket." He held out a small plastic bag containing a piece of collegiate lined note-book paper. "Looks like a suicide note."

Detective Ellison removed the note from the bag and quickly perused it. Emily tried to get a look, but the detective had been quick to refold the note and slip it back into the bag and into her notebook.

"Thank you," the detective said to the men. "You can take him out now."

Short 'n Chunky started to zip the body bag.

"I'm sure your medical examiner will log that small abrasion near the rope mark," Emily said. Now she had the satisfaction of watching the detective and the two men lean forward to see what she was talking about.

"Yes." The detective's words were clipped. "I'm sure he will."

Just then the police photographer appeared in the stairwell doorway. "I think I'm done up there," he said. "The fingerprint guys are still working, though. Is the ME still around?"

"He went ahead to his truck." Ellison nodded at the two attendants to take the body out. "Thanks, guys."

"Are my husband and daughter here?" Emily asked the detective once Short 'n Chunky had pushed the gurney out into the street.

"This way." The detective ushered Emily into the sanctuary of the church.

"Mom!" Megan jumped up from the bench she was perched on.

She, Stan and another, tall, thin man all sat together inside one of the high box pews, looking like errant school children. A uniformed policewoman stood in the aisle, arms crossed. Megan flung herself out of the pew and ran to hug her mother. "Oh, Mom. It's so awful."

Emily wrapped her arms around her daughter. The younger woman began to shake, tears filling her eyes.

"I'm s-sorry. I w-wasn't c-crying bef-f-fore..."

"I know. It's okay." Emily squeezed her tight and brushed the hair out of Megan's eyes.

Stan stepped out of the pew, his face ashen and weary, but he was keeping it together quite well. Emily knew he felt a need to stay strong for their daughter.

"We found the body. Roger's. He was...hanging..."

"Perhaps we should all sit down again." Detective Ellison motioned to where the bell master still sat, head in hands.

"Of course." Emily said.

The detective ushered her family back over to the cubicle and stood over them like an overbearing school marm.

"So, Mr. Remington," she leaned back against the wall of the box pew. "Tell me again why you were in the bell tower this afternoon."

As she went through her list of questions, Emily could tell by the exasperated expressions and tired responses that this wasn't the first time the three had recited the sequence of events and described their ties to the victim.

"I don't know what else to say," Obadiah Garde blurted. "I knew he had an appointment to meet them." He waved in Stan and Megan's direction. "But he never showed up. I only took them up into the tower so their trip wouldn't be wasted. He wasn't terribly reliable, you know."

Ellison asked Megan, "You said you work with his wife?"

Megan nodded. "Her name is Rhea. Oh my god, who's going to tell her?" Her eyes filled with tears. Emily reached into her pocket for a tissue, but Ellison beat her to it, setting her notebook down on the pew and fishing one out of her own pocket.

"That's my job," she said.

"When can I get back to my bells?" Garde asked, his hands clutched tightly against his chest.

"We'll let you know. My men are processing the crime scene now."

"May I go with you?" Megan asked. "She should have someone she knows there. Someone who..."

"I can go along, too, if you think that would help," Stan offered.

"I think it would be a good idea for Mrs. Barnett to go with me. But I don't want to overwhelm the widow during her initial shock and grief. I appreciate your offer, though, Mr. Remington."

Stan nodded.

"Can I go now?" Garde asked. "I've developed the most horrendous headache, and I still have things to take care of before I go home."

"Of course," Detective Ellison said. "But be aware that we may have more questions."

Without even a backward glance, he hustled out.

Detective Ellison now focused on Stan. "Mr. Remington, this is the second dead body you and your daughter have discovered in the past forty-eight hours."

"Second? You mean that woman in the park?"

"I understand you also found a body in Wisconsin last fall."

Emily and Stan both stared at the woman in surprise. Emily was impressed. This detective did her homework and she did it quickly.

"That's true, but that murderer was convicted."

"That's what I hear."

Emily held her breath, hoping Stan wouldn't give in to the temptation to expound upon the death of Father Vic. She had an uneasy feeling that it would just complicate matters to bring up the details of that weekend in the infamous Death's Door Straits again. To her relief he said no more. He simply sat with a forlorn look at having painful memories resurrected.

"You don't make a habit of discovering dead bodies when you travel, do you?" the detective asked.

"Of course not!" Stan said, suddenly angry. "That was my good friend that we found. It wasn't a lark. It was horrible what happened to him."

Ellison nodded. She studied Stan thoughtfully for a moment longer then stood up.

"Mrs. Barnett, we should go to see Rhea Hollinger." Ellison stepped out of the pew. "Before it gets very late." Megan nodded and followed her. "Mr. and Mrs. Remington, would you like one of my officers to give you a lift somewhere?"

"I left my car in the park-and-ride lot at the end of the Red Line," Stan said. "If we could get a ride there, that would be helpful."

"No problem."

"But what will Megan do?" Emily asked. "Her husband and children are out at the campground."

"I noticed a coffee shop near the park-and-ride," Stan offered. "We could wait for you there." Then to the detective, "Could you drop her off when you're finished at Rhea's?"

"Of course. It shouldn't take too long." The detective escorted Megan out of the church and into an unmarked police car.

Once they had left, Emily was grateful to climb into the backseat of a nearby squad car with Stan and to forgo the crowds of the subway system and even the city's taxis.

CHAPTER 12

PHILIP and the girls were huddled around the fire pit when Emily, Stan and Megan drove into the camp site. It wasn't quite dark yet, but Emily found the flickering fire welcoming.

The drive from the park-and-ride lot had been unusually quiet; no one seemed inclined to conversation. In fact, Stan had been even more introspective than usual while they waited in the coffee shop, stirring and stirring his coffee, but he seldom brought it to his lips. He did give Emily a brief description of the horrible scene inside the church tower, but he didn't say much else.

They'd only waited about an hour and a half before Detective Ellison dropped Megan off. Emily was worried about how tired her daughter appeared. Her face was pale with deep shadows under her eyes. In the car, when Emily asked how Rhea took the news, Megan just shrugged and bit her lower lip.

At the campsite Megan didn't have much time to seek solace. As soon as she climbed out of the car, the twins charged her with cries of "Mommy!" Megan gave them an appreciative hug and kissed each of them. "Have you had anything to eat?"

"Pizza," Philip said apologetically. He gestured toward the

boxes on the picnic table. "There's some left over, if you don't mind it cold."

"Cold is good," Stan said.

Emily realized that she was hungry, too. "I could go for a slice."

Stan took a bite, but then immediately looked as if he regretted it.

"A beer to go with that?" Philip offered.

"Could use something stronger. I've got a bottle of brandy inside."

"Pour me some, too, Daddy." Megan shuddered at the sight of the pizza.

"That bad, huh?" Philip put an arm around her.

"Worse."

"I'll go get it," Emily said.

"No, no. You sit down. I'll go." Philip squeezed Megan's shoulders then beckoned to the girls. "Allyn, Annabel, let's get you into your pajamas. Wynter, you, too."

Wynter looked suddenly frantic. "Mom?" It was hard to tell from her voice whether she was upset at being sent to bed or was worried about her mother.

"It's okay, baby." Megan held out her arms and Wynter moved into her embrace, letting her mother linger over her. "Maybe Daddy can put on a movie before you all go to sleep. I'll come kiss you goodnight in a little while."

Wynter pushed her mother away. "Not another stupid Disney movie! Can't I stay out here? Please?"

But at her father's tight-lipped scowl, she harrumphed and stomped into the RV.

Emily observed the mini-drama play out and was reminded that she'd seen this exact behavior before, only it was Megan doing the harrumphing. She suppressed a grin as Megan shook her head and stomped off to fetch wood from a pile near the back of the RV. Accepting the logs from his daughter, Stan placed them into the smoldering remains of the spent fire. Sparks flew up into the boughs of the overhead pines. Before long, the dying fire roared back to life.

"You okay, Dad?" Megan asked.

He nodded and gave her a gentle kiss on the forehead.

It wasn't until she turned to her mother that the tears came. Emily wrapped her arms around her daughter and Megan began to sob. Emily held her daughter in the dancing light of the flames until the weeping subsided.

"I'm s-sorry." Megan hiccupped. She wiped at her eyes with the back of her hand.

"Nothing to be sorry about," Emily said. She nudged her daughter toward the camp chairs; the two women nestled in close. "You witnessed something very traumatic today. And you were very brave and very caring to be there for Rhea when she learned about it."

"I didn't feel brave. I felt like it was my fault. Like I had caused it."

"That's a natural reaction. But the fact that you and your Dad found Roger's body is nothing more than a coincidence."

"That detective told Rhea it was a suicide."

"They did find a note."

Megan sat stared into the fire. "How do you do it?" she asked after a moment.

"Do what?" Emily asked.

"You know, deal with dead bodies. Deal with people whose family members have just died. Do you get used to it?"

"You never get used to it."

Stan put down the stick he'd been using to poke at the fire and sat next to Megan.

"Doesn't it bother you?" she asked him. "About Roger. You know, what we saw today?"

Stan didn't say anything at first. Emily held her breath. She sensed that her husband's emotions were still raw, even months after Vic's death. This new tragedy scraped the wound even deeper.

He reached over and put his hand on top of his

daughter's. His voice was a bare whisper. "More than you can know, baby. More than you can know."

Philip appeared with glasses and the bottle of brandy. "Sorry 'bout that. The girls were still arguing over the movie. Had to make an executive decision." He poured a glass for each and handed them around.

"Drink up," he told Megan. "I'll drive home." He reached for Stan's stick and stirred the fire even though it didn't need stirring.

"You don't have to go," Emily offered. "You can stay here tonight. Sleep in the big bed in the RV. The girls will all be on the pull-outs, and Stan and I can sleep in the tent." She ignored the sideways glance Stan threw her way.

"Thanks, but I have to work in the morning. I'm just glad you're willing to keep the girls again tonight," Megan said.

"Call in sick," Philip said. "No one expects you to go to work after what you've been through today."

"I can't. We're short staffed. Charlie's on paternity leave. And Rhea obviously won't be there. She'll likely be out until sometime after the funeral. Besides it'll be good for me to keep busy. Mom, we can still meet for lunch tomorrow. You and Dad are still going to go see the USS Constitution with the girls, right?"

"That's the plan," Stan said.

"How'd she take it?" Philip added another log to the fire. "Rhea. When she learned the news?"

"Oh, god." Megan grasped her glass with both hands. "It was awful. She never saw it coming."

"It must have been some comfort to have you there," Philip said.

"She clutched my hand so tightly, my fingers went numb. Especially during the questioning. That detective really grilled her."

"It's her job," Emily reminded her.

"I know. But to find out your husband is dead, that he killed himself, and to learn it happened in such a horrific way?"

"So they're sure it was suicide?" Stan asked.

"There was a note. Apparently they found it on his body. And on top of that, the police think he did it because he was having an affair. I thought poor Rhea was going to need sedation."

"Was that in the note, too?" Emily said. "About the affair, I mean."

"According to Detective Ellison, yes."

"It's got to be a crappy thing to hear that kind of news under the best of circumstances," Philip said, refilling Stan's outstretched glass. "Then to find out he was cheating on her?"

"Yeah, but that's the thing. Rhea swears there was nothing going on between Roger and any other woman."

"Oh, honey. That's to be expected," Emily said. "There's always denial at first."

"I suppose. Crap. It just stinks." Megan's eyes filled with tears again. Philip went over to her, helped her to her feet and into his embrace.

When they'd sat down again in the creaky camp chairs, Emily asked Megan, "Did you know him well?"

"Roger? I'd only met him a couple of times. He seemed nice enough. And he was always attentive to Rhea. But who can tell from that?" She stared into the crackling fire for a moment before blurting out, "Why do people do it, anyway? Commit suicide. And why would he do it there of all places? It's all so bizarre."

"In my experience there's no rhyme or reason when something like this happens," Emily answered her daughter. "It seldom makes any sense."

The sun refused to stay behind the curtain, teasing Emily and insisting that she wake up to face the day. Finally, she stumbled out of the small bedroom. It took her a moment to make sense of the disarray in the living area—bodies were sprawled throughout the cabin. The twins lay akimbo on the sofa sleeper, while Wynter had made a nest on the floor. *Oh, yeah, we're in the RV.*

Emily wished she'd had a little less brandy the night before. She searched for a bottle of ibuprofen in the kitchen cupboard and poured herself a cup of the coffee Stan, thankfully, had already brewed. Stan. Where was *he?* She was pretty sure he'd been in their bed all night. *Oh, wait…*

She squinted at the note on the fridge: "Gone for a walk – S."

Really?

Walking alone first thing in the morning—walking at all first thing in the morning—was out of character for him, but she suspected he needed time to work through his feelings.

She rolled her shoulders to work out the kinks—the RV bed just didn't feel like the one at home—then carried her coffee out to the picnic table. Should she wake the girls up for another session of Tae kwon do? She was amazed how good she'd felt after the workout yesterday, even though it was modified to fit her young grasshoppers. Maybe in a few minutes. In the meantime, she'd enjoy the solitude and quiet before the girls joined her with their clamor.

Stan had hiked about two miles before his legs started to protest. The problem with going for walks was that starting out felt good, but about the time you realized you'd gone far enough, you had to reverse direction and traipse back the same distance. He didn't mind so much when he was with Emily, but walking alone wasn't nearly as much fun. Regardless, he'd needed to get out of the RV.

He was surprised at how quickly he'd fallen asleep the night before, considering the day's events. But then he woke up about three thirty and that was it for the night. Typically he would simply give in, get up and read, sometimes even fall back asleep in his recliner. But he didn't have his recliner, and the girls were sprawled everywhere. He had slipped outside, where he sat under the stars for a while. He must have dozed on the chaise lounge, because when he opened his eyes the stars were gone and the sky was a pale gray, waiting for the sun to poke its rays through the boughs of the pines.

Finally, he made coffee and after downing a cup, he tacked a note to the fridge and headed out to see what the rest of the campground looked like at the crack of dawn. Surprisingly there were quite a few people out and about enjoying their morning brew or on their way to the public latrines. *Tent campers?* A waft of bacon frying reminded him that he hadn't eaten the night before.

He wondered how Megan was doing. Had she slept? He considered calling her, but then decided it was too early. He wondered if she was as haunted by the image of Roger's body hanging in the church steeple as he was. He had this creepy, illogical feeling that none of this would have happened if he hadn't been so excited to tour the church. That it was his fault his daughter had to witness something so horrible. Deep inside, he knew the man's suicide had nothing to do with him. The problem was death never seemed very logical when it wasn't connected to the natural rhythm of life. That woman in the park, her death was logical. Maybe not the most auspicious location for a heart attack, but at least she hadn't died in a location where her body would go unfound for days on end.

Stan shuddered then took a deep breath. His thoughts were rambling, he knew. Leaving the campsites behind, he followed the path into the forest. Sunlight glinted off water beyond the trees. At a fork, a small sign pointed down a well-traveled path marked "Meditation Point." He took the other, the one less traveled. *And that has made all the difference,* he mused. He strolled along the overgrown path to a small, languid stream. A stump of a fallen tree beckoned, and he was grateful to sit and let his leg muscles revive.

He sniffed the air. What was that scent? Suddenly he was ten years old again, riding with his father along back-country roads with the car windows rolled down, sniffing for blueberry patches. They tended to grow where forest fires had denuded the landscape. Stan peered through the trees, looking for the blueberry patch. They tended also to be the favorite dessert of bears, though. He decided he could wait until he got home to eat.

Picking through stones scattered at his feet, he found a couple of smooth ones to toss into the water. With each plop rings formed, then flowed lazily downstream. *Kind of like my life right now. Floating away into nothingness.* Okay, that wasn't true. He did have the book deal. And opportunities to speak at conferences. It surprised him how disconcerting it had felt not to have a class schedule to adhere to and papers to grade. The last few years he'd looked forward to retirement, to the freedom to read, research, and write. But when the time actually came, it was harder to get a rhythm going to his day than he'd imagined. He'd even brought his laptop and research notes along on this trip, but the distress of the last couple of days overshadowed any work he'd hoped to get done.

Although that trip to the Longfellow House with Wynter was something he would treasure for a long time. Hell, he knew all along that she just wanted to get away from her sisters, and—yeah, Megan was probably right—that her intense interest in the tour was because she was all eyes for that young college student. But still…

A scream ripped through the air. Stan jerked, his body tensing to flee or fight, eyes and ears straining to locate the source. Then, a scolding call from somewhere up above. There it was. Perched high on the tip of an ancient pine tree. With another screech, the red-tailed hawk took flight. Stan watched it soar in the morning light, dipping and diving as it hunted for its breakfast. But his nerves were on edge now, still raw from his close encounter with death the day before, and he decided to head back to the campsite.

"Grandma, did you start without us?" The twins stood sleepy-eyed in the doorway of the RV.

"Just warming up," Emily assured them from under the awning. "Do you want to join me now or have breakfast first?"

"Tae kwon do! Now!" they shouted, tripping down the steps.

"In your pajamas?"

"Oh." The girls giggled sheepishly at one another.

"I'm just kidding!" Emily laughed. "You can do Tae kwon do in anything. In fact, look what I made for you." She reached for two long strands of white terry cloth that she'd cut from a bath towel she had decided to sacrifice. To the girls' delight, she tied the strands around their slender waists. "There, now you've each earned your white belt. And you are ready for bigger challenges."

By the time she saw Stan ambling back up the road toward their campsite, Tara and Amy had joined Emily and the twins; they'd even brought along Marion from the Flxible, who told her she was already up to her orange belt. *That pops my stereotype.*

"I'm feeling antsy as a cat in a room full of rocking chairs," the woman declared. "And what I need is a good workout."

The four women and two girls worked up a sweat, kicking, thrusting, and blocking. Emily beamed as her husband approached the group and settled into a chair to watch them finish up the session.

"I think you may have found your passion," he said to Emily as she waved goodbye to her three adult "students" striding off down the camp road.

"Hmm. I think I worked up an appetite." She smiled at him.

"Grams! Gramps!" Wynter yelled from the door of the RV an hour later. "Someone stole my earbuds!" She stormed over to the picnic table where Emily, Stan and the twins were digging into heaping plates of French toast.

Allyn perked up. "I'll bet it was the witch!"

"What would a witch do with earbuds?" Wynter asked.

"She's a thief! She'd do whatever it is thieves do with stuff like this," Annabel insisted.

"Yeah, right." Wynter crossed her arms and glared at her sisters. "She is not a thief, and she didn't take anything."

"Who's not a thief? Who are you talking about?" Stan looked confused.

"The cat lady," Annabel informed him. "She's a witch."

"Vinie's not a—oh, for goodness sake," Emily was frustrated. "Wynter, look in the car. Maybe you left them there. Then everyone, let's get dressed because we're taking the train into the city."

"Are we gonna have lunch with Mom?" Allyn asked.

"Are we gonna see that old ship?" her twin inquired.

"We're going to do both," Emily answered. "Let's get moving. We've got another big day ahead of us."

CHAPTER 13

THE girls burst through the doors of the Coolidge Corner library like a trio of cyclones. Patrons scattered throughout the library looked up from their books and newspapers, some with scowls, others with amusement, some with shrugs of indifference quickly burying their noses back into their pages.

"Hi, Mom!" they said in unison, waving to Megan at the front desk. Megan smiled and waved back.

Emily was just about to say something to quiet the girls down when she realized they had already dispersed and settled themselves into their favorite reading nooks. Wynter slid into a chair in front of a computer. Allyn grabbed a martial arts book off the shelf and curled up on an overstuffed couch. And Annabel plopped herself down in the middle of the picture book section, amid a group of excited preschoolers. It was obvious to Emily that this was routine for the girls. Most of the patrons ignored them and went back to their reading. One old graybeard frowned and shook his head. But he didn't seem surprised, just annoyed in the way one is annoyed by something very familiar.

Emily waited by the front desk until a plump woman had finished checking out her books. Megan looked tired but happy to see her.

"Give me ten, okay?" Megan asked. "Then I can take my lunch break. Where's Dad?"

"He found an electronics store up on Beacon Street. He'll catch up with us at the restaurant."

"Dad at an electronics store? He passed up an opportunity to come to a library?" Megan greeted a young mother approaching the desk clutching a toddler in one hand and DVDs in the other.

Emily wandered over to the magazine rack where she picked up a travel magazine with an RV on the cover. Settling herself into an armchair near where Wynter sat, she thumbed through the magazine, searching for tips to make their travels less harrowing.

A few moments later Megan, bright purple purse over her shoulder, approached. "Wynter, tell your sisters it's time to go."

Wynter let out a big sigh, and pushed herself away from the computer. "Annabel! Allyn! Mom says we have to go," she called in a voice loud enough to make Emily wince. But by then the other patrons had stopped paying attention, even the graybeard.

They found Stan already waiting at a little sandwich shop just around the corner from the library. The girls slid into a booth next to the window and immediately switched on their iPods. Emily pointed to a nearby table, and the three adults sat down.

"What did you buy?" Megan asked, pointing to the small bag Stan had set on the table.

"Earbuds. For my darling Wynter."

Wynter emerged from her texting. "You bought me new earbuds?"

He took two sets out of the bag. "And for me!"

"Cool, Gramps! Thanks!" She accepted the gift, ripped open the package, popped them in her ears, and turned back to her own table.

"Wynter!" Megan chastised. But her daughter couldn't

hear her. Or perhaps simply ignored her.

Stan beamed in satisfaction as the waiter brought menus and water. It didn't take long for their orders to come up.

"How did the girls sleep?" Megan asked, lifting the edges of the toasted focaccia bread to examine the interior of her sandwich. She dug out the slice of onion and laid it on the side of her plate.

"Like bears in winter. Not going to eat that?" Stan speared the onion slice with his fork and added it to his already bulging sandwich.

"How about you?" Emily wanted to know. "How did you sleep?"

"Thank God for sleeping pills." Megan lowered her voice and checked to see if the girls were listening. "It made the paper. And all the local morning news shows." She shuddered as she licked mayonnaise off her fingers.

"I'm not surprised." Emily, keeping her voice low, reached for the ketchup. "You can't find a body in a building as famous as the Old North Church and not have it be news. Hopefully it will have a short shelf life."

"The thing is, even with the pills, it seemed like every time I closed my eyes, I could see him hanging there."

"Yup." This from Stan. He grimaced at the sandwich in his hand and set it back down on his plate.

They sat in silence for a moment, the clink of plates and the chatter of other diners filling the empty space, as if to say that for some people, this was nothing more than another normal day. Emily tried a few bites of her spinach salad. It was good, but her appetite was waning.

Finally Megan looked up from the fries she was pushing around on her plate. "Mom, did you have your heart set on going to the USS Constitution with Dad and the girls?"

"Why? Do you have something better I could be doing?" Emily poked Stan with her elbow. She knew that he knew she'd give anything to get out of visiting a dusty old ship.

"As a matter of fact…" Megan took a deep breath. "I

called Rhea this morning. You know, just to check on her."

"How is she doing?"

"Not good. Her sister will be coming in a couple of days. That's something, I guess. Mom, she's still insistent that Roger didn't commit suicide."

"Oh, honey. I don't know what to say. The police know what they're doing," Emily batted away an errant fly. "I think Rhea is just going to have to accept the inevitable. And you will, too."

"I know, I know. But, Mom, there is just something about how sure she is. I...I told her I'd ask if you would talk with her."

"With Rhea?"

"That detective yesterday was sympathetic and all about the whole thing. But still, it was like she was suggesting Rhea didn't know her own husband."

"Oh, honey, I can't interfere with an investigation."

"You wouldn't be interfering. Just listening. And maybe giving Rhea some perspective. Some peace of mind."

Emily sighed. Stan didn't say a word, but Emily knew what he was thinking: stay out of it.

"Please, Mom. Dad, you don't mind going alone with the girls, do you? I've traded shifts. I'm off for a few hours, before I have to go back. I told Rhea that one way or another I'd stop by. God knows she needs a shoulder to cry on right now."

Emily looked into her daughter's own water-filled eyes. "Whose shoulder are you talking about? Yours? Or mine?"

"Request permission to come aboard, sir!"

Stan saluted the young ensign standing at attention at the foot of the gangway. He noted with an historian's eye that the navy uniform the sailor was wearing—mid-19th century blue jacket over a middy blouse, white trousers and black brimmed hat—was historically accurate down to the gold buttons.

"Permission granted. Welcome aboard the USS Constitution." The sailor saluted back and winked at the three girls giggling behind Stan. "I will need to see identification first, though. I'll accept if you'll vouch for your charges." He indicated the girls, the twins now bouncing from foot to foot.

As the young officer studied his driver's license, Stan shielded his eyes and gazed up at the three tall masts that dominated the deck of the old frigate. "Did you know that Constitution is the oldest commissioned warship in the U.S. Navy?" Stan asked.

"As a matter of fact I did, sir."

Chagrined, Stan swiveled and saw that his charges were already at the top of the gangway, shoving at one another to be the first on deck. "Yes, of course you did. I was talking to the—oh, hell! Wait for me!" he called, but his voice was lost in the wind and the cries of the gulls swooping overhead. He huffed after the girls.

Panting, he made his way to the top of the ramp. The three girls stood impatiently waiting for him.

"Hurry up, Grandpa. You're so slow," Allyn admonished.

Then the twins dashed toward the bow of the ship, their footfalls clomping over the wooden deck. Wynter hung back with her grandfather, who seemed singularly unaware that her sudden reticence to chase after her sisters was due to the number of young handsome sailors milling around the deck.

"Please join your tour group over there." A petty officer pointed to a small group of visitors gathered under the forward mast.

Stan put two fingers up to his teeth and whistled for the twins.

"Gramps!" Wynter hissed. "Please!"

The sailor, waiting for the group to assemble, frowned at first, but broke into a grin as the nine-year-olds came galloping up. Once the small crowd had assembled, she introduced herself to the group as Ensign Erin O'Malley. "We'll start our tour here on the spar deck, which gets its name from the masts and the yardarms which hold the sails; collectively they're called the spars. The USS Constitution is a wooden-hulled frigate originally commissioned to fight against the Barbary pirates off the coast of Africa. When she was first deployed in October 1797, she carried a crew of four hundred and fifty."

"Did the pirates catch them?" Annabel asked.

"Pirates tended to keep their distance. Constitution typically carried as many as fifty-four cannons. Twenty up here on the spar deck and thirty-two on the gun deck just below us."

"That's only fifty-two," Wynter said.

"Yup. There are two more called bow chasers up here as well."

"Grandpa! Look at that hat!" Annabel pointed at a tall, slender man in full period dress and wearing wire-rimmed glasses, who saluted the group, his hand barely touching the brim of his black felt, hump-backed hat.

"Let me introduce Lieutenant Commander Nelson, our executive officer," Ensign O'Malley said. "He is—as am I—dressed in the uniform that was adopted by the U.S. Navy shortly after the war of 1812. His hat is called a bicorne or cocked hat. He wears it in the fore-and-aft position as was common in navies around the world in the nineteenth century." She saluted as the executive officer strode past. "Now, if you'll look forward you can see the foremast, which stands at a hundred and ninety-eight feet tall."

All heads craned to look up at the configuration of masts with its webbing of ropes, slapping in the breeze. One lone seagull perched atop a yardarm, squawking at them.

"Do people climb all the way up there?" Allyn asked.

"Affirmative. The only way to maintain and repair the sails is to get up close and personal."

"Cool!"

"No. You can't go up," Stan chided his granddaughter with a teasing shove against her shoulder. "Both feet on deck at all times."

"Aww."

"Join the navy when you grow up then you can climb them," the ensign said to the little girl. Then to the group, "Those masts carry over forty-two thousand square feet of sail when under full power, capable of moving the ship at just over thirteen knots, or nearly fifteen miles an hour. Fast enough to catch pirates." She winked at the twins. "She has been in thirty-three engagements and has won all thirty-three."

"Boston's only undefeated team!" a young man in a beard and Red Sox hat quipped, holding his cell phone high in the air to catch the entire tour on video.

"Absolutely," the ensign chuckled. "Of course her most famous conflict was the War of 1812, where she took on and defeated four British warships, earning her the nickname, Old Ironsides." She gestured toward the hatch. "Ready to go below, mates?"

Stan had many more questions, but the twins were already scrambling to be first down the hatch. "Wait for me!" he yelled.

He waited as first Allyn, then Annabel, and finally Wynter descended into the bowels of the ship. Twisting his body around, he gripped the rope rails tightly and climbed backward down the steep wooden stairs, more a ladder really, to the gun deck.

"Grandpa, you're such a slowpoke!" Allyn called out. And before Stan's foot touched the deck, she and her sisters were running toward the cannons.

Another sailor greeted them below and gave a talk on the ship's arsenal and the life of sailors in the 1800's. Stan raised his hand once, to ask about the weight of artillery, but Annabel grabbed his sleeve to drag him over to look down the hatch to the next level.

A little later, back up on the spar deck, Stan wandered about taking in the sights, sounds, and smells of history. The twins had chased off to explore on their own; he could hear their shrieks of laughter from across the bow of the ship. Wynter stood at the rail in a self-conscious pose, staring out across the harbor as if searching for a lost ship, occasionally casting furtive glances at a nearby sailor chatting with an elderly couple. Stan breathed in deeply, smelling the salt air. The cries of the gulls swooping overhead sounded ageless. No doubt the sailors of old had heard their same plaintive calls. He stood under the mizzen mast, closed his eyes and imagined he could hear the commander shout orders to his crew.

"SIR!"

Stan whirled around to see a sailor, hands resting lightly on the shoulders of Allyn and Annabel.

"Do these girls belong to you?"

Stan nodded, confused.

"You'll have to keep them with you, sir. They're not allowed below decks without an adult accompanying them."

"Below decks? We were just…" Stan reddened as he scowled at the girls. "How did you get back below?" His voice was harsher than he intended, but he glared at them until they hung their heads. "I'll take it from here," he told the young man in a low, growly voice.

The sailor nodded and strode off.

"Sorry, Grandpa."

"It's time to go," Stan barked at Wynter, who was still looking wistfully out to sea.

"Do we have to?" One glance took in the two girls, one held firmly in each of her grandfather's hands, and the grimace on his face. "Oh." Without another word she followed them off the ship.

"Grandpa, slow down!" Allyn protested as he marched them down the gangway. "Why are we going so fast?"

"Keep moving. Just keep moving."

"Look at all the seagulls!" Annabel put the brakes on, causing Stan to just about crash into her.

A colony of seabirds had taken up residence on the pier and the pilings. The girls stood and gawked as several of the gulls raised their huge wings, lifting off with eager cries. Watching the sea birds soar high above their heads, Stan forced himself to relax, to let go of his irritation at having his moment on the ship ruined. As the girls pointed and chattered, he could feel his blood pressure settling back down. The day was glorious after all. He took in a deep breath, tasting the salty tang of the sea air, feeling the sun warm the bald spot on his head.

"Grandpa, look out!" Wynter shrieked.

A wet, sloppy, burning mass splattered onto the bald spot on his head.

"What the—?" He jumped, letting go of the girls' hands, but it was too late. The seagull that had let loose on him cawed as if laughing.

"Grandpa! That seagull pooped on you!" Allyn put her hands over her mouth in exaggerated horror.

"Grandpa!" Annabel exclaimed in wide-eyed astonishment, a snicker bursting forth despite her efforts to suppress it.

Stan turned in a circle, not knowing what to do about the smelly, wet mess, the seagull poop sliding down the side of his head.

"Handkerchief, sir?" The young sailor stationed at the bottom of the gangway came running to help out.

Stan accepted the spotless white cloth with its perfect creases. Dabbing at the mess, he realized that all three girls were staring at him with their hands over their mouths. Wynter's nose wrinkled in disgust. But Annabel snickered again. Stan glared at his granddaughter, but she giggled despite his look. The sailor bit his lip. Then Wynter giggled, tried to suppress it, sniggered and broke out into a guffaw.

"That bad, huh?" Stan's grimace morphed into a sheepish grin, laughter finally sputtering from his lips.

"I have some water you can use. If it's helpful." The

young man offered his bottle of trendy spring water.

Stan accepted the bottle, unscrewing the cap, and—all of them laughing like crazy now—he bent over and dumped the water over his head, dissolving the worst of the poop. The young man with the Red Sox hat stopped and held out his bottle also, and Stan found himself showering with offerings from the small crowd that had gathered around.

"Damn! That shit is hot," he sputtered.

"Grandpa!" Annabel admonished, her hand in front of her mouth again, this time in shock.

"I'm going to tell Grandma on you," Allyn announced.

CHAPTER 14

"I'M so sorry for your loss," Emily said.

Rhea Hollinger nodded and invited them into her house. Emily hated that phrase. It was what police personnel always said to people who were grieving the death of a loved one. Polite but impersonal. But Emily was retired from that life now, and she regretted not finding more compassionate words for this woman who was dealing with the sudden loss of her husband to an apparent suicide. "This must be very difficult for you," she said. "I wish I had more helpful words to offer."

Rhea gave a weary smile. "Do you mind leaving your shoes at the door." She indicated the white carpeting behind her.

"Of course not." Emily and Megan slipped off their shoes and padded after the tiny bird-like woman ushering them into the living room.

"Please have a seat." Her voice was soft and Emily had to strain to hear her. "I was just about to pour myself a cup of coffee. May I pour one for you too?"

"Black, please."

"A little milk in mine."

Brushing her hands on her capris, Emily perched on the

edge of the pristine white sectional, while Megan took the fuchsia chair across from her.

Rhea nodded in approval as they settled themselves, holding her hands tightly in front of her. She wore crisply pressed jeans with a turquoise silk blouse. Silver bracelets jangling at her wrists, she walked briskly through a contemporary, but elegant, dining room, straightening a chair as she went, and into the sparkling white kitchen beyond.

Emily studied the room around her. It was impossibly clean. Not a speck of dust. Emily resisted the impulse to do a white glove test. Two abstract paintings, both with fuchsia coloring, hung on the wall over the sofa. A sculpture of an elephant dominated the glass-topped coffee table. Fresh cut, bright pink roses adorned the dining room table, their scent delicate and sweet. A black lacquered Asian sideboard stood on one wall of the dining area. An antique?

"Are you comfortable?" Rhea returned carrying a serving tray with white mugs, a plate of chocolate chip cookies, creamer and sugar bowls.

No way would Emily dare to eat a cookie in this room. Chance smearing chocolate on the sofa? She gave Megan silent credit for chancing it then gave her full attention back to the grieving widow who had sat down next to her.

"How are you doing?" Megan asked, holding her cookie in a delicate white paper napkin.

"I'm in shock. I don't know what to think. The police think Roger committed suicide." She set her coffee cup back down on the tray. "That's impossible. I don't know how to get them to understand that."

"There was a suicide note," Emily said in a kind voice.

"Did you see it?" Rhea asked.

Emily shook her head.

"They claim it said he was having an affair." Rhea's thin lips tightened, and she clutched her hands in her lap.

"Do you think that could be the case?"

"No. Absolutely not."

"Mrs. Hollinger. Rhea. I don't mean to be insensitive, but that old adage, the wife is the last to know? It's not entirely unfounded." Emily looked to Megan for reinforcement, but none came.

"But you don't understand," Rhea pleaded. "He couldn't have been having an affair."

"Why do you say that?"

"He's…he was…my husband. I know that sounds lame for an excuse. But I knew him…intimately. I would have known. Despite the adage." Rhea's eyes filled with tears. "Megan said you were a cop. I thought you were here to help me."

"Yes, of course we are." Megan's eyes pleaded with her mother to say something helpful.

"Rhea, you need to understand there's nothing I can do. I am no longer active duty. And even if I were, I have no jurisdiction in the Boston area."

Rhea reached for a tissue from a perfectly placed decorative box. "I know. It's just…I had hoped…I don't know what I had hoped for. All I know is that Roger didn't kill himself and the police won't listen to me."

Emily set her own coffee cup down on the tray. She took a moment, composing her words carefully.

"They are going on the evidence. The note they found tells one story," Emily said as kindly as she could. "Without evidence to the contrary, that's the only story they know. Is there anything you can think of that would point the police in a different direction?"

"Like what?" Rhea seemed befuddled.

"Well…if he didn't commit suicide and a person doesn't end up hanging in the belfry of a church by accident…"

"Then someone murdered him." Rhea twisted her hands even tighter. "But who would do that?"

Emily shook her head. This was not a road she wanted to go down. But it was too late. "Think about the people he knew. Was there anyone he had a conflict with?"

"No. He got along with everyone."

"What about at work?" Megan asked. She glanced at her mother, and Emily nodded in approval. "Was he having any problems with his boss or maybe one of his clients?"

"He never mentioned anything like that to me. No. He really seemed to enjoy his work."

"What did he do?" Emily asked.

"He was an appraiser. For an auction house. He specialized in old literary documents."

"Did he ever bring work home?"

"Sure. A lot of his clients were overseas. With the time difference, you know, he was on the phone at all odd hours. And on his computer. He has a…had an office in our spare bedroom. Would you like to see it?"

"Did the police process it? Did they go through his home office?"

Both Rhea and Megan shook their heads. "The only one who came by was Detective Ellison. Yesterday with Megan. She showed me the note. Asked me if it was his handwriting. She never suggested it was anything other than suicide. I was so upset I never thought to press the issue. But when I called her later, she just kind of blew me off. Politely. But she said it was an open and shut case."

"So…you saw the note. Do you remember exactly what it said?"

"To be honest, it's a blur. But I do remember thinking this doesn't sound like him."

"But you confirmed it was your husband's handwriting?"

"It did look like it. Yes."

Emily stared at Rhea, confounded. "I'm sorry. I don't know what to say. If it was his handwriting, why do you think it doesn't sound like him?"

"It was the words in the note. Words like 'my beloved wife.' He would never call me that. And then the tone of his apology. So cold."

Emily thought a moment. In her experience people who

attempt suicide were not in their usual frame of mind. That could explain the tone in his final note. But she couldn't see harrying Rhea over it any further.

"Could we see his office now?" she asked, thinking that if nothing else, maybe she would find something in Roger Hollinger's personal effects that might convince his wife that the police knew what they were doing.

Roger Hollinger's den was a study in contrasts to the home he had shared with Rhea Hollinger. His widow opened the door to the room carefully, hesitantly, as if expecting bats to swoop out into the hall. It was a man-cave in the classic sense. An antique desk sat at right angles to a window with a view of the backyard. Oak bookshelves, swollen with leather bound books, well read, apparently, lined three of the walls. Piles of file folders and magazines toppled from a worn burgundy leather arm chair and matching ottoman that dominated the corner opposite the window. The chair likely hadn't been used to sit in for quite some time. Several Persian throw rugs were scattered about the scuffed hardwood floor. Emily shuddered, remembering the Persian rug that had tumbled off the roof of her RV several months earlier. An old, heavily carved library table dominated the center of the room, its surface stacked with papers.

Rhea picked up a newspaper and several manila envelopes from the floor but seemed at a loss as to where to put them. Finally, she stuffed them into the already full mesh trash can.

"The mess never seemed to bother him," she said apologetically. "I tried straightening up for him a couple of times, but it just irritated him. He said he couldn't find things after I'd put them away." She gave a short, rueful laugh. "I have no clue how he could have found anything in this mess."

Megan opened the blinds to let in more light. "He certainly didn't like to throw anything away, did he?"

"Let's just look around and see if anything turns up. Correspondence, maybe. Photographs. A diary or journal?" Emily began poking through the piles on the desk. "Megan, can you go through that stack of mail on the table over there? Rhea, at this point, it's probably better if you don't throw anything out."

Rhea nodded. She hovered as if hesitant to violate her husband's personal space.

"Maybe you could go get some baskets. I think it will help if we at least sort things as we go," Megan suggested.

Rhea seemed relieved to have an assignment and hustled out of the room. Emily and Megan bent their heads to task.

"So, Mom, what exactly is it we're looking for here?"

"Honestly, Megan, I don't have a clue. It's unlikely that the police are wrong about Roger. But I suppose we should at least help Rhea to feel like she did everything she could to set the record straight."

"All I see here are magazine renewals and credit card come-ons. Oh wait. Here's a credit card statement. On the TV crime shows, they always use those to prove the victim had been in some incriminating place or other."

"Credit card statements can be a good record of restaurant visits and hotel stays. What does it say?" Emily looked up from the pile of envelopes she was examining.

"He bought some books at Barnes and Noble. And computer paper at an office supply store. And he paid for his monthly Netflix fees using his Visa card. That's about it. Pretty boring." Megan set the statement in a pile separate from the junk mail.

Emily reached into one of the half dozen cubby holes on the desk and discovered a stack of business cards. Flipping through them, she noted they were mostly from museum directors and antiques collectors. She set them aside, thinking someone might want to note the names, if it happened that Rhea's hunch was correct.

"There's something buried under these magazines. It's a day planner." Megan leafed through the pages.

"Anything?"

"Dunno," Megan said. "A dentist appointment. With Dr.

Carey. How apropos. Dental 'Carey?' And a phone conference with a magazine editor. This one is odd…"

"What's that?"

"Hard to tell. It's pretty cryptic. 7-4 Mtg. DC at ONC re: Bell."

"Hmmm…" Not very promising, Emily surmised.

"What's weird is that most everything in the datebook is pretty well spelled out. Except this one entry. Do you think it means anything?"

By now Emily was peering over her shoulder as Megan pointed to the entry.

"It is out of character, isn't it? So I wouldn't dismiss it. What's that?" Emily pointed.

"B. Carter," Megan read. "An appointment of some sort. Scheduled for this week. There's a phone number under it."

"B. Carter?" Emily twirled a lock of her hair thoughtfully.

At that moment Rhea returned with a half dozen small wicker baskets in hand. "If you don't mind, I'm going to sort things while you go through them."

"Rhea, what do you make of this?" Megan held the day planner out to Rhea and pointed to the cryptic references.

Rhea frowned. "I don't know. It's not like Roger to use shorthand. He was always very precise with his notation. Even when he was adding items to my grocery lists."

"There's a reference to a B. Carter," Emily said.

Rhea shook her head indicating she was clueless.

"And here's another notation, from about a week ago. 'Call Idiot in Italy.'"

"That's clearly spelled out," Megan quipped. "I wonder who the idiot is?"

Rhea blushed. "Oh, dear. I'm guessing that would be Alberto Forcina. I suppose there's a business card for him around here somewhere. He's an agent in Milan that Roger worked with over the past year."

Emily reached for the stack of cards and found the one for Alberto Forcina. It was ornate, gold embossed with embellished calligraphy. It announced Forcina as an independent agent of literary antiquities and listed an overseas phone number.

"Any idea why Roger was so unhappy with Mr. Forcina," Emily asked.

"There was one phone call I remember. About a week ago. Roger was particularly upset over a sale he had made through him. I don't know the details." Rhea thought a moment. "I had walked into the room just as he was saying something about a forgery. But when he saw me, he ended the conversation, saying 'You tell that Italian idiot what I said.' And then he hung up. When I asked what was going on, he said it was nothing I needed to be concerned about. I shrugged it off. Could this have been important?"

"I don't know. It's hard to say. Did you mention it to the police?"

"I didn't think of it. And they didn't ask about anything that would have brought it up."

"Was he easily upset by his business dealings?"

"That's just it. He never got upset. Over anything. He just always kind of went with the flow. So when I heard him yelling on the phone…"

"Who is this?" Emily asked, pointing to a name in the daybook. "Drysdale?"

"Not a who. A what. That's the auction house where Roger worked."

"That would be as good a starting place as any. Could you give me the address?"

"Then you'll look into it?" Rhea's face lit up, suddenly hopeful.

"I have to be honest with you, Rhea. The police are almost always right in cases like this. I know that's not what you want to hear. And I don't want to raise any false hopes. But a phone conversation that's out of character right before a person dies is always worth looking into."

"Oh, thank you!"

"May I take the day planner? I'd like to examine it a bit more thoroughly. Then I'll get it to Detective Ellison."

"Of course. Would you like something to put it in? A plastic bag, maybe?"

"How about a Ziploc bag?"

"I think I have something big enough. I'll be right back." She flitted away again, this time eager to be of help.

"Do you think there's something here to go on?" Megan asked.

"It's hard to say. But it can't hurt to ask a few questions."

Megan gave her mom a spontaneous hug. "I love it when you do stuff like this."

CHAPTER 15

STAN shook the last of the water off his head and swiped at the spot one last time where the burning gull droppings had splattered. Self-conscious, he held the dirtied handkerchief out to the young ensign who'd been so helpful. The sailor held his hands up as if to ward it off.

"You keep it. I'm good."

For a moment Stan considered stuffing it into his own pocket, but the once crisp regulation handkerchief was gross beyond belief. Spotting a trash can at the end of the pier, he tossed it in with a sheepish grin.

The small crowd that had been so generous with their water bottles began to disperse, and the girls—Wynter and the twins—had settled into occasional giggling interspersed with hiccups.

The sailor gave a perfunctory salute, evidently to avoid the usual good-will handshake, and went back to his duty post.

"Let's go wait for your grandmother," Stan said to the girls.

At that moment the guitar riff from his phone caught his attention. When he saw it was Emily, he brightened.

"Hey, Hon. Perfect timing. Where are you?"

"Just leaving Rhea's house." Emily's voice sounded

130

apologetic. "Something's come up. Megan's heading back to the library, but I thought maybe I would stop in at the police station and pay a visit to Detective Ellison."

"Really?" Stan looked up to make sure there weren't any other gulls floating overhead. "I was kinda hoping to get back to the park. I could really use a shower about now. I—"

"It won't take long. You and the girls go ahead and catch the train to the park-and-ride. Isn't there an ice cream parlor right next to that little coffee shop? I'll meet you there."

"I thought you weren't going to get involved. You were just going to comfort the grieving widow and assure her the police had made the right call."

"Thing is, I'm not so sure they did."

"Emily? Come on. It was clearly a case of suicide. I was there, remember?" Stan closed his eyes against the image of the body hanging in the dark bell tower that insisted on permeating his brain even in the bright sunlight bouncing off the waters of the harbor. "And there was the suicide note."

"Look, we'll talk about it tonight. See you at the ice cream shop."

Stan sighed, imagining all the ice cream lovers wrinkling their noses at the smell of him in the brightly lit shop. "Okay. But you don't get any ice cream cause we're leaving as soon as you get there."

"Ice cream!" The twins shouted in unison, bouncing and clapping their hands.

"That's the plan." He stuffed the phone back into his pocket.

"Eww, Gramps! Are you sure?" Wynter wrinkled her nose.

Stan touched the top of his head tentatively. "Still there?"

Wynter shook her head. "No. I guess you'll pass for clean. Maybe I'll just have a coke."

Forty minutes later, they stood gazing into a glass case containing a dozen flavors of ice cream. Wynter had apparently forgotten her disgust at her grandfather's recent encounter with the seagull; she ordered a double scoop of raspberry cheesecake ice cream.

"I want chocolate chip banana," Allyn said to the girl in a white cap behind the case. "In a waffle cone." Her nose was pressed up against the glass, leaving a smudge when she backed away.

"Allyn, I was going to have chocolate chip banana," Annabel pouted, crossing her arms.

"Can't. I picked it first."

"Okay, okay," Stan interrupted. "She'll have the chocolate chip banana, too."

"Uh uhn. I want the chocolate peanut butter stripe. In a sugar cone." She stuck out her tongue at her twin.

"Something smell odd in here?" the young vendor asked, scooping the little girls' cones and handing them over the counter to Stan.

"Grandpa got hit by a—"

Stan thrust the cone of chocolate chip banana ice cream into Allyn's lips.

"Wynter, do you want a cone or a bowl?" he asked the older girl

She was staring at a college-aged boy who had just come in from the back room, tying a clean white apron around his waist and setting his white cap at a rakish angle onto his massive blond curls.

"You can head out now," he said to the girl behind the counter, who left with an appreciative nod.

Stan tugged at his granddaughter's sleeve. "Wynter?"

She blushed and stammered, "Can you, uh, change mine to the, uh, Paul Revere tracks? Please?"

The curly-haired young man grinned at her. "No problem. What did you say? Cone or bowl?"

"Cone." Her words were barely perceptible.

"Waffle or sugar?" He was already digging into the ice cream.

Wynter's color rose even more deeply. "Waffle," she

muttered looking intently at the crown of his head.

"Sorry?" He looked up with a smile.

"Wynter, you have to speak up," Stan admonished. *What is wrong with her anyway?* He hoped she wasn't getting sick.

"Waffle!" she shouted, then clasped her hand over her mouth.

"Sure thing. And you?" he said to Stan, handing the ice cream cone over the counter.

"Just a scoop of plain vanilla."

"Sorry, there's no plain vanilla. Classic French? Vanilla with pomegranate swirl? Or triple treat vanilla bean?" the young man asked.

Stan sucked in his breath. "French. Classic. In a bowl. One scoop." It took every ounce of restraint not to touch his rancid, balding head as the young man wrinkled his nose. Thankfully the lad had the courtesy to keep his comments to himself. "You don't sell brandy here, I don't suppose?" Stan fumbled in his pocket for his wallet.

"We've got a Brandy Manhattan with Cherries Jubilee flavor."

Stan's face lit up. "That's what I'll have. And put it in a cone. Make it a sugar cone. You got a real cherry you can put on top of that thing?" He handed over the money.

"That's not enough," Annabel said, as the young man held out the change.

"What do you mean?" Stan asked, looking at the bills and coins in his hand.

"You gave him a fifty dollar bill. He only gave you change back for a twenty dollar bill."

"Really?" Stan said.

"Really?" the young man asked, checking his change drawer. "Oh, geez, she's right. Sorry, sir." He handed Stan some extra bills.

"Good catch, Annabel," Stan said.

The nine year old shrugged, her tongue delicately twirling around her slowly dripping ice cream.

"I'm sorry, Ma'am, but I told you that Detective Ellison is busy and can't see anyone right now."

Emily studied the uniformed officer behind the bullet-proof glass, a young woman who appeared to be nearly nine months pregnant. Emily remembered what it felt like to be assigned to desk duty in those last months, knowing it was best for the safety of the baby, for your partner, and for all concerned, but feeling like you'd been put out to pasture for the duration.

"Officer Nakoma," she read from the young policewoman's I.D. tag. She worked to keep her rising impatience in check. "I need to talk to the detective about an ongoing murder investigation. I'm sure she'd—"

"I told you she's busy."

"—see me. If you'd just give her my card—"

But the desk officer had already turned her attention to the older man standing behind Emily. "How can I help you, sir?"

Resisting the inclination to politely step aside, Emily fumbled in her daypack and produced a tattered looking business card—Sgt. Emily Remington, Department of Public Safety, Escanaba, Michigan. It was, of course, out of date, but the woman behind the glass didn't need to know that. She scribbled a few words on the back of the card.

"Excuse me," she said to the man who had wedged his way in front of her. Shoving the card through the slot in the glass she said, "I'm sure she'll take a moment to see me."

Officer Nakoma took the card, glanced at it briefly and punched a few numbers into the phone console then spoke quietly into her headset. After a moment, she buzzed to release the door lock. Emily stepped into a small reception room, its scuffed tan concrete bricks, dirty institutional linoleum, and orange molded chairs reminiscent of both the stations in Escanaba and of the campus department in

Madison where she'd begun her career. The quiet of the entry foyer was replaced with a steady hum of undercurrent conversation from the twenty or so people sitting and squirming in their seats. A fatigued looking woman jiggled a fussy baby on her lap. A scruffy man, smelling of showerless weeks, gazed morosely at his feet.

Emily slid onto one of the orange chairs, immediately regretting having sat down. These chairs were obviously designed by someone in hell and her back would pay for it later. Uniformed officers jostled in and out of a door at the far side of the room, escorting waiting people into the bowels of the building where distant telephones jangled and keyboards clicked. After a ten-minute wait, one of the officers called, "Sgt. Remington," from his post at the door. Emily stood and followed him into a dimly lit hallway. He stopped at a door marked "Det. Ellison" and rapped, then stepped aside for Emily when a voice said, "Enter."

The tall black woman stood behind a gray metal desk. She peered over reading glasses at Emily, looking more like a stern librarian telling a patron to shush than a crack detective.

"Mrs. Remington. This is an unexpected visit. Is there something I can help you with?" She pronounced each word clearly and precisely.

Emily opened her mouth. "It's…" For a moment her confidence slipped. Detective Ellison presented an imposing figure, wearing a grey pinstriped pant suit with a lacy, deep mauve shell under the jacket. Her thick tightly braided black hair was pulled back into a no-nonsense pony tail, her make-up carefully understated. She tapped long manicured fingernails impatiently against the desktop. Emily flashed back to every commanding officer she'd ever stood in front of, though none of them had ever sported salon-styled nails or corn rows.

"It's about the death of Roger Hollinger. I have—"

"The suicide in the Old North Church."

"Yes. So they're calling it. I've come across some evidence

that calls that theory into question. I have here—" Emily tugged at the neck of her t-shirt. The summer heat had invaded the small office.

"Theory? Are you questioning my investigation, Officer Remington? Remind me—you're retired, not off-duty?"

Damn! She's pulling rank. A warm flush rose on her face and sweat beaded her forehead. Ellison offered an amused smile that said, "I've got your number," and Emily was immediately irritated that the detective would assume she was nervous, when in fact it was just those damn hormones acting up again.

"Yes, of course. Retired. It's just that—"

"Look, I've got three men out on sick leave, a pickpocket gang harassing tourists in the North End, some idiot taking potshots at city busses, and the mayor on my back about security for an African prince who wants to go pub hopping with his favorite consort. The last thing I need is for you or anyone else to start second-guessing a clear suicide—one with a note in the victim's own handwriting, by the way—and creating a media frenzy of speculation that there's a phantom murderer stalking our most popular tourist attractions."

"But I have—" Emily slipped her daypack off her shoulder but stopped when the detective held up the business card she'd given to the receptionist.

Ellison tapped the rumpled card against her fingers. "I don't see anything here about your being retired." Those black eyes glaring at her over the glasses again.

"No. I apologize. I just grabbed the first one—" Emily felt heat rising to her face again, and this time it had nothing to do with hot flashes. Defensiveness quickly evaporated into anger and determination, however. "Hear me out," she said. "Mrs. Hollinger asked me to look into her husband's death. She doesn't believe he committed suicide."

"Are you a licensed investigator now?"

"No," Emily conceded. "But when it comes to seeking the truth—"

"The truth is that he committed suicide. His wife ID'ed the handwriting on the note. He was having an affair and she's having difficulty accepting that truth. And you have no license to practice in the Commonwealth of Massachusetts. Now I have work to do."

At that moment an assistant rushed in, thrusting a thick file at the detective. "This is all I could find on that jewelry heist," he said.

"Thank you. Will you escort Mrs. Remington out?" Not bothering to look up from the sheaf of papers she'd started flipping through, she said to Emily, "You're lucky I don't arrest you for impersonating an officer."

Emily stormed out of the building, her daypack slamming against her back. At the corner, waiting for the traffic light to change, she took a couple of deep, centering breaths. Waves of heat rose off the pavement, reminding her of her humiliation at fighting off a hot flash during her encounter with the detective. *What did I expect? Flip the roles around and I would have been standing there saying it was an open and shut case.* But now she wasn't so sure. Should she have been more persistent about presenting Roger's daybook? Or was it better that she didn't have an opportunity to turn it over, just to have it tossed into an evidence box on a closed case?

The light changed and she hurried to the T stop, glancing at her watch. Stan would be antsy by now. What was that about wanting to take a shower in the middle of the day? *What did he do? Fall overboard? A close encounter with a diarrheic seagull?* Pushing through the turnstile, she trotted down the steps toward her train.

Waiting on the platform, she slipped Roger's black leather-bound book out of her day pack and examined it again. Gold leaf edges caught the light from the bare bulb overhead. Roger Hollinger must have had expensive taste. Or, given his pre-occupation with old books, perhaps he just liked the feel of leather and how it would last. Paging through the book, she re-read some of the entries. It all seemed pretty routine, except for that mysterious "7-4 Mtg. DC at ONC re: Bell." But then her eye caught the other one. B. Carter. Carter?

On a hunch Emily flipped open her phone and dialed Stan, stepping away from a noisy family waiting near her.

"I'm on my way. Listen, do me a favor. Can you do a reverse look-up on your phone?"

"Yeah, of course," Stan said. "Why? Who?"

"*Who* is what I'm trying to find out." She read the ten digit phone number printed in tiny tight script under B. Carter's name. The platform under her feet began to rumble. The light of an oncoming train bounced off the tunnel walls of the opposite track. Moments later, the train squealed into the station drowning out Stan's voice.

"Wait, I can't hear you."

She tapped her foot impatiently, waiting for the people on the platform across from her to board and the train to rumble out again.

"Okay, say that again?" She held a hand over one ear and sidestepped, trying to avoid the growing crowd jostling for position on the platform.

"I said...the number belongs to a Belle Carter. The address is listed as being in Brighton. Emily, is that the same woman Wynter and I met at the Longfellow House, the one we found dead in the park? Why do you have her number?"

"That's the question of the day. Gotta go. My train's here."

After pushing her way onto the train, she dug through a small zippered pocket on her pack, searching for the card that Detective Ellison had given her earlier at the pool. She flipped open her cell phone again.

"Hello? Whitman Carter? Hi, my name is Emily Remington. I'm the one whose family found your mother in the park the night of the fireworks. A police officer gave me your card the other day and said you were interesting in meeting me."

CHAPTER 16

STAN was about ready to strangle his darling granddaughters by the time Emily arrived at the ice cream shop. Allyn's chocolate chip banana ice cream had somehow ended up in Annabel's hair, and Wynter had locked herself into the small shop's restroom, refusing to come out until her grandmother got there.

Through the teen' teary tirade, he took it she was having an unexpected feminine disaster, and not knowing what to do about it, he tacked an "Out of Order" sign scribbled on a napkin to the bathroom door to ward off disappointed customers. He himself had run into the men's room three times, to re-wash the spot on his head where the seagull's offering had landed.

"Grandma!" the twins shouted as she pushed through the glass door, the jingle bells at the top announcing her arrival.

"Grandpa's mad at us."

"And Wynter won't come out of the bathroom."

"And I gotta go bad!"

"And my hair's all mushy and sticky."

"And where's Grandpa going?

"And how come everyone holds their nose when he—? "

Stan let the shop door slam shut behind him as he stalked

off to where he'd left the car parked earlier that morning.

An hour later they were back at the RV park. Finally showered, Stan popped open a beer and settled onto the chaise lounge next to Wynter. He had appreciated how quickly Emily had gotten the girl calmed down and her teenage feminine needs taken care of. He was even more appreciative when she offered to take the two younger girls to the pool to splash off some yet unvented energy. He took another sip of the cold beer, before nodding off in contentment.

"Daddy?" Wynter sat up.

Stan opened one eye. Was that Philip in the Chevy Suburban maneuvering a pop-up camper into the site next to theirs? And was that Megan sitting next to him, grinning like a Cheshire cat?

Giving up on his nap, Stan helped them get the camper positioned and unhitched from the car. After they chocked the wheels and leveled and stabilized the unit, Philip cranked the roof up. Then he and Stan cranked out the bed ends, and Stan went inside to install the door.

"Daddy! Daddy! Where did you get it?" Allyn asked, running toward the popup. She and Annabel and Emily were just coming up the camp road, wet towels wrapped around their waists.

"Yeah, Philip? Where did you get a popup big enough to hold its own toilet?" Stan laughed, poking his head through the door of the camper that was big enough to sleep the entire family. He held the door wide as they all trooped into the mobile tent.

Wynter eyed the small commode with skepticism after Philip proudly lifted the lid of a storage unit in the center of the camper, exposing the small toilet seat. "I'm using Grandpa's bathroom," she announced.

"Hey, it's got a privacy curtain," Philip chuckled.

"Cute," Megan said. "I'm using Dad's bathroom, too."

"I'll use it!" Allyn announced, sitting on the toilet seat with her swimsuit still on.

"Not in front of everyone. Let's put the lid down." Megan nudged her daughter off the unit and set the lid back onto the commode. "I'm going to help Grandma get dinner ready. Annabel, Allyn let's get you over to the RV and out of those wet swim suits." She gestured to the twins, who had quickly made themselves comfortable in the miniature dinette. Wynter had flopped onto one of the beds and was on her back looking at her phone.

"Philip got a great deal for the weekend," Megan informed her father.

"So what's on the menu for tonight?" Philip asked. "Camping makes me hungry."

Later, after the dinner of bar-b-cue chicken and potato salad had been cleared from the table, Stan held up a double deck of cards, "Who wants to learn to play Hand and Foot?"

"I do! I do!" the twins shouted.

"Wynter?" he invited.

"I guess." The older girl slid onto the picnic table bench next to her grandfather and across from the twins.

Philip worked on building a teepee of logs in the fire pit, while Megan dragged lawn chairs into a circle around it. Emily wandered back and forth across the lot, stooping to look under the RV, inside the car, under a pile of towels. She straightened up with one sandal in her hand.

"Anyone seen my other sandal?"

"Nope."

"Not me."

"Did you look in the RV?" Stan asked, dealing the cards.

"That was the first, third and seventh place I looked." Emily sounded exasperated. "I've searched everywhere."

"I bet the witch stole it," Annabel said, her voice a bare whisper.

"I heard that, Annabel," Emily chastised. "She's not a

witch. We've been through this."

"Who's not a witch?" Philip asked.

"The cat lady." Allyn said. "She's been stealing stuff all week."

"She didn't steal anything," Emily admonished.

"Like what? What did she steal?" Philip prodded.

"My earbuds, for one thing," Wynter informed him. "I can't find them anywhere."

"My goggles," Allyn said. "And my beach towel."

"And now Grandma's sandal." This was Annabel.

"But what would she want with one sandal?" Wynter asked. "It doesn't make sense."

"It does if she needs it to cast a spell," Allyn said.

"Nobody is casting spells," Megan said. "You girls are being unkind again."

"Sorry," Annabel and Allyn said together.

Wynter smirked. "Maybe she needed it for the cats to chew on."

"Sounds like someone to keep an eye on," Philip said.

"Don't encourage them," Megan chided.

Emily sighed. "I'll wear my tennies. The sandal will show up sooner or later."

The sun had set and the light was beginning to fade. Stan got up and fetched a battery-powered lantern from the RV and set it at the end of the picnic table so he and the girls could still see their cards. An hour later, after Megan had put the yawning little ones to bed in the pop-up camper, Stan stirred the fire, satisfied when it blazed back to life. Wynter had pulled her chair close to his, even though her eyes were glued to the tiny glowing screen in her hand. He tousled her hair and nestled into the chair next to her, the Brandy Manhattan Philip had made for him cooling his hands.

"So...tell me more about your visit with Rhea this afternoon," he said to Emily and Megan.

"Oh, Dad! Mom is so awesome! She's agreed to help Rhea figure out what happened to her husband."

Stan raised an eyebrow. "Yeah, what's up with that, Em? We're on vacation here."

Emily twirled her vodka and tonic, studying the way the light of the fire bounced off the liquid in the glass. "Yeah, well, the thing is…something isn't adding up."

"What exactly isn't adding up? And what was so important you had to bother Detective Ellison?"

"Did you give her the day planner?" Megan asked.

"Not yet."

"What day planner?" Philip asked.

"Roger's appointment calendar. We found it when we were going through his things," Megan said, then to Emily, "You still have it? I thought you were going to turn it over to the police?"

"I was. I am." Emily caught Stan's look. "I will."

"You're withholding evidence?" Philip asked. "Something that's important to the case? You could get into a shitload of trouble for that."

"Yes, you could," Stan chimed in.

"I can't believe this. Mom, what were you thinking?"

"I was thinking that Detective Ellison has already decided the outcome of her investigation. And that if I gave her that calendar book now, it would get plunked into some evidence box and stuck on a shelf in a storage room where it would never see the light of day."

She looked at Stan, not so much for affirmation, he knew, but just to be sure he wouldn't keel over in a fit of apoplexy. So when he spoke it was in a quiet, matter-of-fact voice.

"What is in that book that makes it worth you risking your reputation and possibly going to jail?"

"Jail?" By now even Wynter had shut off her phone. "Grandma could go to jail?"

"No one is going to jail. It's just that Rhea is convinced that her husband didn't commit suicide and that he hadn't been having an affair."

"C'mon, Em. You're the one who always says—"

"The wife is the last to know. I know, but..."

"But what?"

"I'll show you." She went into the RV and moments later came out with the plastic zippered bag.

"Is that it? Let me see." Philip reached to take the book from her hands.

"Wait. You probably don't want to get your fingerprints on it," Megan said.

Philip held the bag up by one corner, trying to peer inside.

"I've got just the thing." Stan opened one of the storage compartment doors under the RV, dug into a large plastic tub, and produced a small box.

"You travel with disposable gloves?" Philip asked as Stan ripped off the top.

"Never want to hook up the black water hose bare handed," Stan pontificated before passing the box around.

Everyone solemnly gloved up so they could take a peek at Roger's day planner. Emily laughed at the sight of them. "I've already handled it, so I'm not going to worry about gloves," she said, moving to the picnic table under the lantern. The others crowded around.

"This is kinda creepy going through a dead man's calendar, don't you think?" Wynter said with a delighted shiver.

"It's all part of police work," Emily said, watching Philip page through the book with gloved fingers.

"Pretty mundane stuff in here," he declared.

"Look ahead a few pages. There. Look at that." Megan pointed to the cryptic letters: 7-4 Mtg. DC at ONC re: Bell. "What do you think that means?"

"DC...dental clinic?" Stan offered.

"How about Downtown Crossing?" Megan suggested.

"What?" Stan was puzzled.

"The T station," Philip said. "Okay, how about this one?

DC, like in Washington, DC?" He seemed to be enjoying the guessing game.

"But look here," Emily said, pointing to another notation. "This looks like an appointment for later this week."

Stan read the notation. "B Carter. Belle Carter? That's the number you had me Google this afternoon." He rubbed his chin. "You got it from Roger's daybook?"

"Belle Carter?" Philip asked. "Isn't she…?"

"The lady who died in the park," Wynter finished his sentence in a hushed voice. "The one Grandpa and I met at the Longfellow House. Why does Mrs. Hollinger's husband have her name in his calendar book?"

"Pretty big coincidence, if you ask me," Philip commented.

"Most likely a business connection," Emily said. "It turns out he was an appraiser of literary documents."

"Really?" Stan raised an eyebrow.

"Anyway, I called Belle's son. I have an appointment to meet with him tomorrow morning."

"Her son?" Megan asked. "Mom, how did you—?"

"When Detective Ellison stopped by the pool the other day, she gave me his card."

"Ah, okay. I remember you saying something about that."

"His name is Whitman Carter. He had wanted me to call anyway. I guess to say thanks for finding his mother."

"Maybe she's the one Roger had the affair with," Philip suggested.

"I still don't believe he had an affair. Even if there was a note," Megan disagreed.

"What if he didn't write it?" Wynter asked.

"Rhea confirmed it was his handwriting, honey," Emily said.

"So, maybe he wrote it under duress," Philip guessed.

"Someone forced him to write a note saying he had had an affair then strung him up in the bell tower?" Stan asked.

"Stranger things have happened."

"Still. Highly unlikely." His eyes met Emily's. "You're determined to meet this Whitman Carter tomorrow? The son?"

"It seems the least I can do to help Rhea out. Would you be willing to tag along?"

CHAPTER 17

WHILE Stan stood in line to order their coffees, Emily claimed a small table for three near the window. Situated across the street from the Boston Common, the incredibly busy little café Whitman Carter had recommended appeared to be *the* place to go on a summer morning.

Whitman had seemed pleased to get Emily's call. However, she was feeling guilty and a bit regretful at giving up precious time with her daughter and granddaughters. And Stan wasn't happy that she was pursuing this interview. On the upside, Megan had been so appreciative of Emily's willingness to help her friend that Emily felt a bit mollified. And early that morning, before they'd headed into the city, she'd had the pleasure of conducting another Tae kwon do session with the twins. She still hadn't been able to coax Wynter into joining, but had been energized when Amy, Tara, and Marion showed up eager for a workout.

Stan set two steaming cups on the table then swiped at his cell phone and sat down to check his favorite news apps.

"Damn!" He threw the phone down on the table.

"What?"

"No Wi-Fi."

"Really?"

Emily eyed the room. Of course. The usual huddles of students sitting over their laptops and netbooks were missing. Instead, people were chatting or reading. Emily quickly brought her coffee cup up to her lips to hide her grin.

"There's a newspaper stand by the counter."

With a grunt, Stan got up to fetch a copy of the *Boston Globe.*

Emily inhaled the aroma of the hazelnut brew as she watched him make his way through the crowd of tables. Certainly she could have met Whitman Carter by herself, but despite Stan's disgruntlement, she was grateful that he was willing to come along in case the man turned out to be something other than just a grieving son. Blowing across the hot liquid, she took a tentative sip. This might just qualify as the best coffee she'd had in a decade.

Stan trooped back, plopped himself in his chair and opened his paper with a deliberate rattle. Emily bit her lip to keep from smiling, then sat back to take a survey of the people around her, a habit she had developed as a small town police officer. The old man shuffling in with a walker to order coffee black and a bagel with cream cheese, toasted please. The woman with too many shopping bags searching for an empty seat. The college students engaged in an intense debate at a crowded table tucked into the back corner.

A swirl of black fabric swooped past the window. The door of the shop flew open and a young man strode in, dressed in black cape and tri-corner hat, sporting a wooden cane. All eyes tracked the figure, even those of the over-caffeinated college students.

Stan glanced up from his paper in momentary confusion, but then broke into a wide grin. "Is that our tour guide from the Freedom Trail?"

The man swiveled, his cape flowing around him as he eyed the patrons in the shop one by one. He spotted Emily and Stan by the window and immediately headed in their direction. Whitman Carter?

He doffed the tricorn with a flourish and, putting one foot behind him, bent into a bow from the waist. "Mr. and Mrs. Remington, I presume!"

Amused, Emily greeted him. "Whitman Carter?"

Stan immediately rose to shake the man's hand.

"It's so good of you both to meet with me." Carter straightened and furrowed his brow, studying Stan's face. "You look familiar. Have we met?"

"Coupla days ago," Stan said. "On the Freedom Trail."

"Ah! The wonderfully knowledgeable history buff! And you were with the two—or was it three—delightful girls?"

"You're the cobbler," Emily said, reaching to return the handshake he offered her.

"Cordwainer," Stan corrected her. "And it was three. Delightful depends on mood and cycle of moon."

Whitman pushed his cape aside and sat on the wrought iron chair across from Emily.

"Is this purely a coincidence? Or did you join the tour because you knew my mother?"

"A coincidence, I'm afraid. We'd never actually met your mother. Well, that's not true. Stan did."

Whitman Carter appeared confused.

"Only once. I had an appointment with her at the Longfellow house," Stan explained.

"But they told me you were with her when she died?"

"It's a sort of six degrees of separation situation. We weren't so much with her as we found her," Emily said. "Would you like some coffee?"

"I'll get it." Stan jumped up. "What would you like?" He hustled off.

"This should be quite a story," Whitman said to Emily, a bit sadly.

"You appear to be the storyteller. How did you happen to become a Freedom Trail guide?" Emily asked.

"I'm a teacher. A history teacher. So yes, a storyteller. This is my summer job. Do I remember correctly that you're from the Midwest?"

Emily nodded. "We're from Upper Michigan. You know about the two peninsulas of Michigan?"

"Indeed, I do." Whitman positioned his hands to create the lower mitten and upper fox-like peninsulas of the Midwestern state. "I've even been across that grand bridge of yours. The Mackinac."

"Stan's a history teacher. Was. He's retired now. We both are. But he still writes. He's got one book out on Great Lakes shipwrecks, but now he has this bug in his ear about George Washington. Hence the visit with your mother." Emily paused as Stan handed a cup to their guest.

"A fellow storyteller. I knew it from the moment I first met you, sir." He accepted the coffee with an appreciative nod.

Stan produced his business card and happily accepted Whitman's. Kindred spirits, Emily mused.

"I want to thank you both," Whitman said, tucking Stan's card into his shirt pocket, "for…you know, for being with, or rather, finding my mother. At the end." He blinked, fighting encroaching tears. He busied himself stirring his coffee, sipping, stirring some more.

"I'm so sorry for your loss," Emily said. Those words again.

Whitman nodded.

"I had only met her that one time," Stan said. "But she seemed like a wonderful person. Kind and helpful. Extremely knowledgeable."

Whitman grabbed for his handkerchief and blew his nose. "Sorry. So, how is it that you happened to find her? There in the park."

Stan shifted uncomfortably in his chair. Emily knew this was the sort of situation where he preferred to let her take the lead.

"Our family was sitting just a few feet away from her chair. It was actually one of our granddaughters who…who discovered that she was dead."

"How horrible for your granddaughter! Is she okay about it?"

"It doesn't appear to have caused any trauma. Your mother, well, she seemed to have died peacefully," Emily reassured him.

"The Medical Examiner told me it was most likely a heart attack. They have an autopsy scheduled." He grimaced. "Standard procedure, I guess." Emily nodded. "But it just seems so odd." He bit his lip and shook his head.

"Odd in what way?"

"For one thing, she didn't have any heart problems that I was aware of. In fact, she'd had a physical not too long ago."

"Heart attacks can happen to anyone," Stan said tapping his own heart. "Even to people who appear to be healthy."

"That's what my brother keeps saying."

"Your brother?"

"Tennyson. Mother raised the two of us by herself. My father left us when we were quite young."

"I'm sorry. This must be doubly hard on you." Emily hesitated for a moment. "I know this must seem like a strange question, but was she seeing anyone? Did she maybe have a gentleman friend?"

Whitman laughed. "Mom? No." He set his coffee deliberately on table, pausing to find the right words. "She'd had relationships. But not with 'gentlemen.' Not since Dad left anyway."

Emily was perplexed.

"She had started dating women when I was in high school," Whitman explained.

Emily hiked her eyebrows, and she exchanged a glance with Stan.

"She'd been in a serious relationship with one woman for several years. Evelyn. Not quite a second mother, but she'd grown to be part of my family. They'd even talked on and off about getting married under Massachusetts' new law."

"It sounds like they were no longer together?" Emily queried.

"Evelyn moved out a couple weeks ago. No explanation. Mom wouldn't talk about it. I even tried calling Evelyn once, but she wouldn't take my call."

Emily hesitated again before asking, "Do you know a Roger Hollinger?"

Whitman was silent for a moment, then shook his head. "Never heard of him. Why?"

"He died the day after your mother did."

"Shit. Really? How? What's the connection? I assume there's a connection or you wouldn't have mentioned it."

"The police think his death was a suicide. There was a note." Emily searched the man's face, but he didn't react. "The note made reference to an affair he was supposedly having."

"And you think it was with my mother?" Whitman looked almost amused.

"No, not necessarily. But her name and phone number were listed in his daybook. It appears he had a meeting scheduled with her for this week."

"I see." Whitman scratched his head. "Actually, I don't see. Couldn't it have been a business meeting?"

"Most likely it was."

"And…how do you happen to know what is in this Roger what-ever-his-name-was' daybook."

"Kind of a long story. But I've been asked to make enquiries."

"By whom? Why? Are the two of you some sort of investigators?"

"I'm simply helping out a friend."

"She's a retired police officer," Stan said. "She's had quite a lot of experience with things of this sort."

Now their guest seemed at a loss for words. Emily suspected that didn't happen often.

Finally, he blurted out. "Damn! That is just too bizarre."

Then after a moment, "Suicide, you said? This Roger fellow?"

"Quite possibly."

"Is there some doubt?"

"When someone dies unexpectedly there's always room for doubt."

"Is there room for doubt in the death of my mother? Is it possible she died from something other than a heart attack?"

"What do you think?"

"I think I need something stronger than coffee."

"Are you saying my mother committed suicide?"

Whitman Carter was now sitting across from Emily and Stan nursing a whiskey neat. He had taken off the black cape, folded it, and set it next to him on the bench of the secluded booth they'd commandeered in a quiet, little tavern just a block from the Public Garden. His tri-corner hat sat on top of the cape, his cane lay across the bench seat behind him. On the walk over from the coffee shop, he'd dialed up his tour company and called in sick for the rest of the afternoon.

"I really have no idea what the circumstances of your mother's death were." Emily poked at a Cobb salad. "What I do know is that someone she may have worked with at one time or another killed himself, and no one knows the real reason why."

"I mentioned that I'd met with her recently. At the Longfellow House." Stan dipped his spoon into a thick creamy cup of clam chowder. "I was hoping she could point me in the direction of some of George Washington's papers from his time in Boston."

Whitman reached into his pocket for his cell phone. A couple of taps on the screen brought up a photo of a woman dressed in a park ranger's pants and shirt with a Smoky Bear hat on her head. He held it out to Emily.

"I'm confused," Emily said. "Didn't you say she was a historian?"

"A literary historian," Whitman corrected her.

"The Longfellow House is a national park," Stan said. "She was also a park ranger."

"Her area of specialty was Longfellow," Whitman explained. "About five years ago she lucked into the park ranger job at the house in Cambridge. You would have thought she'd died and gone to literary heaven."

Emily regarded Stan for a moment. Given a different path in life, he would have had the same reaction.

"Mom had finished her PhD just a year before. Her dissertation, I'm sure you can already guess, was about Longfellow and his poetry. More recently she started talking about some new find she had made through her research. She kept saying it was going to turn everything around for her."

"In what way?"

"You see, Mom...she struggled financially when we were growing up. Tenny wasn't much help. He liked motorcycles and graduated to fast cars. Was always hitting her up for money to buy his next big toy. And it didn't help that all three of us were paying off student loans of one sort or another."

Emily and Stan both nodded sympathetically.

"Anyway, a couple of years ago, Tenny got involved in some sort of financial scheme and came away solvent. Or so we thought. Then—surprise, surprise—he needed money again. And Mom, you know, she handed over the cash without question. Never complained. But I think she was living on the edge again. It was pretty hard on her relationship with Evelyn. I won't kid you. Mom seemed to feel that this new find—whatever it was she found in her research—would somehow bring her a real cash bonus. She believed she could bail him out and still have enough to do something nice for herself and Evelyn. But to be honest, I have no idea what it was she found or how it was going to help her financially."

"Would your brother know?"

"Hell, I doubt it. All he cared about was getting bailed out. He didn't pay much attention to where the money came from.

Tried to hit me up, once I got a job with a year-long contract, but…listen, you're not interested in brotherly hoo-haws. Point is, as far as knowing anything about my mother's research, Tennyson is likely a dead end on several levels."

Whitman's voice was getting louder and louder, his clenched fist pounded the table. Emily and Stan sat in awkward silence.

"It kills me that she never seemed to be able to get ahead!" He stopped. "Sorry. Don't know why I'm bothering you with this."

Emily reached over and touched his hand. "You've just suffered a deep loss. Please don't feel like you have to apologize." She hesitated a third time. "Would it be okay if we talked with Evelyn? About your mother's research?"

"I don't see why not," Whitman said softly. "Actually, that would be a great idea. Let me give you her number. You might want to talk with the people at the Longfellow House, too. One of the rangers maybe? And there was this other guy. A judge of some sort, I think she said. He might have been connected with one of their fundraising groups. I got the impression he was a sort of mentor to Mom."

"Do you know his name?"

Whitman shook his head.

"That's probably Judge Calderwood," Stan said. "He was with Belle when Wynter and I met with her."

Emily asked Whitman, "Is there anything else you can think of that might shed some light on her research?"

"Not really. She did some guest lecturing over at Simmons College. Maybe you could find someone there to talk to?" He checked his pocket watch. "I've taken up too much of your time." He signaled for the check. "This one's on me."

"Oh, hey, that's not necessary," Stan protested.

"No, really. It's the least I can do. For…you know…being there for my Mom. Calling the authorities. That sort of thing."

"So, Whitman," Emily said while they waited for the

check. "That's a rather unusual first name."

"Mom named me after Walt Whitman."

"The poet?" Stan said.

"And my brother Tennyson…"

"Let me guess," Emily said. "Alfred Lord Tennyson."

"You know your nineteenth century lit." The young man left cash on the table.

"My life isn't all murder and mayhem." Emily smiled.

He picked up the tri-corner hat and plopped it on his head. "I'm just glad Mom didn't discover how much she loved Henry Wadsworth Longfellow until after I was born."

"Or you'd be Longfellow Carter?"

Whitman laughed softly and eased out of the booth. "Or maybe Wadsworth Carter. Kids in junior high would have had some real fun with that one. Look, hate to drink and run, but I do have to go."

Emily spoke quietly. "Whitman, what does your gut say about how your mother died?"

He shook out the cape and swung it over his shoulders, reached for the cane. Then he looked her directly in the eye. "My gut says she didn't die of a heart attack. And she certainly didn't commit suicide."

With a nod to Stan, he spun and strode out of the tavern, his cape swirling behind him.

CHAPTER 18

"NICE guy," Stan said stepping out into the sunlight.

Whitman had disappeared down the street. Stan and Emily headed off in the opposite direction, toward the Public Garden. Stan had to work to keep from huffing. It bothered him that Emily was in better shape than he was. He wanted to blame it on his heart, but he knew it had more to do with his waist line.

"Glad we met him?" she asked.

"Yeah, of course. He is an historian after all."

"But...?"

They stopped at the cross walk to wait for the light to change. "But obviously Belle Carter wasn't the one Roger Hollinger was cheating on his wife with."

Emily shrugged. "It was a long shot anyway. It's not like he would have written the name of his lover on his calendar for his wife and the rest of the world to see."

"I dunno. Men do some pretty stupid things when they get in the cheatin' mood."

"And you know this how?" They started across with a crowd of other pedestrians and entered the park.

"It's a guy thing. Being stupid. It's why I never cheated on you. I'm not stupid." He paused to admire an enormous bronze statue of George Washington astride a magnificent horse, mounted high on a pedestal.

Emily shaded her eyes to stare up at the graceful general who gazed out over the Garden with a sense of victory and satisfaction. *"That's* why you never cheated on me?"

"That and the fact that I'm still crazy in love with you after all these years."

"Why, Stan Remington! That's the most romantic thing you've said since…the other night." She nudged him in the ribs and then kissed him right there in the park in front of everyone.

"Okay…that was nice. Very nice!" He grabbed her arm to pull her out of the way of a pair of roller bladers. They started off down the path again toward the lagoon. "So what now?"

"I dunno. I suppose we tell Rhea that it's looking like Roger's death was suicide after all. I'm not seeing any evidence to the contrary. I really hate letting her down, but..."

"Yeah, I know. Shall we head back to the campground?" Stan asked hopefully.

They strolled across the century-and-a-half-old miniature suspension footbridge spanning the lagoon with its famous swan boats.

"On the other hand, it might not be a bad idea to talk with Belle's friend first. Her partner. Friend. Whatever. Evelyn."

"Why?"

"Gut feeling. I still think it's too much of a coincidence that the phone number of a woman we found dead in the park shows up in the calendar book of the man you found dead in that church."

"So now you're thinking Roger didn't commit suicide?"

"No. But the bigger question is why would he do it? Maybe Evelyn can shed some light on what the relationship between Roger and Belle was, if it wasn't an affair."

He followed her to a bench on the other side of the bridge, still feeling uncomfortable about pursuing a death investigation, but he had to admit that meeting with the cordwainer had piqued his curiosity. Breathing in the fragrances of the garden, he was grateful for the chance to sit for a few minutes while she searched for the number Whitman Carter had given her.

"Hello, Ms. LeBlanc? My name is Emily Remington."

Stan contemplated the half dozen graceful swan boats, filled with rows of happy children and their parents. That couple over there looked more his age. Grandparents, likely. He regretted not having gone with Emily and the twins the other day. However, he wouldn't have given up that time on the train with Wynter for anything. He tapped his phone and brought up the photo she had taken. He wondered if he could talk his eldest granddaughter into coming to Michigan when the time came for her to go to college. College. What was it Whitman Carter had said? Stan hit the browser app on his phone and typed in a name. An entry popped up with a link to an office phone number. He tapped the link.

"Hey! Associate Professor Timothy Frazer here. Not in at the moment. Check my web page for office hours or leave a message. Chat with you soon."

Stan waited for the beep. "Hey there yourself, Prof. This is full Professor Stan Remington, the guy who gave you the D minus on that western European history exam then let you take it over so you wouldn't flunk the course and lose your scholarship. I'm in Boston for a few days and thought maybe we could catch up. Call me back if you're still around for the summer." With a shrug of disappointment, Stan pocketed his phone just as Emily was finishing her call.

"She's agreed to meet with us this afternoon," Emily told him. He could hear the suppressed anticipation in her voice. "But she isn't free until about four o'clock. Who were you talking with?"

"Whitman had mentioned that his mother did some guest lecturing over at Simmons College. Do you remember Tim Frazer? A former student of mine?"

Emily shrugged.

"He's teaching at Simmons now. I called him on the off chance that he knew her."

"Good idea!"

"Yeah, well…went straight to voice mail. I left a message. It's a long shot that he'll even get back to me. Okay, so what do we do 'til four?"

"I know what I'd like to do."

Stan grinned thinking of how sweet that kiss felt then realized she wasn't talking about an afternoon liaison. His smile faded.

"The bell tower. You did a great job describing what you saw when you and Megan found Roger, but I really need to see the scene for myself."

"No. Emily, no." He stood up and strode away. Emily rushed to catch up with him.

"You wouldn't have to go in. You could wait outside. Or in the gift shop. They must have a gift shop. Right? Filled with wonderfully historic books that you could spend hours getting lost in. Not that it would take me hours to look around. Really, I get that you don't want to go up there again. But you wouldn't have to."

Stan stopped to face her, causing her to almost bump into him.

"Damn it, Emily! Don't give me that look. We're getting way more involved than we should be, just talking to that dead woman's son. And to be honest, I'm having second thoughts about whether we should even be meeting with this Evelyn woman. And as for that bell tower…"

He was shaking now. Emily grabbed his hand.

"You don't understand," he said, his throat threatening to close up. "That church is the closest I've ever come to…to…touching something, breathing in something that existed in the time that my heroes were alive. And now, every time I close my eyes and think of it, I see…him. Hanging there. In the dark. Emily, what if I can never go inside that church again? What if I can never touch the very steps that Paul Revere climbed? Or sit in the seat he sat in? Because of…because of…him. That man. His body, hanging there." Stan blinked back tears he was determined not to let form.

Emily squeezed his hand. "Then maybe you should go back inside. Now. With me. Maybe you should confront that fear. That feeling."

"I dunno."

"Let's walk over there. You can decide when we get there. If you don't want to go in, that's okay. You won't stay out of that wonderfully historic place forever. I know you won't. But let's go and see what happens."

He knew that what she was saying had nothing to do with her "investigation." It had everything to do with her belief that you had to face your demons. And he was grateful she was there to support him in whatever he decided he needed to do.

He wrapped his hand around hers and they headed across the Common and toward the North End.

But twenty minutes later, as they walked up Hanover Street and entered the Paul Revere Mall, he caught sight of the white-washed steeple stabbing the clear blue sky. His heart began to pound. And he knew it had nothing to do with being out of shape.

The yellow tape was gone. A sign that the police accepted the verdict of suicide, Emily decided. They had traversed the Paul Revere Mall with its own larger-than-life sculpture, this one of Paul Revere high on a grand steed. Dodging a crowd of tourists scrambling off a red open-air trolley, they worked their way up the sidewalk between the church and the annex building.

Approaching the red double doors of the church, Stan hesitated, sweat beading his forehead. His face paled as he stared up at the gleaming white steeple. Maybe this wasn't such a good idea, Emily mused.

"I can't." His voice was barely a whisper.

"It's okay. We don't have to go in. It was a bad idea. We'll find someplace to hang out for a couple of hours then catch a cab out to Evelyn's house."

Just then a guitar riff emanated from Stan's pocket. "Hello?" Putting his phone to his ear, he stepped aside to avoid another tour group and edged along the wrought iron fence to get away from the crowd.

Emily followed him, glad for the bit of shade. As Stan continued his conversation, the color came back into his face and he was smiling again.

"Sure. We can come right now," he was saying. "We'll catch a cab. Shouldn't take long to get there. Thanks so much for calling back." He thrust his phone into his pocket.

"That was Tim Frazer. He got my message after all. Turns out he's free for a couple of hours and invited us to come to the campus."

"You just said you didn't want to pursue this any further," Emily said.

"I wouldn't mind catching up with him. He did return my call."

Emily squinted up at the steeple. "I wonder if you'd mind going on your own? It'll just be a lot of academic talk anyway, right?"

Stan followed her gaze upward. "You're still determined to go up there, aren't you? You don't even know if you can get in. It's likely locked."

"Maybe I can find a tour group going up. Didn't you say they give regular tours of the building? The crypt, the tower?"

"I thought you wanted to find out about Belle Carter. If I go to see Tim by myself, how do I bring it up?"

"You're a researcher. I'm guessing you could get far more information about Belle Carter from one simple conversation with a former protégé than I ever could interrogating him."

Stan scratched at his ear uncertainly. A cab stopped at the

curb to drop off an older couple in front of the church.

"If you're going to go, you'd better catch that cab," she said.

He hesitated, but only for a moment. "Okay. But don't do anything stupid, okay? Text me that woman's address and I'll meet you there at four." He waved to catch the cabby's attention. "Nothing stupid, got that?"

"Got it!" Emily waved him off as he slid into the back of the cab.

The taxi lurched off and she jogged back toward the church. Walking past the historical marker embedded into a brick post, she stopped. "The Old North Church," she mouthed silently. "Old North Church…O…N…C…" The initials in Roger's daybook. Could this be what he was referring to when he wrote, "Mtg. DC at ONC"? She touched the plaque as if it held the answer she was looking for. It would make sense. But then who was DC?

The church felt cool inside, compared to the heat of the midday sun. Following a group of stragglers into the sanctuary, she paused to get her bearings. The room was bright, filled with sunlight gleaming off the white walls, pillars, and boxed pews. She remembered Stan and Megan sitting in that last pew like school kids with Detective Ellison hovering over them.

She surveyed the altar with its pulpit high overhead then shifted her gaze up toward the choir loft. What a thrill Stan must have felt being in this building! His sense of history was so visceral. She could image what his reaction had been when he spotted the octagonal clock high up on the balcony wall. *I'll bet that's been there since the days of Paul Revere.*

After dropping a five dollar bill into the donation jar at the reception desk, she stepped back out into the small foyer. A sign listed the times of the scheduled tours. Nearly an hour until the next one. She didn't want to wait that long. And she doubted the tour would take her exactly where she wanted to go anyway.

Approaching the bell tower door, she grasped the knob and tried to turn it; but it was locked, just as Stan had said it would be. Digging for a small fingernail file in her daypack, she waited for an older couple to move past her and into the sanctuary of the church. The foyer was empty now, but only for a moment. She quickly inserted the file into the key hole, jiggled it a bit and felt the tumbler move.

A young couple came in through the front door, a pair of toddlers tugging at their hands. The family paid no attention to her, rushing past and into the church. Emily took advantage of the empty foyer again, quickly opened the door, slipped inside, and shut it behind her. The stairwell was dark and smelled of old polished wood. She flipped open her phone to provide just enough light to navigate the creaky old steps. It helped that the walls were white-washed and reflected even the little light she had.

As she rounded a corner at the top of the stairs, she found herself in an open chamber. She flipped a switch on the wall and lit up the room. The wall to the right was filled with cupboards and drawers. She remembered Stan saying something about an archival room. This must be it.

She crossed the room to another stairwell, this one with unfinished brick walls. She needed the light from her phone again. The rough-hewn steps curved up and into an even larger chamber with brick walls. Two round windows with two-foot casements, one on either side of the room, let in a surprising amount of sunlight. Hanging in a circle from the ceiling was a collection of ropes, each knotted about five feet off the floor. The ringing chamber.

She stepped to the opposite wall and gazed up and into the gloom of yet another stairwell. Nothing for it but to keep going. Realizing she needed something more than her cell phone screen, she dug into her daypack and found her mini-mag light. Taking a deep breath, she started up again, this time climbing two full flights.

The beam of her flashlight bounced off a large massive

object hanging just off to the side—a bell. This must be where Stan and Megan and the bell master had found Roger Hollinger's body. Swinging her flashlight in an arc, she noticed even more steps, these ones steeper than what she'd just come up, almost ladder like. She was thankful she didn't need to climb any further.

She surveyed the interior of the steeple where the large bell hung, wishing she had more light, but she'd have to make do with what she had. Based on Stan's description of where he'd seen Roger's body, she deduced the location, but there was no rope, no evidence of anything having been amiss. The only sign that anything had happened up here was the residue of dusting powder on the rail around the bell casing.

Taking her time, she examined the entire area thoroughly, noting the details of the wooden structures around her, and wondered what would drive a man to do what he did. When she was satisfied there was nothing more to see, she headed back down the stairs to the ringing room again. A voice boomed out.

"What are you doing up here?"

CHAPTER 19

STAN paid the taxi driver and, hurrying toward the distinguished-looking administration building, ran smack into a young woman walking backward, followed by a small crowd of bewildered looking teenagers and their anxious parents.

"Oh! Excuse me!" she said to Stan, then, "People! People! Stay with me. We'll finish up our tour back inside the Main Campus Building."

Waiting for the group to shuffle through the door behind their perky young guide, Stan studied the façade of the classical old building, its white pillars dominating the main entrance and the ubiquitous—at least in Boston—spire overlooking the campus. Following them inside, he nodded sympathetically at a middle-aged couple who seemed to be calculating the cost of the next four years. The guide and her entourage veered toward the bookstore while Stan headed for the elevator.

He breathed in deeply. Campus life. He hadn't realized until this very moment that he missed it. The sounds, the smells of an academic building. There was a latent energy that Stan always felt on a college campus. Something about the undercurrent of inquiry, learning, and research that the students and the professors engaged in—Stan found it invigorating. He didn't have any other word to describe it. Maybe he'd have to see if he could pick up an adjunct class or two when he and Emily got back to Michigan.

Stepping off the elevator onto the third floor, he studied the numbers on the office doors and knocked on the fourth one down.

Tim Frazer had been one of the few students, Stan reflected, who had taken a real interest history instead of just biding time in a required gen ed course. Now here he was an associate professor in the archive management program at Simmons.

"Nice digs," Stan said, poking his head through the doorway.

"Professor Remington!" Frazer jumped to his feet and grasped Stan's hand in both of his. "Man, it's been a long time." The younger man beamed from ear to ear to see his old mentor.

"Hey, hey, Stan to you, *Professor* Frazer."

Frazer laughed and bent to free a chair of the flotsam of papers and files for Stan. The small office was crowded with heavily laden bookshelves reaching toward the high ceiling. A desktop fan wafted the sultry summer air, swirling dust motes and rustling page corners.

"I see you're making quite a name for yourself. I've read a few of your articles on cultural and personal bias in war document archiving. Intriguing insights."

"That's kinder than what some in the academic community have said." He was a thin man, but muscular, and had lost most of his hair in the years since Stan last saw him. Dressed in jeans and a Red Sox t-shirt, he could have been mistaken for a student. Except for the bald head.

"You always were one to challenge the existing mindset. I remember a few exuberant discussions with you in class." Stan plopped himself into the proffered chair which squeaked loudly at his weight.

"I was pretty much an arrogant ass!" Frazer grinned apologetically. "Now that I'm in your position, I understand how tiresome I must have been."

Stan laughed. A knock sounded and the door opened to a trio of shy, giggling coeds, two brunettes and a blonde representing three different continents.

"Oh! Sorry, Dr. Frazer. Is this a good time?" one of them said, studying the schedule taped to the door.

"Would you mind coming back in an hour or so?"

"Sure! No problem." The girls did an about face and trooped out.

Stan raised an eyebrow at his former student. "So how is it you managed to land a job at an all-women's college?"

"Turns out only the undergrad department is all female. The graduate programs have gone co-ed. What are you doing in Boston?"

"Visiting our daughter Megan. You remember Megan?"

"Yeah, sure. Sort of had a crush on her way back when. An awfully cute girl."

"She's married to an accountant now. Has three kids."

"The good ones always go fast," Frazer said. "So, when you called you said you were on a mission. What can I do to help?"

Stan was pleased that such an easy opening presented itself. "I'm trying to find out about a woman whom I understand had been doing some guest lecturing here at Simmons. Did you happen to know Belle Carter? She was the literary historian over at the Longfellow house."

"Yes, I knew her quite well as a matter of fact. She is— was—a mentor to me." Frazer's voice broke a bit on that. "She died just a couple of days ago. Why are you asking about her?"

"Unfortunately, it was my family sitting near her at the fireworks when she was found." Stan briefly explained their part in the evening's traumatic conclusion.

"It's just such a shock," Tim said, shuffling papers that didn't need shuffling. "I mean one minute she's alive and vibrant, and the next she's gone. A heart attack, I guess."

"That's what they're saying."

"But that still doesn't explain why you've come to me."

Stan gestured helplessly. Just how much should he tell the young man of what he'd been through in the past couple of days? He shifted his position and crossed his leg, eliciting an unhappy squawk from the chair.

"Kind of a habit, I guess. Always looking for the story behind the story. My wife and I had lunch with Ms. Carter's son earlier today, and he mentioned something that piqued my curiosity."

"Oh, yeah? What was that?"

"It had to do with her research on Longfellow. I was wondering if you knew of anyone here at the college who might have been privy to what she was working on."

"Actually, I'm probably the best person to ask. She and I developed a friendship after I attended one of her lectures and stayed afterward to challenge her on her interpretation of the ending of one of Longfellow's poems."

Stan smirked. "Same old Timothy, eh? Still can't pass up a worthwhile argument."

"Somebody has to keep you old profs alert and accurate. Anyway, we went out for coffee afterward, and it turned into a weekly get-together. She eventually offered to read a draft of a paper I was working on and made some very helpful suggestions." He paused, blinking. "I'll miss her insights."

"So what was she working on?"

"Longfellow—always Longfellow. He was an obsession with her. But I still don't understand why you're asking."

Stan hesitated a moment. "Did you see the news about the fellow that was found dead in the Old North Church?"

"Oh, god, yes. Suicide of all things. It was all over the morning news." Tim leaned back in his chair. "Is there a connection between that guy and Belle?"

169

"Seems they found a note on him. Implied that he was having an affair with someone."

"With whom? With Belle? Not likely. She's…" Tim paused.

"A lesbian? Yes, that's what I've heard. I guess I'm just looking for a connection—any kind of a connection—between her and the man with the suicide note."

Tim looked at him, puzzled. "I wish I could help you, but I don't know who he is. They haven't even released his name."

"Hollinger. Roger Hollinger."

Tim's eyes went wide. "How do you—?"

"It's a long story. But, the short version is that Megan knows his wife. Works with her."

"Geesh! You always did have a habit of getting involved in convoluted relationships."

Stan sighed.

"Look, I don't know whether this is useful or not," Tim said. "Actually it's kind of creepy. But if that's the guy I'm thinking of, I'm the one who brought them together. A while back, Belle mentioned she was puzzled about some papers she had come across at an estate sale. Actually, she was pretty hush-hush about it—closing and locking the door to my office as if she was afraid someone might overhear us. It was a bit out of character. She said she'd found a lost manuscript in Longfellow's hand, a stanza of the Paul Revere poem. She wanted to know if I knew someone who was an expert in authenticating literary manuscripts, someone not connected with Longfellow House. I didn't think I could help her until I remembered an appraiser I met at the Antiquarian Books Festival last fall. I had to dig around, but I finally found his card in my stash—it was Hollinger."

"He worked for Drysdale's Auction House."

Tim nodded. "But why would he claim to have had an affair with her? Unless maybe he tried to…you know, and discovered…"

"That she wasn't inclined toward men?"

Tim shrugged his shoulders.

Stan's phone vibrated. It was Emily's text giving him Evelyn LeBlanc's address. "I shouldn't keep you from your students." He stood up.

"Maybe you should talk to the people she worked with at the Longfellow house." Tim Frazer shook Stan's hand in farewell. "There was one guy on the board of directors that she used to mention once in a while. A mentor of sorts, from what I gather. I think his name is Calderwell. No, Calderwood. I'm sure you could get his name and contact off their website."

"Actually, I've met him." Stan reached for the door. "It was nice seeing you again."

"Hey, yeah. Let's keep in touch," Tim said.

"And thanks for the info. This whole situation is puzzling, but I'm guessing it's not going to amount to much of anything."

"Who let you up here?" Obadiah Garde, the bell master, hovered over her like an avenging angel. Emily gripped her mag light a little tighter, glancing quickly around to see what else she could use as a weapon if she needed it.

"I don't know if you remember me, Mr. Garde. I'm Emily Remington," she said, moving to the middle of the room.

"I know who you are. You were here afterward. After that awful episode. The day…" He seemed to hesitate before blurting out the name. "…Roger died."

"Yes. You were giving a tour of the steeple to my daughter and husband when you found his body. How are you doing?"

"Miserably." He stepped over to one of the bell ropes, unknotted it, then re-looped it.

"I'm sorry."

"Everything has turned to bedlam. My ringers are

distraught. The television reporters will not leave us alone. And the tourists…the tourists! I can't get anything done." He shifted from rope to rope, unknotting and retying each. There were eight of them, Emily noted.

"I'm sure it's been very difficult," she sympathized, backing out of his way.

"You haven't told me what you're doing up here." He glared at her.

"Stan, my husband, has had difficulty sleeping since it happened," Emily lied. "We thought perhaps if I came here, I could gain an understanding of what he is going through. Help him through it."

"Good luck with that. If I didn't know better, I'd swear Roger planned the entire incident simply to get notoriety," Garde said with a sneer.

"Why do you say that?" Emily asked, backing up again.

"He certainly wasn't happy with my stepping into the Ringing Master position. He coveted it for himself."

"He did?"

"Oh, yes. He fancied himself an expert at change ringing, just because he'd rung for Church of the Advent before coming here. I'm not surprised he killed himself. I'm just surprised he did it here, of all places."

"You think that's what happened? That he killed himself?"

"What else could it be? I mean, my goodness, he left a note."

"The note. Yes."

"And it's beyond the pale that he would cheat on his wife that way! I'd met her once or twice. A lovely woman." He knotted another rope then surveyed the room, frowning.

"Did he ever speak of another woman?"

"To me? Heavens no. We didn't have that kind of relationship."

"What kind of relationship did you have?" Emily asked.

The light from the deeply encased round window illuminated the side of his face, casting the other side into dark shadow. "Roger Hollinger was an egotist and a bully. We spoke to each other as little as possible. Except that he was always questioning my choice of methodology."

"Methodology?"

"I insist my ringers learn to listen, to feel what the bell is doing." Garde grasped the last rope. "To feel the rhythm. It's a unique kind of awareness that is totally sensory." He caressed the rope, bringing it in close to his face. "Mr. Hollinger was constantly advocating that I allow the ringers to engage in rope-sight, an imprecise methodology at best. I found him to be…exasperating. That's the only word I can think of." He twisted the rope into a fierce knot.

"I see," Emily said, though she didn't really.

He turned to face her. "And on top of it, he seemed to feel it necessary to entertain the ringers, making jokes and whispering asides, causing them to laugh when I most needed their attention."

"It must have been very difficult for you," Emily had to work to keep from feeling exasperated herself.

Garde sighed and walked over to a set of black three-ring binders lined up across a small shelf. "It was my burden to bear." He opened each as if to inspect the contents, but then closed and replaced them one after another. "I have ambitious goals for this group of ringers. I intend to restore their reputation to the caliber our group had once enjoyed." He shoved the last binder into place.

"Has the reputation of the ringers faltered recently?" Emily prodded.

"I'm afraid so. As a direct consequence of Mr. Hollinger's antics."

"You said he wanted to be Bell Master?"

"Oh, he lusted after the position! When he learned that I had been appointed Ringing Master and Steeple Keeper for Christ Church—you as a tourist know it as the Old North Church—he was beside himself. But I made sure he understood his place and that if this group was going to evolve and improve, everyone—including Mr. Hollinger—would have to acquiesce to my leadership."

"And did he? Acquiesce?" Emily asked.

"Hardly. In fact, I have it on good authority that he was lobbying to have me removed and replaced."

"Replaced by whom?"

"Himself, of course. Oh, I do have great sympathy for his wife, of course, but I am not sorry that he is no longer a thorn in my proverbial side." He pushed past her brusquely. "Now if you'll excuse me, I have work to do here."

CHAPTER 20

EMILY texted Stan that she was on her way and to let him know where to meet her. Stepping out into the sunshine, she sidestepped to avoid another tour group pushing their way into the church.

"Excuse me," she mumbled, bumping shoulders with a tall woman. "Oh!"

It was Detective Ellison.

"Mrs. Remington." The detective arched her eyebrows quizzically.

"Just took the tour," Emily lied. "This place is awesome. Awash in history!"

"History."

Emily tapped her wrist where her watch usually sat. "Gotta go. Running late." She hustled off down Salem Street, looking back over her shoulder once to see the detective still standing in the doorway, scrutinizing her with bemusement.

Damn! Ellison was the last person Emily expected to see. And she wasn't quite sure why she had reacted the way she did, except that she had a feeling the detective wouldn't be happy to find out she'd been interrogating a key person of interest in the Roger Hollinger case. She admitted to herself that she had stepped over the line in confronting Obadiah

Garde, but then again, she didn't have much choice. He was blocking her exit from the bell tower. Although she knew she shouldn't have been up there in the first place. A locked door is a clear sign that you don't belong. She understood full well that the detective could accuse her of interfering with the investigation. But up until this very moment, it had seemed that Ellison was dismissing Roger's death as a suicide. Apparently she was following up on leads after all.

Emily took a couple of deep breaths and slowed her pace. She wondered what direction Ellison's conversation with Garde would take. The man was certainly a very odd individual. What was that he'd said about Roger Hollinger coveting the bell master's position? It sounded like Garde was more than a little paranoid.

Stepping into the street, she waved to catch the attention of a Metro taxi rounding the corner. She was eager to meet up with Stan and switch her attention to questioning Evelyn LeBlanc. *What would she have to say about Roger's suicide note?*

"Brighton," she told the cabbie. "Strathmore Road."

"You're not going to believe who I ran into," Emily said to Stan as she paid her taxi driver. She scanned the street to get her bearings. The densely residential neighborhood not far from the Chestnut Hill reservoir was clotted with parked cars, walkers, joggers and bikers—a conglomerate of college students, yuppies and retirees. "Detective Ellison."

"Where? Why?" He put a hand on her back as they headed up the narrow walk together toward a building with a maroon awning.

"At the church. And I don't think she was going in to pray."

"You didn't—"

"Do anything stupid? No. But I did get a chance to talk with Obadiah Garde. Now there's a piece of work." She pressed the buzzer and the front door opened almost immediately. "The proverbial bat in the belfry—and I'm talking really batty. We need to talk."

The apartment they were looking for was on the third floor. No elevator. By the time they'd climbed the three flights of stairs, Emily could hear Stan huffing behind her. She waited for him to catch his breath. Then said, "How'd it go with Tim Frazer?"

"Great! We had a nice chat. He's an associate professor now."

"Did you get around to asking about Belle Carter?" she rapped on the door to Evelyn LeBlanc's flat.

"Yeah, as a matter of fact I did. We'll want to talk about that later, too. Um, you do know that this is *her* address?"

Emily looked up at the house number. "Belle Carter's? But didn't Evelyn move out?"

When the door opened, they found themselves confronted by a tall willowy woman in her late forties with tired, questioning eyes.

"Evelyn LeBlanc? I'm Emily Remington. I'm the one who called you earlier. And this is my husband, Stan."

"Sure. C'mon in. Pardon the mess."

They stepped into a brightly lit, if narrow, great room cluttered with packing boxes.

"I'm just gathering some of my things." Evelyn shrugged. "I've been staying with my sister for a while."

"I'm sorry for your—I'm so sorry," Emily said. "This must be a very difficult time for you."

Evelyn reached for a pack of cigarettes and lit one, blowing the smoke up and away from her guests. "I gave this up ten years ago." Her hands trembled and she took another long drag. "Do you want something to drink? Coffee? Tea? A shot of bourbon?" She held up a nearly empty bottle of Wild Turkey.

Emily shook her head.

"I'm good," Stan said.

"Go ahead. Sit down." Evelyn picked up a half-filled glass

and drained the bottle into it.

Emily and Stan moved boxes and bags off the couch and sat side by side while their host wrapped glass figurines in tissue paper and arranged them in a brightly colored cardboard carton.

"I talked with Whitman after you called," Evelyn said. "He told me there may be a question as to how Belle died."

"It's unclear to us exactly what happened," Emily said. "We were hoping you could shed some light."

"How would I know? I wasn't with her that night." She reached for the glass again and threw a swallow of bourbon into her mouth.

"Whitman said that you and she had had a falling out?"

"That's a polite way to put it." She snorted, grabbing a second box. "I won't go into the details but it wasn't pretty. I told her I'd had enough and left. How would you like it if you found out *he* was cheating on *you*?"

Stan's ears reddened when she jabbed a cigarette-laden finger in his direction.

"She was having an affair? With…another woman?" Emily asked.

"Hell no! That I might have forgiven her for. She was cheating on me with a shitbag of a man. No disrespect intended," she said to Stan. "But I don't need that kind of crap in my life."

She drew on her cigarette again, then stubbed it out in an over-filled rose bud shaped ashtray.

Emily was careful to keep her tone neutral. "Do you know who she was seeing?"

Evelyn shook her head, her gray-streaked ponytail swaying back and forth. She blinked rapidly, anger melting into hurt and grief. "I found a condom in her purse. Who did she think she was fooling? She didn't even try to deny it." Now the tears fell freely. She reached for the bourbon glass again.

The sound of a key jiggling in the front door caught their attention. A burly man of about thirty-five, wearing a frayed sport coat and slacks, strode in. He stopped short, looking from one to the other in confusion.

"What the hell are you doing here?" he demanded of Evelyn. "And who are they?"

"I live here, Tenny. This is my home, too." Evelyn reached for another cigarette. "These are…friends of Whitman. They came to pay their respects."

Stan rose and extended his hand. "Stan Remington. This is my wife Emily. Are you Belle's other son?"

Tennyson Carter surveyed Stan suspiciously. He resembled Whitman, except he was heavier, his neck thick and his stomach sagging over his belt. Carter gave a perfunctory handshake before turning on Evelyn. "You have no right to be here. What are you doing with my mother's stuff?"

"I'm not interested in her 'stuff.' I'm taking what's mine before I cancel the lease."

Whitman picked up a glass figure of an elephant. "This was my mother's. I gave it to her for birthday."

"My mistake." She took it from him and set it back on a shelf. "What do you want?"

"I need to find her insurance papers and her medical records. The medical examiner is saying she didn't die of a heart attack after all."

"What?" Emily and Stan said together.

"What exactly did he say?" Emily asked, standing to meet the man eye to eye.

"It was an allergic reaction to some drug she took. I'm gonna sue the damn pharmacy that filled that prescription. There's no excuse for that kind of mistake."

"Are you saying she died of anaphylactic shock?" Emily asked.

"What business is it of yours?" Tenny thrust a thick finger at her chest and she took a step back, startled.

"Hey, hey! No need to get riled here." Stan quickly stepped between them.

"Nobody's getting riled. My mother just died, and this bitch here…" now he was pointing at Evelyn. "…is helping herself to stuff that rightfully belongs to me and my brother. And now you two…" He jabbed a finger back in Emily's direction. "…are sticking your noses where they don't belong."

"Mr. Carter, I am very sorry about your mother," Emily said. "But circumstances have led us to be involved."

"What circumstances?"

"We're the ones who found her on the Esplanade that night," Stan said.

"You?" Tennyson seemed taken aback.

Stan nodded.

"So…what? You're here looking for a reward or something?"

Stan threw his hands up in incredulous disgust.

"Not a reward," Emily said. "Answers."

"What do you mean? What kind of answers?" Tennyson said warily, eyeing her then Stan.

"It's possible her death is related somehow to the recent death of a…a friend of our family."

"Someone else died?" Evelyn brought her hand up to her mouth. "Who? Not that man she was having an affair with?"

"My mother? What the hell is going on here?"

"We didn't think there was anything between them," Emily said to Evelyn. "But now, to be honest, I don't know."

The distraught woman plunked herself down onto a straight-backed chair. "But why? How?" She shook her head in shock. "Do the police know about this?"

"Whoa! Wait. You're not bringing the police into this." Tennyson clenched his fists.

"Why not?" Evelyn asked. "If something awful happened…"

"My mother died of an allergic reaction. I won't have her dragged into the spotlight. This is exactly what those cable news shows would love to get their mitts on. A woman seduced by a lesbian, falls in love with a man, and gets killed for it." Suddenly he stopped and pointed at her. "Unless you had something to do with it. With her death."

"What are you saying?!" Evelyn stared at him in horror.

Emily stepped between them. "No one is saying anyone had anything to do with anything."

But Tennyson glared right past her at Evelyn.

"We don't know what happened," Emily insisted.

"How exactly did this guy die, this 'friend of the family?'" he asked.

Behind him, Stan shook his head in warning.

"That's unclear," she said.

"I'll tell you what is clear. You and him…" He pointed at Stan. "…are not wanted here." Now he glowered at Evelyn. "And you got one day to get out."

Stan caught Emily's eye and beckoned toward the door. She nodded, but on a whim asked, "Evelyn, how much was Belle's life insurance policy for?"

But before Evelyn could say anything, Tennyson growled, "Don't answer that."

Evelyn shrugged. "I really wouldn't know." Then she looked up at her lover's son with a worried expression. "I think you should go, too."

"One day…" He shook a thick finger at her. "You can leave the key on the table when you go." Then he spun toward the door. "After you," he said to Emily and Stan with a flourish of his hand and a sneer on his face.

Outside, Stan and Emily trotted down the front steps and past a Mazda MX with its top down parked at the curb.

"Nice ride," Emily observed.

"Yup."

Behind them the car door slammed and the engine revved. Tires squealed as Tennyson hit the gas and roared away.

"So what are you thinking?" Stan asked.

"I'm thinking I'd like to know more about that man." She frowned, noticing a black sedan roll past them from up the street and stop in front of Evelyn's apartment building.

"Isn't that...?" Stan turned to stare.

"Keep walking," Emily said. "I'm not ready to talk with the detective yet."

CHAPTER 21

WHEN Stan and Emily arrived back at the campground, Stan was pleased his son-in-law had thrown several thick steaks on the grill and had dinner almost ready. The sky was clouding over and he could hear the rumble of thunder off in the distance.

"She's at it again," Allyn said in a conspiratorial whisper, once they'd all gathered around the picnic table.

"Who's at what?" Stan asked.

Annabel looked at him with solemn eyes. "The witch."

"Are you talking about the lady with the cats again?"

"They think she stole one of their lawn darts," Wynter said.

"It is odd that things keep going missing." Megan motioned for Stan to pass her the steak sauce.

"Could it be that you girls need to be more responsible and not misplace things so often?" Emily asked.

"What about your sandal, Grandma?" Allyn asked.

"Yeah, Em." Stan poked her in the ribs. "You walking lop-footed these days?"

"It's in the RV somewhere. I probably kicked it under one of the kids' piles."

They were just digging into a desert of raspberry shortcake when the first drops began to fall. Everyone scrambled to clear the picnic table; Stan was the last to step into the RV just as a streak of lightning split the sky and the roar of thunder ushered in torrents of rain.

The twins shrieked.

"Hey, hey!" Philip yelled.

"Why don't you start a card game with them while Megan and I finish the dishes," Emily suggested. "Then we can put a movie on for them in the bedroom while we talk."

Forty-five minutes later, after a rousing game of Hand and Foot, the three girls were curled up on Stan and Emily's bed entranced with Harry Potter. While Stan fetched the cribbage board, Philip made Brandy Manhattans for the guys and a vodka tonic with a twist of lime for Emily. Megan carried a bottle of pinot grigio and a wine glass to the tiny dining table where Stan was already shuffling the deck.

"Sounds like you two had a busy day," Megan said, filling her wine glass. "You were gone a lot longer than I expected. Not that I'm complaining," she hastened to add. "So how was Belle Carter's son?"

Stan dealt the cards, five to each of them. "Turns out he was somebody we knew already. He was our guide when we took the girls on the Freedom Trail tour. The cordwainer."

"You're joking!"

"That's quite a coincidence," Philip said, scooping up his cards and sorting them by suit. He tapped them on the table waiting for the play to begin.

"What did he tell you?" Megan asked.

"Basically that he didn't know Rhea's husband," Emily said. "And he thought it was highly unlikely that his mother and Roger were having an affair."

"Why?"

"Because she's a lesbian," Emily said, sorting her own cards.

"What?" Megan blinked in surprise.

"That scuttles that theory," Philip tossed a card to start the crib.

"Except…" Stan discarded a lone six of clubs.

"Except what?" Megan picked a card at random from her hand and held it in mid-air, waiting for Stan to finish his sentence.

"Her partner, Evelyn, said Belle *was* having an affair. With a man."

"Wait, wait, wait…! You talked to Belle's lover?"

Stan nodded.

"This just keeps getting better and better," Philip said.

"It apparently caused quite a rift between them." Stan tapped the deck for Philip to cut, then flipped the top card over.

"Four." Philip tossed out the first card.

"She and Belle were living in Brighton," Stan said.

"You went all the way out to Brighton after you met with Whitman Carter? Uh…seven." Megan put a three of hearts on the table.

"Not right after. Your dad stopped by Simmons College first to see an old student of his. Nine." Emily threw her card onto the table.

"You remember Tim Frazer?" Stan asked. "Fifteen for two." He moved his peg.

"Yeah. Had a crush on him way back when. He had the most awesome curly chocolate brown hair."

Without thinking, Stan brushed a hand across his own balding head. "Not anymore."

"Really?" Megan laughed. "But why Tim?"

"You had a crush on one of your dad's students?" Philip faked a scowl, tossing his card down. "Twenty."

"Twenty-five." Emily threw her card onto the table. "Whitman had mentioned that his mother did some guest lecturing at Simmons, so your dad arranged to meet with Tim, who, it turns out, knew Belle—"

"And introduced her to Roger. Thirty-one for two!" Stan

185

moved his peg again.

The others laid their cards out to tally up points, while he scooped up the crib and jumped a few extra holes.

"So they *were* having an affair." Megan pushed the spent cards into a pile and shoved them toward Philip.

"Hard to say," Emily said, sipping her vodka and tonic. "Oh, and we met Belle's other son. Tennyson Carter. He showed up at the apartment while we were talking with Evelyn."

"Not a happy camper." Stan frowned as a gust of wind and rain buffeted the awning outside.

"What do you mean?" Megan asked.

"That he was rather surly would be putting it nicely," Emily said.

"Seems Belle didn't die of a heart attack," Stan informed them. "According to Tennyson, she overdosed on some medication she was allergic to."

"That sounds pretty suspicious," Philip said, "given everything else that's been going on. Twenty-two for six!" He slapped a card onto the table and jumped a peg.

"He must have been pretty upset over his mother's death," Megan said.

Stan set down another card. "Yeah. But more than that, he was pretty pissed off at Evelyn, for being a, well, you know... sort of like he thought she'd led his mother astray."

"And Evelyn was pissed with Belle over the affair," Emily added. "I'd have to say the energy in that room was pretty negative at that moment."

"I can't believe you two went through all of that for Rhea. You are so awesome."

"Don't count us awesome, yet," Emily cautioned. "I think we created more questions than what we got answers to."

"You said Dad went over to Simmons College to meet with Tim. You didn't go with him?"

"Your mother felt the need to see where Roger died for herself."

"You went back to the church?" Philip tapped the deck sitting in front of Emily. "C'mon, deal."

She picked up the cards and shuffled them slowly and deliberately. "As a matter of fact, I had a rather fascinating conversation with the bell master." She began dealing.

"He is one creepy guy," Megan observed

"Obadiah Garde," Emily said. "Seems he and Roger didn't get along."

Philip snorted, throwing his card into the crib. "Obadiah? Creepy name, too."

"He was convinced Roger was conspiring to replace him as bell master. Said he wasn't at all sorry to see him dead."

"Roger wanted to be bell master?" Megan seemed surprised.

"According to Garde he did. But I have no idea if it was paranoia speaking or Roger presented a real challenge to his ego."

"Mom, do you think Mr. Garde had something to do with Roger's death?"

"I don't know, honey. But I'm beginning to think that maybe Rhea's instincts aren't so far off after all. Your play."

Megan poured herself another glass of wine before playing her card.

Stan said, "You always say there has to be means, opportunity, and motive."

"With that Obadiah guy maybe there was opportunity and motive," Philip said. "But that begs the question of means. I've met Roger. He was a pretty big guy."

"I saw Garde pull those bell ropes during the rehearsal," Stan said. "We're talking, what? Roughly half a ton of bronze alloy each?"

Philip nodded his agreement.

"He made it look like he was flicking lights on and off with a chain switch. I'm telling you, the man's got biceps."

"Still…" Emily reached for her drink. "The man may be loony tunes, but if Roger met with foul play, Garde's a shaky suspect at best."

"This is all so horrible," Megan said. "I can't believe that detective wouldn't listen to you."

"She might be rethinking the situation. I ran into her today, too."

"No wonder you were so late getting home! What did *she* say?"

"I didn't really stop to talk. Everything is so nebulous right now. I feel like we need more information."

"So you're willing to keep working on the case?" Megan sounded hopeful.

"Let's take a look at that day book again," Emily suggested. She got up to fetch it from the bedroom, squeezing past Wynter on her way to the tiny bathroom. "Did anyone see where I put it?" she called out.

"I thought it was on the nightstand," Stan answered.

"Allyn, Annabel, did you take that book from my nightstand?"

"What book?" Allyn asked.

"The one in the zip-lock bag?" Annabel said. "It was there last night."

"I bet the witch…"

"Don't go there, Allyn," Emily warned. She stepped back into the living room. "Did someone move it?" She lifted a cushion. A moment later, everyone joined in the hunt. "This is so odd."

"Could somebody have gotten in here?" Philip asked.

Wynter emerged from the bathroom. "What's going on?"

Megan looked at her parents and husband with a worried expression. "You don't think somebody broke in and stole it, do you?"

"Stole what?" Wynter asked.

"Oh, Philip, what if somebody did get in here?"

"There's no evidence of a break-in," Emily reassured her daughter. "The lock hasn't been tampered with, and nothing else is amiss."

"But where did it go then?" Stan asked.

"The w—"

"No, Allyn!" all four adults said at the same time.

"Okay," Philip said, trying to sound like the voice of reason. "If someone did take that book, I don't think it has anything to do with the other things that have gone missing. One way or the other, someone got into this RV."

Megan shuddered and put her arms around her little girls. "I don't like this."

"Calm down," Emily said. "No one is in any danger."

Stan nodded in agreement, but mentally he ran through all the locks he would check after his family was in bed for the night.

"So, what about the investigation?" Megan pursued. "You can't give up now."

Stan hesitated, then plunged ahead. "Tim did tell me Belle had found a manuscript she thought might have been an original Longfellow draft. She was pretty excited about it. The reason he steered her to Roger was to authenticate it."

"That's right," Megan confirmed. "Roger did work for a literary auction house. Here in Boston."

"I'm thinking it might be worth a trip to that auction house to see if anyone there knows what Belle found," Stan said.

"Mom?"

"Both Whitman and Tim suggested we talk to the people at the Longfellow House," Emily said. "There's a guy there who'd been mentoring Belle. I guess if you and the girls don't mind us going back into the city for another day, your dad and I could follow up on those two leads."

"Of course we don't mind. In fact, I need to go into the city with the girls anyway. I totally forgot the twins have dentist appointments. We can drop you off."

"Sounds like you've embarked on a regular investigation," Philip said.

"Just asking questions. I'll leave it to Detective Ellison to do the investigating. But it never hurts to ask questions."

"There's one other question I'd like an answer to," Stan said. "If Belle Carter didn't die of natural causes..." He paused.

The other three leaned forward waiting.

He arched his eyebrows dramatically. "Who are the beneficiaries on her life insurance?"

"That's the question of the day, isn't it?" Emily responded.

Then Philip spoke up. "I might be able to find that out for you." He stood up and grabbed his cell phone, moving to the front of the RV. "Hey, Charlie!" they could hear him saying. "Phil here. How ya doing? Listen I got a favor to ask..." He lowered his voice. A few minutes later he returned to the table. "Charlie Pearlmutter is a golfing buddy of mine. We play eighteen every Wednesday. He's also the state insurance commissioner. Said he can have an answer to our question in the morning."

The rain stopped and a stretch of sky in the west began to clear, allowing a hazy orange sun to paint the horizon with a golden glow.

A knock at the door made them all by jump. Stan eased himself out of the tight booth he'd been sitting in to answer it. Alvina Pendergast, swathed in a lime green rain poncho, brandished a bright blue lawn dart. Behind her, a swarm of cats traced figure eights on the Persian carpet, shaking their paws at a puddle of water.

"It's her!" Allyn whispered.

"I take it this belongs to your darling brood." Vinie smiled, holding the lawn dart up for all to see. "I found it under my picnic table. I think someone needs to work on their aim." With a dramatic change of expression, she pouted out her lower lip. "If one of my precious kitties got injured, I'd hate to think of the consequences." Then she broke into a broad smile again and look from one twin to the other. "You'll want to take care, dearies."

"We're sorry." Stan took the offending dart from her. "Thank you for returning it. I'll make sure it doesn't happen again."

Vinie marched back down the steps and across the road to her own RV, the cats leaping like jumping beans behind her to avoid more puddles.

"Looks like we solved part of your mystery," Stan said to Allyn.

"Don't touch it! Use your handkerchief," the little girl said in response.

"What?" Stan was befuddled.

Annabel spoke up for her twin. "It might have fingerprints on it. We need to test it."

Stan stumbled from the bedroom into the RV's miniature bathroom, groggy from a restless night's sleep. It had been too wet for a fire after the storm and in fact the rain had pattered on the roof of the motorhome on and off throughout the night. He'd dreamed intermittently about the Old North Church and fireworks. During his waking moments, he couldn't shake the idea that somehow Tennyson Carter had something to do with his mother's death. Maybe it was just an accidental overdose, an allergic reaction, but there'd been too many coincidences the past couple of days. And somehow Stan felt like it was he who'd set the chain of events into motion that ended in the deaths of two people, even though he knew that was illogical. But that meeting with Belle Carter at the Longfellow House stuck in his head like a movie that someone had attached the wrong ending to.

Staring at his reflection in the mirror, he debated whether to shave or not. Not. So he squeezed himself into the narrow shower and grabbed for the shampoo. Twenty minutes later, he padded past his softly snoring granddaughter, grabbed a cup of coffee to join Emily out under the awning.

Thankfully the twins had opted to sleep with their parents

again in the pop-up tent. He loved the little girls, but the RV just wasn't big enough to have them underfoot for very long. They were always in motion.

He stood for a moment in the doorway and surveyed the rain-soaked campsite. The trees had grown coats of bright green lichen on their trunks. The air smelled fresh and earthy after the rain. He breathed in deeply.

"Good morning," Emily greeted him.

"A bit chilly out." He noticed she had her sweatshirt on, even though she was wearing shorts.

"It'll warm up soon enough."

Settling into the lawn chair next to her, he asked, "So, what are you planning for today?"

"I don't look forward to going back into the city, but I feel like we can't stop asking questions now."

"You thinking Belle Carter didn't die of natural causes?"

"I'd be really surprised if she did, the way events are shaping up."

They sat and sipped at their coffees for a moment, enjoying the warming breeze carrying with it the scent of pine and honeysuckle. A dog barked a couple of campsites away. And Stan could see Alvina Pendergast's cats basking in patches of morning sun.

"What was your impression of Belle's other son?" he asked.

"Tennyson? Personality-wise, you wouldn't know they were from the same gene pool."

"How could a man be so angry at his mother's lifestyle that he'd behave the way he did?"

"Are you suggesting that maybe Tennyson had something to do with Belle's death?"

"I dunno. Could he have?"

Emily let out a deep sigh. "In my experience…anything is possible."

Her cell phone trilled.

"Who?"

Emily squinted at the caller ID. "Detective Ellison."

She set the phone down on the table as if it were burning her fingers.

"Shouldn't you answer it?"

She looked at him with a half-guilty expression. "I'm not ready to talk to her."

"You said that yesterday."

"Uh huh."

"Emily, two days ago you made me wait in an ice cream shop with three sugared-up girls and seagull shit on my head so you could take a side trip to see that woman, and today you don't want to talk with her?"

She picked up the phone again and hit the voicemail button, then the speakerphone.

"Mrs. Remington, this is Detective Dayanna Ellison from the Boston PD. I see you've been doing a bit of off-the-grid sight-seeing in my town. Evelyn LeBlanc told me that you and your husband had stopped by. And I know why you were in the church. What I don't know is how you found Evelyn or what you think you are doing. We need to talk. Please call me back right away."

She shut the phone off again.

"Well? Aren't you going to call her?"

"My battery died."

"Emily!"

"Okay, okay." She tapped on the back of the phone three or four times with her index finger. "But I think we should check out that auction house first, like we talked about. There's a set of dots here that are begging to be connected. I just can't quite figure out what picture they're trying to make. Once we have a better idea of how Roger and Belle are connected, we can make a case to Detective Ellison."

"So, what do we do?" Stan asked. "Just walk into the place and start asking questions? I can't imagine they'll give us the time of day."

"We just need to come up with a good story." She reached

out and ran her fingers along his chin. "You probably should shave."

CHAPTER 22

STAN resigned himself to the inevitable and reached for the electric razor while Emily conducted a thirty minute Tae kwon do workout with her usual ladies and the twins. A delighted Megan joined them, as well as a young couple, newlyweds who were tenting at a nearby site, and Lyle, the Hulk Hogan who rescued them from the exploding faucet.

Stan was always amazed at how easily Emily drew people to whatever activity she was doing. And he was relieved she'd found something to be actively involved in—something other than investigating dead bodies. Or he'd hoped. But here they were, deep in the middle of another mystery.

He ran a comb through the fringe of his hair then stepped outside. He noticed Wynter sitting off to the side, watching the group from the comfort of the chaise lounge. *A girl after my own heart.* He smiled and sauntered over to the chair next to her.

As soon as Emily had finished and showered, Stan helped herd the kids into the SUV. Emily motioned for him to go ahead and sit up front with Megan; she climbed into the back with the girls. Just then, Philip emerged from the camper, cell phone in hand, and waved them down. Stan rolled down his window.

"I just heard from Charlie," Philip said. "Belle Carter was insured for a quarter of a million. Her sons are the beneficiaries."

"That's a sizeable chunk of change!" Stan said. "None of it goes to Evelyn?"

Philip shook his head. He slapped the side of the car twice, indicating that Megan could take off.

"Thank your friend for me," Stan called out through the window.

"What does that prove?" Megan asked.

"Kind of takes Evelyn out of the picture as far as money goes. I suppose she still could have killed Belle out of spite and anger."

"She seemed quite devastated by Belle's death," Emily noted.

Stan nodded. "Whitman didn't seem to be hurting for cash. He has the summer job, but a lot of teachers work second jobs in the summer. Tennyson, on the other hand…"

"Might have gone off the deep end financially, if what Whitman said about him is true," Emily finished his sentence. "But to kill his mother?"

Stan shrugged and turned his attention to the Massachusetts scenery rushing by. He wished they could figure this thing out. He found himself growing increasingly unhappy about the way this vacation was turning out. His dream of sitting in the shade of the RV's awning with a good book—preferably one about George Washington or one of his other Revolutionary War heroes—seemed to be fading as fast as the freeway signposts going by. He liked Boston well enough, loved all the history embedded in the city, but traipsing around trying to solve a murder wasn't his idea of relaxation.

But he had to admit he was intrigued by the connection to Henry Wadsworth Longfellow. Imagine if he were to find a long lost manuscript written in the poet's own hand! It was just too bad it was all bound up in the death of two people.

He glanced over at his daughter; her hands clenched the wheel. Even in profile he could see that her jaw was set tight. He resisted the urge to ask what was going through her mind right now. Maybe later, when the girls weren't around, he could have a heart to heart with his baby.

In the back seat Emily was laughing and singing "Ninety-Nine Bottles of Milk in the Fridge" with the twins. He was glad she was able to enjoy this time with them, even if it just for the forty minutes or so it took to drive into the city.

Battling city traffic like a pro, Megan—Stan was relieved he wasn't the one behind the wheel—dropped him and Emily off on Boylston Street.

Eyeing the gilded street numbers on the dark red awning over the carved mahogany door, Stan rubbed his jaw. *Good thing I shaved.* A smaller sign to the left of the door discreetly affirmed the name of the establishment: Drysdale's Auction Galleries. Gold embossed lettering beneath the name listed their specialties: furniture and decoratives, art, rare books and manuscripts. He grasped the brass door knobs suspecting that he and Emily were woefully underdressed, even in their summer slacks and Bahama shirts.

He hesitated, suddenly unsure whether they should go in or not. "What do you think?" he asked his wife.

"Let's do it," she said.

Inside, they were surprised by how busy it was. People wandered the reception area, browsing the various bays and examining centuries old framed paintings, antique books, old maps, hand-written orchestral music, and even several antique cigar boxes. Stan's eyes lit up at the assemblage of historic memorabilia. A collective murmur of approval drifted from an open set of glass doors. Then a single voice began to chant in a rhythmic patter.

They crossed the hardwood parquet floor to peer into a large gallery where a man stood on a dais at the far end. An audience of about two hundred people sat in neat rows, nearly filling the room. Around the edge of the room were more displays of literary collectibles.

"Twenty-four...Twenty-four five...Twenty-five..." the auctioneer intoned, gesturing first to the right, then to the left, pointing toward individuals with numbered paddles held aloft.

Stan raised an eyebrow at Emily, who nodded and followed him in. A perfectly coiffed young man in a three-piece suit motioned them to a pair of empty seats. He offered a numbered paddle, but Emily politely shook her head.

"Thirty...thirty-one..."

Emily leaned over to ask in Stan's ear, "Is he talking dollars or hundreds of dollars?"

"Likely thousands," Stan whispered back.

Emily looked taken aback. "For an old book?"

People on either side craned their necks to frown at her. She'd spoken too loudly. Pursing her lips together, she folded her arms and leaned back against her chair.

"Thirty-four five..."

Along one side of the room a dozen formally dressed representatives listened intently to cell phones clamped tightly to their ears, occasionally holding up a finger or signaling the auctioneer with the slightest of waves.

"Forty..."

"Don't touch your face!" Emily hissed into Stan's ear as he reached to scratch an itch.

He slipped the offending hand back into his lap. Emily was right; he'd hate to accidentally buy something he couldn't afford.

The auctioneer cocked his head toward a woman in the second row. "Will you give me forty-one?"

She raised her paddle. Then he gestured toward another woman, this one in the back, just a few rows in front of Emily and Stan, who let her paddle flutter almost imperceptibly when he asked for "forty-two."

Since all the others had dropped out, he began talking

directly to the two bidders, "Forty-two five," making eye contact with each in turn, subtly urging them on. The sense of competition between the two women was palpable, if silent on their parts. The bid rose higher. And higher. Finally, one of the women dropped her head.

"And the sale goes to number six-four-seven-one for fifty thousand dollars," he said, tapping his gavel on the lectern and acknowledging the winner with a quick flourish of his hand.

The crowd offered a restrained applause. Several people stood and wandered back out to the reception area. The auction house personnel rushed to wheel the display table with the much sought after book away from the dais, and wheel another—this one featuring a pair of hand-carved book-ends—to take its place.

Emily nudged Stan. Reluctantly he followed her out of the gallery.

"That was so cool!" He was grinning like a school boy.

"Yeah, well, don't get any ideas. We'd have to sell the Winnie and mortgage the house."

"Might be worth it."

She ignored him as they wove their way around small clots of people chatting in low murmurs. On the far side of the lobby, they found a receptionist sitting at an S-shaped black lacquered desk with a glass and chrome top. Overhead, a nouveau art chandelier dangled precariously; Stan realized he was staring at it, jaw agape, only when Emily elbowed him.

The receptionist, a young Asian woman with short-cropped black hair greeted them with an indifferent smile. The simple grey skirt and peach satin blouse she wore contrasted oddly with her pierced nostril and eye-brow.

"Did you want to register to take part in today's auction?" she asked.

"Actually, no. We, uh," Stan stammered, "we'd like to see Roger Hollinger." He flushed. Lying was harder than he'd imagined, but he was determined to follow the script he and

Emily had devised that morning.

"I'm sorry, but Mr. Hollinger is not available." The young woman said this so matter-of-factly Stan wondered if she knew Roger was dead.

"We have a book he's agreed to look at," Emily said, without missing a beat. With a nod of her head, she indicated the Longfellow book Stan was grasping in his hand.

The young woman tapped her computer. "Do you have an appointment?"

"No. But I have his card." Stan fumbled in his shirt pocket for the card Tim Fraser had given him. "I—uh—met him at the Book Fair last fall and he said we could stop by anytime to have it appraised. The book. Do you know when he'll be in?"

"I'm sorry, but Mr. Hollinger is no longer with us."

With us, as in he left the company? Or as in with us in spirit but not in body, gone to that great auction house in the sky? He wondered what, exactly, this self-possessed young woman knew about the circumstances of Roger Hollinger's absence.

"Is there someone else we could talk to?" Emily asked. "Someone else in his department, perhaps?"

"All of our appraisers are busy at the moment. Because of today's auction. You could leave the book with me and I'll see that it is directed to the first available appraiser. However, it may take several weeks before someone could get back to you."

"We don't live in the area," Emily said. "We're only in Boston for a few days."

They were interrupted when a dark-haired woman wearing a Drysdale name badge strode up to the desk.

"Priscilla," she asked impatiently. "Do you have those notes that Roger had written up for his Nantucket client?"

"Hello," Emily interrupted, addressing the woman. "Are you an associate of Roger Hollinger? We were hoping to meet with him and he's apparently no longer here. Would you have time for us?"

"Excuse me?" The woman looked startled.

Priscilla raised her eyebrows in exasperation. "I'm sorry, Ms. Singh. I told them all the associates are busy at the moment. They say they have a book they want appraised."

"Actually," Stan said, "we have a situation that involves Roger Hollinger."

"I told you. He isn't—"

"It's ok, Priscilla, I'll handle this." The woman had quickly recovered her composure. "Why don't you come back to my office? I'm Vidya Singh, an associate of Mr. Hollinger. And you are?"

"Stanford Remington. And Emily Remington."

Vidya Singh gestured toward a hallway and began walking briskly, her spiked heels clicking on the wood floor. She was dressed smartly in a gray tailored business suit softened by a blue silk blouse and scarf. Her skirt brushed her legs just a tad below the knees.

She ushered them into her office, but didn't invite them to sit down. "I assume you know that Roger—Mr. Hollinger— passed away several days ago?"

"Yes. We've come on behalf of his wife," Emily said.

"Rhea?"

"She has questions concerning the manner of his death. She asked us to look into his business dealings."

"Are you private investigators? May I see your licenses?"

Stan glanced at Emily in sudden panic. But she responded without concern.

"No. We're friends of the family. Stan is an historian and researcher."

He began to relax as soon as she said that. *When you think about it, an auction house that specialized in old manuscripts is nothing more than a purveyor of history.* He nodded. "I'm a retired professor from a college in Michigan. My focus now is on research and writing."

"Ms. Singh, I'm sorry we didn't phone ahead for an appointment," Emily said. "But we are following a line of inquiry and took a chance that someone in Mr. Hollinger's place of employment might be willing to help."

Stan cringed at the formality of Emily's language. But it seemed to be effective. Ms. Singh studied them for a moment, then walked over to her desk and picked up the phone. She pressed a single button. "Hello, Rhea. This is Vidya." She eyed the Remingtons, daring them to bolt. "How are you doing? This is just so awful, about Roger. Everyone here is devastated." She listened for a moment then, "I am so sorry to bother you. But do you know a Mr. and Mrs. Remington? You do?" She listened again, tapping her finger on the desk, still not taking her eyes off Stan and Emily. "Yes, of course. I will. Please take care of yourself."

She hung up the phone and held their gaze for moment longer, as if unwilling to believe what she just heard. But then her eyes softened, and she sighed.

"How can I be of help?"

CHAPTER 23

"CALL me Vidya, please."

Vidya Singh was an incredibly beautiful woman in her late thirties. She wore her raven black hair long over her shoulders. The Drysdale associate motioned Emily and Stan to a round walnut inlay table just a few steps from her desk. The three of them settled into comfortable leather-backed chairs.

"I take it you're not really here about that book," she said with a sad smile, indicating the copy of *In the Harbor* Stan had placed on the table.

He shook his head. "It's just a prop. Something Emily found at a garage sale. For a minute I hoped maybe I had a signed first edition; unfortunately the book was published after Longfellow's death."

Vidya nodded. "I'm sorry. But such forgeries are quite common."

"So I've learned." Stan paused. "Roger Hollinger's death must be very difficult for you and your co-workers. Were you close?"

"He and I had become good friends. I'll miss him greatly. And of course, we've had to re-assign all his clients. It puts pressure on everyone. " Sitting with perfect posture, she propped her delicately tapered fingers into a steeple upon the table. "Even with Rhea's blessing, I'm not sure that I should be talking to you, do you understand? Our firm acts in strict confidence concerning our clients. But as I said, Roger was my friend. We worked together often, and I admired his expertise, his professionalism, and his...how do I put it? His sense of ethics. Plus he made me laugh."

"Is something bothering you about his death?" Emily asked quietly.

Vidya thought a moment before answering. "The man I know would not have committed suicide. I think his wife is right to be concerned."

"Did Roger ever mention a woman named Belle Carter?" Emily asked.

"Actually, I met her once. I believe she works for the Longfellow House."

"We were told she came across a manuscript that she believed might have been an original stanza of *Paul Revere's Ride*, written in Longfellow's own hand."

Vidya sat up even taller and her eyes widened. "If it was authenticated, it could be very valuable."

"Is there any way to know if Roger did in fact authenticate it for her?" Stan jumped in.

"I do have access to his files. Yes. I can likely find out." She spread her fingers out on the table top. "But first there's something I should show you."

She stood and opened a locked filing cabinet next to the window overlooking the street below. Selecting a file, she set it on the table in front of Emily and Stan and opened it so they could see. "I found this as I was organizing Roger's papers."

Emily and Stan leaned forward to see the document in question. It was a bill of sale to a Mario Falluci in Naples, Italy.

"*The Bell of Atri?*" Stan asked after studying it a moment.

"Another manuscript in Longfellow's own hand," Vidya

explained.

Emily gasped when she saw the selling price—more than $200,000. "Was that the auction price?"

"This one wasn't sold at auction. Occasionally an associate will represent something on consignment for a long-standing client."

A typed notation indicated that the client—the seller—had been Duncan Calderwood of Boston.

"Judge Duncan Calderwood," Vidya clarified. "He's active in the Longfellow Historical Society."

"Is that the guy Whitman was talking about?" Emily asked Stan, who nodded.

"He's been a client of Roger's for some time." Vidya slid a clip from the papers and located a hand-written note dated several months earlier.

Stan read the note out loud. "'BC asked me to appraise Bell of Atri ms along with others donated to Longfellow House collection. Why two copies? Look into this.'"

He pointed to the notation. "BC is Belle Carter?"

"Possibly." She shrugged.

"Tell me more about this *Bell of Atri* manuscript," Emily asked.

"The poem was published in 1863 as part of the *Tales of a Wayside Inn* collection," Vidya explained. "The sale item was a draft."

"Is it unusual for there to be two copies?" Emily asked.

"I think Roger's presumption, in this case, is that one of the copies is an exact replica of the other," Vidya said.

"I don't understand. You just said it was a copy."

Stan leaned back in his chair. "Two hand-written copies would never be exactly alike. There'd be small differences in the way a single word is formed, editing differences, changes in wording, that sort of thing."

"So in this case, an exact replica would be…"

"A forgery." Stan finished.

Emily frowned, trying to make a connection. "So this

Judge Calderwood? He didn't know he was maybe selling a forged copy of a Longfellow poem?"

"If that one *was* the forgery. It could have been either," Stan said. "Or both."

"And that creates a problem," Vidya said. "For Roger. And for Drysdale enterprises."

Emily whistled softly. "I would say so. Since we were planning to go to the Longfellow House anyway, maybe we should call ahead and see if we can get an appointment with the judge. I'm curious to see whether he knew about the duplicate copies. Vidya, do you have a phone number for him?"

"I'm sure I can find one for you."

"So, what about the stanza from *Paul Revere's Ride*?" Stan asked. "Do you think Roger had suspicions about that manuscript, too?"

Vidya shrugged. "As I said, he was a man of deep ethics." She slipped the papers back into their folder.

"You said you have access to Roger's office?" Emily asked her.

"Ordinarily I wouldn't do this." Vidya's voice wavered. "But as I told you, I don't believe Roger killed himself. If someone else was responsible…"

Unlike Roger's office at home, this one was remarkably neat and orderly. Emily wondered if Roger kept it that way to impress clients or if Vidya had taken it upon herself to straighten it up as she worked to re-distribute his client files among Drysdale's appraisers.

Vidya closed and locked the door behind them. Rummaging in the top drawer of the dead man's desk, she produced a small key. "If that manuscript he was appraising for Ms. Carter was still in Roger's possession, it would be in his safe."

He keeps the key to his safe in his desk drawer? Who does that?

Vidya opened the safe and shuffled through its contents. After a moment she found what she was looking for—a twelve-by-nine-inch envelope from which she extracted an archival folder with the name "Drysdale" stamped boldly across it. Nesting inside the folder was a single sheet of hand-written poetry, with editing marks, words scratched out and others inserted.

"Is that it? The stanza from the Paul Revere poem?" Stan asked. "May I hold it?" Emily knew that if it were the real deal, few things could make Stan's heart beat faster than touching something that the most famous poet of the nineteenth century had written in his own hand. *If.* It had been Roger's job to authenticate this particular manuscript. Was it something a man could get killed over?

Vidya carried the document to Roger's desk and indicated that Stan should sit. She laid the document in front of him.

"Do I need gloves?"

But she was already reaching into a small chest of drawers for a white cotton pair.

Stan stroked his gloved finger lightly across the top of the page. Reverently, he ran it across a phrase inserted, touched some of the lettering, brushed one of the words crossed out.

After a moment he asked Vidya. "What do you think?"

"I have no idea. I don't see the provenance here."

Emily asked, "Wouldn't he keep the documentation with the manuscript?"

"Yes, of course. I don't know why it isn't here."

"I've been through his home office," Emily said. "I didn't find anything like that there."

"It's not something he would leave lying about," Vidya said. "In our business, allegations of forgery can make or break a career. Most often break it." She picked up the document and slipped it back into its folder. "I'll see if I can find someone who can finish the appraisal. But without the provenance…" She shook her head.

Vidya walked them back to the lobby. Before parting ways with an apology saying she had to get back to the auction, she gave them Judge Calderwood's phone number. Stan immediately placed the call, surprised but pleased when the judge said he had time to meet with them that afternoon.

"Mr. and Mrs. Remington!"

Emily and Stan swiveled in unison to find themselves face to face with Detective Ellison.

"Are you bidding on a book today?" The detective looked displeased to see them there at Drysdale's.

"Oh, hello," Stan said. "No, we, uh…we already have one." He flashed the cover of the Longfellow book he'd carried in, but just as quickly shifted it out of sight.

"Detective." Emily forced a smile. "I'm sorry I wasn't able to call you back."

Stan jumped in with, "We've been rather busy with the girls."

"Are they with you here today?" The detective looked around dramatically, her expression saying she knew full well she wouldn't see any children.

Stan felt his cheeks begin to burn.

"Dentist appointments," Emily said. "We figured we'd check with an appraiser to get the signature in Stan's book authenticated."

"You have a collectable?"

"Found out it's a fake. Look, we hate to bolt again, but we have an appointment this afternoon." She nudged Stan. "I think that's our taxi out there."

She pulled him away from the detective and out the front door before he could say anything more to incriminate them. A quick glance over his shoulder at the angry frown on the detective's face told him they'd crossed a line by coming here.

"Em?'

"Too late to worry about it."

CHAPTER 24

TRAFFIC was gridlocked and Emily was beginning to question their decision to take a taxi to the Longfellow house in Cambridge rather than the T. She cringed when she realized they were back on Storrow Drive, noting that indeed there were no trucks, buses—or RVs—on the riverside roadway.

"What are you thinking?" Stan asked.

"That I can't believe we were dumb enough to almost get caught under a bridge that first day."

"I mean about running into Detective Ellison again."

"Yeah. Not a happy woman, that one."

"Emily! C'mon. She was obviously pissed. It's like we're one step ahead of her the entire way."

"Funny thing that."

"Do you suppose she's there to talk to Vidya?" He checked the traffic tie-up on his phone's map program.

"Oh, I have no doubt about it." Leaning over, she frowned at his tiny screen filled with dotted red lines all up and down the roadway.

"We're in deep shit, aren't we?" he asked.

"We haven't broken any laws. We're just asking questions about two people we encountered under unfortunate circumstances."

"What? Is that a euphemism for 'found their dead bodies'?"

Emily didn't respond. She was already thinking ahead to their appointment with the judge. Stan had googled him while they were at lunch and learned that he was an appellate court judge. He also sat on the Board of Directors of the Longfellow Historical Society, a group whose fundraising efforts drove much of the renovation of the grounds and the house itself.

Thankfully, Stan had the patience of Job when it came to online research. Sitting in front of a computer screen for any length of time made Emily edgy, and she could never seem to find what she wanted, even with the best of search engines. Stan on the other hand…he'd even googled Drysdale's while he was waiting for her to shower that morning. And it was a good thing they'd had a heads up about the auction going on today. He'd also found out some things about Drysdale's business operations that gave her a better handle on just what Roger Hollinger had done for a living. They were becoming a pretty good investigative team, it occurred to her. During her career, she'd developed a knack for getting people to talk; his research skills tapped in to what they weren't willing to say. *No wonder the imperious Detective Ellison was always one step behind.* Emily smiled.

"What about those Longfellow manuscripts at the auction house?" Stan interrupted her reverie. "The duplicate copies?"

Emily tapped her leg, considering his question. "I suspect they're an important piece to the puzzle. If Roger did commit suicide, it might have been because of a perceived threat to his reputation."

"And if it wasn't suicide?"

"If it wasn't suicide—and I'm not convinced it wasn't— money is always a motivating factor. And there appears to be a lot of money at stake with those manuscripts."

Stan frowned at the meter, ticking away the per mile

charge. "I wonder if I should call and tell him we're running late."

But just then the traffic opened up and the driver took advantage of a break in the lanes to gun it. They crossed the river. "We're almost there," he announced.

A broad-shouldered man in his late forties, Judge Duncan Calderwood appeared to be growing a bit of a paunch under his three piece summer suit. He met them in the visitor center with polite handshakes and an autocratic bearing.

"Very good to meet you again, my man," he said to Stan. Then he asked Emily, "Have you had a chance to tour the residence?"

"No, she hasn't," Stan was quick to say.

"Of course, I'm not an official docent," Calderwood said. "But I dare say I am as knowledgeable about our man Longfellow as any of the park rangers. The poet and I share a common ancestor, after all."

"You're related?" Emily asked.

"In a manner of speaking. Distant cousins, if you will. And you," he said, addressing Stan, "you said you're an historian?"

"Born and bred." Stan beamed.

"Then you likely already know there's a double history embedded in this domicile." Calderwood took Stan's elbow and led him down the hallway. Emily purposely let them walk ahead so that she could observe Calderwood.

"Do I remember correctly that you are engaging in research about our man Washington?"

Stan nodded.

"Then you'll be pleased to know that this house contains over six hundred thousand artifacts as well as an extensive archive of letters, books, and documents from the period predating General Washington's stay to the early twentieth century…"

Emily tuned out the ensuing discussion between the two

men as they walked from room to room. *What a pompous windbag!* She noticed the ornate cane he carried seemed to be more for effect than as an aid. She wondered if Stan was picking up on how patronizing the man was. After a few moments, she shifted her focus to her surroundings.

She tried to imagine what it must have been like to live in this house with the ornate furniture and paintings and portraits of stuffy people that made it feel more like an art gallery than a home. Room after room was swathed in garish color combinations and patterns. *Maybe that's the way people liked it back then. But yikes! Fanny Longfellow had the God-awfulest taste in carpeting.* Underneath Emily's feet, bright pink and red pansies fought with a turquoise background for domination.

When they'd finished with the tour, Calderwood suggested they walk over to the Carriage House where they could have a cup of coffee and sit and chat. The outbuilding had been remodeled to house a moderate-size meeting room; the horse stalls were now small office cubbies.

"You said on the phone that you had additional questions about that Longfellow book you discovered?" Calderwood asked, passing Stan the sugar.

"Yes, we were just at Drysdale's with it, and they confirmed what Ranger Carter told me."

To Emily's surprise, Calderwood's face didn't register any emotion at the mention of Belle Carter's name; however she thought she detected a slight stiffening of his body at the word "Drysdale."

Calderwood leaned back in his chair. "So what is it you think I can help you with?" He took a sip of his coffee and stared at Stan intently.

"To be honest," Emily decided to take the lead, "We're here about Ms. Carter. We're hoping you could tell us something about her."

Calderwood frowned. "Unfortunately she passed away earlier this week. Why are you asking?"

"There's been a question raised as to how she died."

"Raised by whom?"

"Her son. Whitman. He thinks that something she came across in her research may have been valuable enough to endanger her life. It was he who suggested we talk to you."

"I was informed she'd died of a heart attack."

"According to what her son said, she had an anaphylactic reaction to an antibiotic," Emily said.

"Really? How awful. But I don't understand why you are involved."

"It's a complicated story. But we've learned that she came across a Longfellow manuscript that she believed could potentially bring a boost to her income. Whitman thought you might be able to tell us something about that."

Calderwood shook his head. "I became aware that she encountered financial difficulties from time to time. But I wasn't privy to the particulars. Do you know her elder son as well?"

"Tennyson?" Emily nodded. "We've met him."

"I must say, that young man is rather a worrisome sort."

"In what way?"

"Based on information she shared with me, I would hazard to say it's entirely possible that young man contributed to her...shall we say, financial situation. To be honest, I found their relationship to be rather disturbing."

"How so?" Emily asked.

"Oh, I couldn't say." He waved a languid hand in the air. "It was little things she let slip." He leaned forward, an eyebrow raised. "I'm not sure I'm comfortable talking about this. You say Whitman asked you to look into the situation?"

"We met with him yesterday," Stan said.

Emily noted that Stan could be just as evasive about the truth as she had learned to be.

"Would you mind terribly if I called him before speaking to you further?"

"Not at all. I have his number." Emily started to reach into her bag.

"That's quite all right. I'm sure we have it on record here. And I'm sorry I can't be of help with whatever you think it is Ms. Carter found that might shed light on why she died. But I certainly hope the police are questioning Tennyson. He's a bad apple, that one, and I have no doubt a conversation with him would shed an interesting light on the circumstances of his mother's demise." He checked his watch, a gold, high-end time piece, maybe a Rolex, maybe something even more expensive.

Emily was amused that someone who'd said he didn't want to speak with them any further kept talking.

"He couldn't seem to reconcile Belle's relationship with the woman she was living with," the judge added.

"Evelyn LeBlanc?"

"You know her, too?"

"We've met," Emily said. "Judge Calderwood, did you know that Belle had a Longfellow manuscript that she'd taken to an appraiser at Drysdale's for an evaluation?"

"To Roger Hollinger?"

"You know him?"

"He's represented the Historical Society in fundraising sales from time to time. What was this piece that Belle took to him?"

"A stanza from *Paul Revere's Ride*," Stan said. "Possibly written in Longfellow's own hand."

"Really?" Calderwood's eyebrows shot up. "That would be quite a find…if it was determined to be authentic."

"Yes, that seems to be the question of the day," Emily said. "However, the provenance is missing."

Calderwood checked his watch again. "I really do have to run, I'm afraid. I have another appointment." He stood up to signal the end of their meeting. "Do call me if you think of any other way that I can be of help." He reached for a gold-topped cane. "May I walk you out?"

Just then Emily's phone pinged. "My daughter." She glanced at the text on the screen. "Perfect timing. She's here to pick us up."

As they followed the sidewalk around toward the front of the grounds, Emily commented on the small garden. "It's beautiful…so peaceful."

"It's a re-creation," Calderwood said proudly. "Quite a bit of research and planning—not to mention fundraising—went into the restoration. In its day it was the center of the Longfellow's social life during the summer months. After he died, his daughter Alice commissioned a complete redesign. It's her garden that we've restored. "

"That yellow rose bush is particularly lovely."

"A Harris Yellow."

"And look at that tree. It's huge!" Emily pointed to the gnarled old linden tree.

"That particular tree, I'm proud to say, has graced the grounds for a full century. Likely not here while the old man was alive, but perhaps planted by one of his children or grandchildren. Is that your ride?" He pointed the tip of his walking stick toward the vehicle waiting in the road just outside the front gate.

"Yes. Thank you so much for your time," Stan said, shaking the judge's hand one last time before the man walked off.

"Listen." Calderwood had stopped and turned around. "I probably shouldn't say this. Gossip and such. But, when you brought up Roger Hollinger's name in regard to our Ms. Carter, it took me quite aback."

Puzzled, Emily waited for him to continue.

"As I think of it, she'd recently said things to me privately that indicated she was, perhaps, having an affair with Mr. Hollinger. Quite scandalous, of course, considering her choice of a life partner. No, I shouldn't be saying anything. Please disregard what I've just said. I'm sure it's nothing. I must say good day. It was very good to meet you." He bowed slightly to Emily and nodded to Stan, then continued walking on down the sidewalk.

"Nothing, my ass," Stan said, opening the door as the two younger girls scrambled into the way back.

"Hey, Mom, Dad. Did you learn anything today?" Megan asked. "Wynter, honey, let Grandma sit up front." But the girl obstinately held her position as shotgun.

"I'm okay in the back." Emily climbed in and slid over to the far seat. "I don't know. There's something about that man…"

"A font of information." Stan slid in next to her.

"I was leaning toward mis-information."

"Exactly."

Megan checked her mirror, then steered the car away from the curb. As they passed the judge striding purposefully up the block, Stan gave a little wave of farewell.

"That man," Annabel said, pointing. "He was at the park."

"What park, honey?" Megan asked, checking her rearview mirror a second time.

"The night of the fireworks. He was sitting with the lady that fell over."

Emily swiveled around to face Annabel. "Sweetheart, are you saying you saw him with the lady that died the other night?"

"Only for a while. He didn't stay the whole time."

"Are you sure?" Emily craned her neck to look out the window, but they were already too far away for her to see him again.

"If Annabel says he was there, he was there," Wynter declared. "She's never wrong about stuff like that."

CHAPTER 25

"ANNABEL, honey, tell me exactly what you saw in the park the other night, just before the fireworks." Emily straddled the picnic bench so she could be eye to eye with her granddaughter.

Annabel scratched at a mosquito bite, her legs kicking back and forth under the table. "That lady...the one that died...she was sitting in her chair almost the whole time the music was playing. And that guy was with her." She reached for her glass of lemonade and took a long slurp, smacking her lips at the sour taste. She giggled when she saw her grandfather mimicking her puckered lips.

Emily scowled at her husband. Megan nudged him in warning.

"What do you remember about him?" Emily asked.

Annabel shrugged. "He was kinda fat, I guess. He walked with a stick, except it didn't curl down at the top like a cane. It had a knob. A gold knob."

Stan was amazed at how observant Annabel was about even small details.

"Can you think of anything else about him?"

"He didn't look like he liked picnics."

"What do you mean?"

"He wasn't wearing shorts or anything. He wore black pants and a button shirt. Like when Daddy goes to work." She swatted at a mosquito flitting around her face.

"Did you see them come into the park?"

"Uhn uhn. They were already there when we got there."

"So much for my powers of observation," Emily said in a wry tone.

"And I was too busy playing with the girls," Stan added.

Annabel slurped her lemonade again. "Am I in trouble?"

"Oh, no, honey," Megan reassured her. "You might have seen something important. You're so good at noticing things."

"You just might be able to help us solve a puzzle," Emily said.

"Like a mystery?" Annabel asked.

Emily touched the little girl's hand. "Yes, like a mystery."

Annabel screwed her face up, trying to remember. "They both were sitting in chairs when we got there. Red, white and blue chairs. But at the end of the music, just as the fireworks started, the man got up and took his chair with him."

"He left the park?" Stan asked.

"I guess so. He didn't come back."

"Did you notice anything about the lady?" Emily asked. "Like, was she having a good time? Or was she angry and upset?"

"I guess she was having a good time. She smiled a lot. I couldn't hear what they were saying." The little girl squirmed on the bench.

"You're sure it was the man from the Longfellow House?" Stan asked. But when she looked at him confused, he amended his question. "From the big yellow house."

Annabel nodded. "Can I go watch the movie with Allyn and Wynter now?" she pleaded with her mother.

Megan glanced over at Emily, who nodded. "You can go now, honey. But it's too nice to be indoors. Why don't you tell them to get their swimsuits on and the three of you can walk down to the pool for a little while."

Annabel threw her leg over the bench of the picnic table and ran up the steps into the RV. "Allyn! Wynter! Get your swimsuits on!! Mom says we can go to the pool!!"

"She notices everything, doesn't she?" Stan commented.

"She's always been that way," Megan said. "Sometimes too remarkable. It's difficult to fudge about things with her."

"Not unlike her mother." Stan winked and Megan stuck her tongue out at him. "So what do you think this all means?" he asked Emily.

"I think it means our judge had some involvement in Belle Carter's life beyond work."

"Could he have had something to do with her death, too?" Megan asked.

"Let's not jump to conclusions," Emily advised. "All we know is that he was with her the night she died."

"And he wasn't with her when her body was found," Stan put in.

Stan tapped at the keys on his laptop. He could hear the girls outside shouting and laughing as they batted the shuttlecock back and forth over the picnic table. The smell of burgers on the grill wafted through the open window making his stomach growl. Emily and Megan hustled in and out of the RV throwing together a salad, filling lemonade glasses, and chopping tomatoes and onions.

"Philip says the burgers are ready," Emily said, rummaging in the fridge for ketchup and mustard.

"Okay. Be out in a minute." He tapped his pencil on the yellow pad next to the computer, staring at the names he'd written. Thoughtfully, he circled "Judge Duncan Calderwood." Then he circled Belle Carter's name and drew a line between the two. Finally, he wrote "Roger Hollinger" and circled that name, drawing lines connecting it to the other two.

"Are you coming?" Emily asked, poking her head back through the door.

"Yup. You bet." He retraced the circle around Roger's name before throwing his pen down. He glanced once more at the Boston Globe article he'd been studying, then he shut the lid of the laptop and followed her out the door.

After dinner, Stan brought his laptop out to the picnic table and went quickly back to work.

"What are you so engrossed in?"

"Huh?" Stan jumped, startled when Philip set a Brandy Manhattan down in front of him. "Oh, thanks! Why is it so quiet all of a sudden? Where are the girls?"

Philip laughed. "They left a half hour ago. Those two gals who've been doing the workouts with Emily in the morning…?"

"Tara and Amy?"

"Yeah, those two. They stopped by and invited the twins on a hike." He slid onto the bench across from Stan.

A moment later Emily and Megan joined them, vodka and tonics in hand.

"What's this about Annabel seeing someone with that lady who died at the fireworks?" Philip asked.

"That little girl of yours doesn't miss much, does she?" Emily touched the ice-filled glass to her cheek.

"Tell me about it. Drives me nuts with all her questions. And a memory like an elephant." Philip swirled his own drink. "So what's going on?"

"Apparently Belle Carter wasn't alone that night on the Esplanade after all."

"So…are you thinking this guy Annabel saw had something to do with her death?" Philip asked. He slapped a mosquito landing on his arm, killing it.

"I honestly don't know," Emily said. "But at the very least, he's a material witness. He was the last person to see her alive."

"So what does that mean?"

Stan shook the ice in his glass, then tilted it toward Emily. "Honey, do you remember what Judge Calderwood said just before we got into the car this afternoon?"

"He said a lot of things just before we got into the car. And before that as well." She waved a mosquito away from her face.

"I mean when he said it took him aback when we brought up Roger Hollinger's name."

"Yeah? So?" Emily batted away another mosquito.

"We didn't bring it up."

"We didn't?"

"You asked him if he knew that Belle had taken a Longfellow manuscript to someone at Drysdale's…"

"And *he* asked if it was Roger," Emily finished. "Good catch, Stan." She popped up, walked over to one of the undercarriage storage compartments and brought back two citronella candles.

"So, what does it matter who said what?" Philip asked, taking the candles from her and lighting them.

"It's not so much who said what as what wasn't said."

Now Philip looked really confused.

Stan tried to clarify. "The judge said Roger had brokered fundraising sales for the Historical Society. But he failed to mention that he himself had been doing personal business with Roger."

Philip pressed, "But didn't you say that your friend at Simmons College introduced Belle to Roger this past year? And how do you know that the judge was doing business with him?"

"We saw the paperwork at Drysdale's."

Emily concurred. "That's an important piece of the picture that he left out. And on top of it, he did seem to be doing a whole lot of finger pointing this afternoon."

"Calderwood?" Megan asked.

Emily nodded. "That bit about Belle and Roger having an affair. And earlier when he was telling us about Tennyson, making sure we knew he was a 'bad apple.'" She finger-quoted in the air.

"Okay, so, I went a bit deeper with the Google search on Calderwood." Stan tapped on the lid of the computer. "He's an appellate court judge," he told Philip and Megan. "The guy apparently comes from old Boston aristocrat lineage. He goes by Duncan Calderwood…" Stan held his glass up in a faux salute. "The Third."

"Hoity toity," Megan said.

"From what I can gather, though, he's pretty much run his family's fortune to the ground. Still lives in a big old house up on Beacon Hill. But it's mortgaged to the hilt."

Philip whistled. "That's a pretty exclusive neighborhood."

"So, is he really a distant relation to Longfellow?" Emily asked.

"I couldn't verify that. Doesn't mean he isn't. He's apparently a document collector in his own right, though. Has some original manuscripts by various 19th century literati— Thoreau, Emerson, Dickinson, Alcott—some of which he inherited as part of the family trust; others he's procured over the past decade or so."

"Married?"

"He has a wife, but her name doesn't pop up much in the society news. Kind of weird, don't you think? Oh, and something else that's interesting. Mr. and Mrs. Calderwood are apparently members of Christ Church here in Boston."

"Christ Church? Isn't that—?"

"The Old North Church," Megan said with a shiver.

"Seriously?" Emily waved at Vinie walking past, a cat under each arm.

"He's an active member of the church's fundraising group. The one that oversees building preservation."

"That means he had access to Roger that night." Emily furrowed her brows.

"Oh geez, Mom. Maybe we should call that detective." Megan was wringing her hands now.

"Whoa! Whoa! Wait!" Philip thrust his hands out. "And tell her what? That our little girl was a witness in a crime that no one knows whether it was even committed or not?"

"Honey, we have to tell someone," Megan said.

"After the grilling we got the night we found that woman, and after what you and," he said, pointing at Stan, "you went through when you found Roger's body…you want to sic the Boston PD on Annabel?"

"When you put it that way." Megan hesitated. "But what about Rhea? She deserves to know what's going on."

"No one is siccing anyone on anybody," Emily reassured them. "And when it's time, we'll talk to Rhea. But Annabel has seen something that may be relevant, something Detective Ellison should know about."

Philip still looked unhappy, but after exchanging glances with Megan, he nodded in resignation.

"I'll call her in the morning."

CHAPTER 26

"YOU'VE reached Detective Dayanna Ellison at the Boston PD. If this is an emergency, please hang up and dial 911. Otherwise, leave a message and I'll call back as soon as possible."

Emily left her name and number then tucked the phone back into her pocket. Sipping her morning coffee, she felt secretly relieved. She wouldn't admit it but, like her son-in-law, she didn't really want that woman or anyone else in the Boston PD grilling her nine-year-old granddaughter. When the time came for Annabel to tell the authorities what she'd seen in the park, yes of course, she'd have to say something, but Emily was glad to put it off, if just for another couple of hours—a couple of hours of pure vacationing. Content for the moment, she stretched out on the chaise lounge.

The campground was quiet after the morning rush of campers pulling up stakes to head home or for parts unknown. Amy and Tara had stopped by early on their way out to thank Emily for the invigorating Tae kwon do workouts of the previous days. Philip and the girls had lured Stan out of the RV and away from his computer with an invitation to play miniature golf.

The sun was rising in a milky sky; the scent of blueberry

and honeysuckle lingered on a teasing breeze.

"Good morning." Megan wandered over from the pop-up with a coffee mug in hand. "Hey, I spotted a poster for a yoga session. Want to go with me?"

"Yoga?"

"Yeah. They hold it at a place called Meditation Point. How cool is that?" At Emily's look of skepticism, Megan added, "I talked to the lady at the camp store and she said you have to hike through the woods to get to there. Who knows, maybe you'll find out you love yoga." Megan lifted one foot and pressed her hands together over her head, moving into the classic tree pose. Shifting her stance, she let loose with a swift, if clumsy, kick. "And I didn't complain about the Tae kwon do."

Emily laughed. "Okay. But if I get stuck in a knot, you'll have to fetch your father to come untie me."

The trail to Meditation Point wound its way through a scrub of white pine, black birch, and hickory. The two women strolled side by side, their feet crunching on the cinder path. Patches of sunlight flickered through the branches. After a few moments they came upon a small meadow lush with Queen Anne's lace, black-eyed Susans, purple coneflowers and blue asters. Butterflies flitted in and out of the morning shadows while bees buzzed to and fro, drunk with nectar. Emily breathed in deeply, enjoying the heady scent of wildflowers. A red-winged blackbird perched nervously on the bobbing globe of a lavender milkweed flower scolding them with a *chak chak chak*.

"So lovely…" Megan murmured.

Emily nodded, reveling in the peace and quiet…until a commanding *ding!* splintered the ambience. Megan shot her mother a disgusted look as Emily scanned the incoming text on her phone.

"AT&T," Emily said sheepishly. "Thanking me for paying

my bill promptly.

"I think this is meant to be a phone free zone," Megan chided.

"Old habits die hard. Sorry. I'll silence it."

"Why don't you just shut it down all together? Enjoy the moment without distractions," Megan said with a tight lipped smile.

Emily nodded and they walked on in silence for several moments, until Megan finally blurted out, "Wynter is driving me nuts!"

Now Emily smiled. *So much for avoiding distractions.* "She *is* thirteen."

"I know. But it's like Philip and I can't do anything right. She's morphed from the sweet little girl she used to be into something straight out of a Wes Craven movie."

"It's part of growing up."

"Oh come on. I was never like that."

"Heavens no," Emily snickered. "You were worse! Much worse."

Megan responded with an exaggerated groan.

"I have noticed she can be a bit petulant at times," Emily conceded, "but she seems to be getting along famously with your father."

"Yeah, I wonder what that's all about. I can't believe she volunteered to go to the Longfellow House with him. If it isn't required to maintain her grade point, you won't catch her near anything remotely historical in the entire city of Boston."

"Seems like that would restrict her travels a bit," Emily said, remembering Wynter's pointed disinterest on the Freedom Trail. "At that moment I think it was the lesser of two evils." She moved her hands up and down as if weighing the options. "Swan boats with her little sisters or a museum with her grandfather. Turns out she hit gold."

"Ah yes, the cute guide." Megan kicked a pebble out of her path. "All she's interested in are boys and what her friends think. And do. And wear. And boys, of course. Do you think she bothered to tell me anything about their excursion? It's as if there's a cone of silence around her some times. And when she bothers to communicate, you can't predict which Wynter you'll get. The morose moody teen or the giddy little girl."

"She'll grow out of it. Maybe not the boys part, though."

"She'd better. If I hear one more complaint that this thing we've said or that thing we're doing is boring, I'm going to strangle her." She grabbed at a dead twig that was threatening to scratch her arm and snapped it in half.

Emily held her tongue.

The trail skirted the edge of the meadow, making its way alongside a narrow brook, glistening languidly in the morning sun. A small wooden footbridge beckoned and on the other side of the brook, they climbed a small embankment into the cool shade of a stand of oak trees.

Spotting hikers ahead, they quickened their pace. Moments later they emerged into yet another small clearing, and followed the others up a small rise to an outcropping of granite overlooking the meadow they had just walked through. Off in the hazy distance they could see the Boston skyline.

"Namaste!" A graceful young woman in too-short shorts and an already-sweat-stained tank top pressed her palms together, fingers pointing to the sky, and bowed her head in greeting. Her thick brown hair was braided into a knot at the nape of her neck. "I'm Julianne. Please, find a spot. We'll start in a moment."

Emily groaned quietly as she settled onto the rock-hard ground and crossed her legs into a semblance of a lotus position, unsuccessfully mimicking those around her.

Julianne tapped a brass bell with a small mallet, signaling the beginning of the session. Emily noted Megan taking deep cleansing breaths and did the same.

Julianne's hypnotic voice coached them through a relaxation exercise. "Breathe in, breathe out…close your eyes and slowly let your body relax as you open your mind to an awareness of the confluence of your body and the ecosphere. Feel one with Gaia, Mother Earth, beneath you…"

Emily grimaced, feeling only the muscle cramp in her left hip. She wiggled to adjust her position.

"Please gently move into Savasana." Julianne, in one fluid motion, slid her body into a prone position, and the eager yoga students followed her lead. "Also known as the corpse pose."

Emily straightened her legs out in front of her in relief and flopped onto her back. She gazed up at a wandering cloud. *Corpse position.* The image of Belle Carter sprawled across the fallen lawn chair popped into her mind.

Julianne took several of her own deep cleansing breaths. "I want you to imagine your body as if there were three parts: the navel, the heart, and the throat…"

Emily closed her eyes. The thick rope wound around Roger Hollinger's throat demanded her attention. *Was it really suicide?*

"As you inhale, I want you to center your thoughts and draw your breath first in toward your belly, pulling it back toward your spine…"

Why did he say he was having an affair with Belle Carter? Emily took a deep breath and pushed her belly out. *It doesn't fit. But Evelyn did think Belle was cheating on her. But with Roger?* In a sudden panic, Emily remembered to exhale. She opened her eyes to a sky striated with clouds.

"Feel the breeze on your face." Julianne's voice was soft and lilting. "Listen to the sounds of Gaia. Breathe in deeply. Notice the fragrance of the wildflowers wafting from the meadow."

Flaring her nostrils, Emily took a deep breath. The scent of the wildflowers was heady. But something else was in the air, vague and smoky. Remnants of last night's campfires. It reminded her of…cigar smoke. *Cigar smoke?* That whistling garage sale vendor had smelled of cigar smoke. *So did the judge,* she suddenly remembered. And the book. She pictured Stan sniffing the open pages and pretending to be able to identify the cigar brand by the left-over aroma. *What ever happened to that receipt?* It went missing right after he showed the book to Belle. Too bad about that signature being a forgery. *Forgery.*

Julianne guided the group to a standing position and then into the downward-facing dog pose. "Adho Mukha Svanasana," she called to the group.

A whole mocha savanna? Emily placed her hands flat on the ground. Glancing over, she mimicked Megan's pose and attempted to walk her hands out until her body became an inverted V and her butt stuck up in the air. She let her breath out with a whoosh, and fixed her eyes on a series of jagged scratches in the rock. They resembled a jumble of foreign letters. *Letters. Forgery.* Rhea had recognized Roger's handwriting in the suicide note, but wouldn't accept that he had written it. She kept saying it didn't sound like him. *What do people sound like in a suicide note?* And what about the Italian connection? And the two copies of the poem about the bells. Was one of those a forgery too? *Seems to be a lot of that going around.*

Emily inched her feet a bit farther apart to keep from wobbling. And then there was that bit about the Paul Revere poem. *What did Vidya Singh say?* Emily squeezed her eyes tight, trying to retrieve memories that insisted on hiding in jumbled fragments. *Something about Calderwood?* She couldn't remember. Calderwood had said he was a collector of Longfellow manuscripts. He also insisted that Roger and Belle were having an affair. Her arm muscles cramped and she began wobbling wildly. As she adjusted her feet and legs to keep from falling over, her phone popped out of her pocket and onto the rocky ground.

She lunged for it, losing her balance, and crashed over with a loud grunt.

"Mom?" Megan broke her pose.

Julianne and several of the students viewed her with

puzzlement.

"Sorry!" Emily said in a loud whisper, brushing her scraped legs off. She picked up the phone and flicked it on.

"Mom!" Megan hissed this time.

"Sorry, Sweetie. I just thought of something. Gotta make a call."

"Here, Kitty Kitty! Where are you, Luna? Come here, sweet kitty!" Alvina Pendergast was frantically pacing in front of her RV.

"Can we help you?" Stan asked. He and Philip and the girls were on their way to the miniature golf course.

"I can't find my precious Luna!" She wrung her hands, then wiped a stray tear from her eye.

"Luna?" Wynter said, looking up from her phone.

"She's under the RV! I can get her!" And before anyone could stop her, Annabel darted to the RV, slid onto her belly, and scooted under. "I got her!" She wriggled out with the calico cat clutched in her hands.

"Thank you! Thank you!" the woman said over and over, between bursts of "Bad kitty!" She hugged the feline to her chest and nuzzled her face in its fur.

"I found these, too." Annabel held out a pair of swim goggles.

"Those are my goggles!" Allyn shouted. "It *was* you. You stole my goggles!"

"What are you talking about?" the woman spluttered.

Allyn grabbed the goggles from her sister's hand and held them up in triumph as Philip rushed to intervene. "You did, too. You're a witch and you stole my stuff. Where's my towel? And Wynter's earbuds?"

"Allyn!" Philip admonished. "I'm sorry," he said to the woman, "but the goggles have been missing for a couple of days."

"Why would I take your goggles?"

"To cast a spell!" Allyn said.

"Excuse me?" Vinie looked even more perplexed.

"We all know you're a witch." The little girl stood with her hands on her hips.

"Don't be stupid, Allyn," Wynter said.

Stan put a hand on Allyn's shoulder. "I'm sure there is another reason why the goggles ended up under your RV."

"Thank the stars Luna is safe." Vinie nuzzled the cat even tighter. "I think perhaps you—my goodness you two look alike." Her eyes flicked from one girl to the other, then she stared directly at Allyn whose glare never faltered. "You need to investigate the situation further before drawing conclusions."

"Huh?"

"She's saying she didn't do it, and we need to solve the mystery of who did," Annabel explained.

"Oh. Okay. Nice cat."

"Let's go." Philip took the girls by the hand and dragged them away. "Sorry," he said one last time to Vinie.

"My apologies, too," Stan said before following Philip and the girls.

"I think she stole Grandma's sandal, too," Allyn said loud enough for all to hear.

A few moments later, as Philip was paying for their golf game, Stan's phone broke into his favorite guitar riff. He stared at it, confused by the unfamiliar number.

"Hello?"

"Mr. Remington?"

"Yes."

"This is Whitman Carter."

"Ah! The cordwainer." He waved Philip and the girls on into the course.

"I tried calling your wife, but it went right through to her voice mail."

"What can I do for you?"

"I'm at my mother's apartment. I've been going through

her personal papers and I came across something...I don't know what to think of it."

"What...?"

"A reference to a manuscript that she was all excited about. A poem in Longfellow's own hand, or so she believed. She was getting it appraised. But she had some reservations about it. I found her notes." He paused. "Maybe your wife, or even you, would be willing to take a look?"

"Now?" Out of the corner of his eye, Stan could see the girls practicing golf swings, waiting for their turn to start the game. He swiped at beads of sweat on his forehead, feeling the humidity increase.

"If you could. I'd really appreciate it. My brother's been going nuts over this estate thing. Of course, it's not like she had any money, but you know what I mean. Evelyn's hired an attorney."

Stan sighed. "Okay. What was that address again?" He walked over to Philip. "Something came up. I really hate to cut out on you like this, but it has to do with that woman's death."

Surprised, Philip said, "Maybe I should go with you. If you're going into the city, you'll want someone who can manage the driving."

"What about the girls? I don't think we should leave them alone."

"Megan and Emily will be back any minute. Wynter can babysit until then," he said to her.

"Will you pay me?" she asked.

"We don't need a babysitter!" Allyn protested.

"Wynter's in charge. And yes, I'll pay you. You can play a couple of rounds of mini-golf here then go back and watch movies in Grandpa's RV. Make sure you keep the door locked, all right?"

The twins quickly forgot to be miffed about the babysitting arrangement once they saw the windmill, bridges, and hazards of the course.

"Wynter, when your mom and grandmother get back, tell Grandma that we're meeting Whitman Carter at his mother's apartment," Stan instructed his granddaughter.

"Who?"

"The cobbler that took us on the Freedom Trail tour."

"Aye aye, sir!" She snapped a sassy salute and herded her sisters off toward the windmill.

"And keep the door locked!" he called after her.

Emily jogged to a shady spot near some birch saplings. *Is it getting more humid or is this another damned hot flash?* she wondered as she switched on her phone. She could hear the yoga instructor's voice intoning rhythmically. Turning her back in an effort to minimize the distraction to the group, she listened to the two voice mails that had popped up in her message window.

"Mrs. Remington, this is Detective Ellison. I'm glad you are no longer avoiding me. We do need to talk. Please call as soon as possible."

Emily nodded as if in agreement, but tapped the button to listen to the other voice message first. It was Whitman Carter. "Mrs. Remington, can you call me back as soon as you get this message? I'm at my mother's apartment with my brother Tenny, and we found something among her papers I think you should see."

She immediately hit the return call button, but to her chagrin it rang a half dozen times before reverting to Whitman's voice mail. "This is Emily Remington, playing phone tag, I guess. Call me back."

Frustrated, she hit the return call button again, this time for the police woman. And of course, it, too, went directly to voice mail. "Damn!" She hung up without a leaving a message. What could she say? Her reasoning was too convoluted to leave any kind of message.

"Mom, what were you thinking?"

Emily jumped at her daughter's voice. The yoga session had just wrapped up and Megan had stomped over to confront her mother. Emily blinked. "That you can't judge a book by its cover. Or a suicide note."

Megan stared in bewilderment at her mother striding down the wooded trail.

CHAPTER 27

PHILIP hit the horn and swerved just in time to avoid a taxi that had braked without warning. Stan was relieved his son-in-law had offered to drive, even as he clutched the armrests on either side of him. Philip maneuvered across trolley tracks and down one way streets with a familiarity Stan knew he couldn't acquire even if he'd lived there for decades. As it was, they drove around the block three times before finding a parking spot—right in front of the building. A car was just pulling out.

"Count your blessings," Philip declared. "This almost never happens.

Moments later they were on the stoop under the maroon awning.

Stan hit the buzzer for Belle Carter's apartment. No response. He jabbed it three more times. Finally he tried calling Whitman on his phone. Still no response.

"What do we do now?" he asked his son-in-law.

Philip contemplated the apartment windows above. He shrugged his shoulders and ran his thumb down the entire line of buttons, pressing each one. After a moment, the front door buzzed and Stan heard a click as it unlocked. Philip quickly grabbed the door and yanked it open.

"That works?" Stan said, impressed.

Philip snorted. "Every time."

Stan took a deep breath and started up the first flight of steps ahead of his son-in-law. He stopped at the first landing.

"You okay?" Philip asked.

"Yeah, I just have to take it slow." By the time his foot touched the final landing, though, his heart was pounding and he had to pause again to catch his breath. After a moment, he led Philip to 3D. Raising his hand to knock on the door, he realized it was already open a crack.

"Hello?" he called, pushing the door an inch wider. "Whitman! Are you in there?"

A faint moan emanated from the room beyond. Philip raised his eyebrows and reached for the door. The two men entered cautiously. They heard it again; this time the moan was louder. Following the sound, they found Whitman Carter sprawled on the kitchen floor, nearly unconscious.

"Where's your car?" Emily asked as they approached the camp site.

"Dunno." Megan peeked into the pop-up camper and shrugged her shoulders. "No one's here." She nodded toward the RV. "Looks like someone's home over at your place."

"Grandma!" the twins shouted as she walked in. They jumped up from the sofa and ran to hug her.

"Mom!" Wynter flicked the remote, shutting off the TV. "What took you so long? I need a new swimsuit."

"Where are your dad and Grandpa?" Megan asked.

"They drove into the city. Can you take me to the mall?" Wynter stood in front of her mother.

"The city? You mean Boston?" Emily reached into the fridge for a bottle of water. "Why did they go there?"

"They left you kids alone?" Megan cried in a sudden panic.

"To meet that cobbler guy. Mom, we're perfectly safe. I kept the door locked. I really need a new swimsuit."

"Why do you need a new swimsuit?" Megan asked. "What happened to the one I bought you a month ago?"

"The witch stole hers," Allyn said. "Mommy, can I have a tonic? Wynter won't let us have a tonic."

"Wynter, honey," Emily found herself straining to keep from losing patience. "Who did you say Grandpa and Dad went to meet?"

"That guy from the Freedom Trail. Huzzah! Mom, the mall?"

"Oh, Honey. I can't go now. I'm fighting the beginnings of a migraine. You probably just misplaced it."

"Did they say why they were meeting him?" Emily asked.

Wynter shrugged her shoulders. "I did not misplace it. Someone took it."

"He called Grandpa," Annabel said, popping open her soda can. "Just when we were starting our mini-golf game."

Emily asked, puzzled, "The cobbler called your grandfather?"

Annabel nodded.

"Mom? The swimsuit?" Wynter demanded.

Grabbing her car keys from the hook over the counter, Emily said to Megan, "I think I'd better go find them."

"What do you mean? Where are they? Do you have any ibuprofen?"

"I think I know where to look. Whitman left me a message while we were out Yoga-ing. In the top drawer in the bedroom."

"My vacation will be ruined if I don't have a swimsuit!"

"Wynter!" Emily said, way more sharply than she meant to. At the startled look on the girl's face, she took a deep breath and centered herself. In as calm a voice as she could muster she said, "Why don't you come with me? We can stop at the mall on the way home."

Wynter threw her arms around her grandmother. "Grams! You're the best!" She threw a haughty look at her mother and raced out the door to the Volkswagen.

"Whitman!" Stan ran across the living room and knelt at the man's side.

Whitman's face was bruised and cut, his nose broken and bleeding. His eyes were almost swollen shut, but he was breathing. He moaned again. Stan could sense Philip hovering over them. "Call 911."

Stan was startled when Carter put a shaky hand on his arm.

"You have to stop him."

"Who? Whitman, who did this to you?"

Whitman spoke through bloodied lips. "Tenny. Tried to talk sense into him. But he got mad at me."

"Why? What's going on?" Stan reached for the towel Philip had fetched from the kitchen and handed it to Whitman.

"I showed him Mom's notebook. He's going after Calderwood."

"Calderwood?"

"Tenny thinks he killed our mother. Poisoned…her." His voice was barely a whisper. He closed his eyes as if he was going to pass out again. When he opened them, they were filled with fear. "Stop him…before he does something stupid."

Or before Calderwood does something to him. Stan was filled with a growing sense of dread. "Where did he go?"

"Don't know…maybe…Longfellow House?"

Stan wavered, looked up at Philip who shook his head in indecision.

"Please…" Whitman gripped Stan's arm with a strength that belied his condition.

The sound of sirens filtered through the windows; revolving red lights bounced off the walls.

Hitting the accelerator, Emily maneuvered the car up the ramp and onto highway. "Try calling your grandpa for me." She tossed her phone to Wynter. "Maybe you'll have better luck."

"It went straight to voice mail, Grams." Wynter's fingers flickered over the tiny keyboard. "I'll send him a text." But before she could finish the message, Emily's phone trilled.

"Is that him?" Emily asked, taking off her sunglasses. *When had the sky become so overcast?*

"It's a Boston number. Hello?" Wynter listened for a moment. "Hi, Rhea. No, it's me, Wynter. This *is* Grandma's phone. We're in the car. Want to talk to her?" She spoke to Emily. "It's Mom's friend."

Emily winced. Thinking of the day planner sitting on the table in their RV, she knew she owed Rhea an explanation of what they had learned about her husband; however, the pieces to the puzzle had not yet locked into place.

"Put it on speaker, Honey."

"Mrs. Remington?" Rhea's quiet voice wobbled a bit as the signal wavered.

"Yes. It's me. And call me Emily. How are you, Rhea?"

"I hope I'm not disturbing you."

"No. It's fine." Emily gave her granddaughter a sideways glance, but the girl had already popped in her ear buds and was fingering her iPod.

"I was just wondering what you had learned about the notes in Roger's daybook."

Emily hesitated a moment. "We talked to Vidya Singh at the auction house."

"Yes, I remember."

"She's researching some of Roger's dealings for us. But it's a little early for me to have anything to report." She realized Wynter was regarding her with a skeptical look.

"Oh. Okay." Rhea sounded disappointed. "By the way, the real reason I called is that I just got off the phone with Obadiah Garde."

239

"Really?"

"He called to say he has some of Roger's things that were left behind at the church. 'Inconsequential items' he called them. A sweater, a couple of notebooks. He wanted me to come and pick them up."

Emily could hear her taking breaths, working to overcome the catch in her throat.

"I want them. But..."

"You'd rather not go into the church right now," Emily finished her sentence.

Rhea sighed. "I can't. I thought of asking Megan, but…"

"No, you're right. Would you like me to go?" Emily offered.

"Would you? It's a lot to ask, I know. You've done so much already."

"I'd be happy to get Roger's things for you," Emily assured her. "In fact, I'm almost to Boston now." This was only a small fib. "I can go right away."

Beep! Emily frowned.

"That's so kind of you! And kind of Mr. Garde to call me, don't you think? He could just as well—*beep!*—have thrown those things out."

Or was his intent to purge the church of anything having to do with his usurper? Emily wondered. *Beep!* "Rhea, my battery's dying. I can't stay on. I'll collect Roger's things for you, and Megan can bring them to the library next week."

"Thank you, Emily! Thank you so much! You're a life sa—" *Beeeeeep!*

The connection severed. Emily groaned and tossed the phone into the door pocket.

Wynter spoke up. "Why didn't you tell her what you and Gramps found out about Belle and all those other people?"

Emily gritted her teeth. How much had Wynter overheard at the campground?

"Doesn't seem very honest to me," the girl concluded.

"Honey, things have gotten complicated. When the time is

right, you can be sure I will tell her everything."

Wynter shrugged and shifted her eyes back to the iPod.

Emily sighed. *Life is so much simpler when you're young.* She wished her granddaughter could retain her innocence forever. But now she had to decide which would be the more efficient route: going to the church first or to Belle Carter's? The angle of the afternoon sun, barely peeking out from behind a dark cloud, reminded her how late it was getting. She opted for the church.

Philip wheeled the car onto Brattle Street and sped toward the Longfellow House. Stan tried for the fifth time to get ahold of Emily. But to his consternation it kept going to voice mail. Exasperated, he clicked the phone off. Philip pulled the car up in front of a No Parking sign and shut off the engine. A distant rumble filled the air as they hurried around to the public entrance at the back of the big yellow house. Panting, Stan tugged on the door. It was locked.

"Closed?" Philip asked.

Stan checked his watch, then looked around, frantic. "Someone's still here." He pointed to a battered Ford Ranger parked in the staff lot. "In there." Striding toward the carriage house, he found a tall, lanky custodian bagging trash.

"We're looking for Judge Calderwood. He's one of the trustees here."

"I know who he is," the man grunted. "Everyone 'round here knows the Judge."

"Do you know *where* he is?" Stan worked to quell the impatience in his voice.

"You're the second person to ask that in the last twenty minutes." The man hefted a large black plastic bag and walked toward the door.

Stan exchanged glances with Philip, who mouthed the words, "Tennyson Carter?"

"And what did you tell the first person who asked?"

"The same thing I'm goin' ta tell you." They trailed the man out the door and to a green dumpster behind the building.

"Which is…?"

"Likely on his way to the Church."

"What church? The Old North Church?"

"What other church is there? At least as far as his Honor is concerned."

"You're sure of this?"

"Would I tell you if I wasn't?"

"Oh for Pete's sake," the words exploded from Philip's lips.

"The Judge always announces when he's goin' over to the Church. Likes folks to know how important he is."

Stan and Philip hurried back to the car, the rumble of thunder growing louder in the distance.

"Not even a word of thanks?" the man shouted after them. He waved them off in disgust as they pulled out into traffic.

CHAPTER 28

"WAIT here," Emily said to Wynter. "I'll only be a couple of minutes."

She considered it a minor miracle that they had found a spot to park on the one-way street less than a hundred feet from the Old North Church. The signs posted required a residential permit, but Emily decided to chance it since she planned to just run in and out. Although she did have a couple more questions for Obadiah Garde, it wouldn't take long.

The air was heavy and humid, and a distant rumble of thunder accompanied her as she he strode through the wrought iron gate and up to the front door of the church. She stopped abruptly at the "Closed" sign on the door. *Damn!* She shrugged her shoulders and tried the door handle anyway. To her surprise it was unlocked.

"Hello?" she called out, stepping into the darkened foyer.

No response. She peeked into the sanctuary, but it was empty. That's when she heard the scuffle and a muffled shout. Frowning, she edged toward the door to the bell tower.

"Stop! Please!" Obadiah's voice.

Emily jogged up the single flight of stairs.

"Please, no! I had nothing to do with it!" He pleaded in a

raspy, choking whisper.

As Emily peered in through the doorway into the archives room on the first landing, she saw Obadiah shoved up against the wall by a man inches taller and considerably heavier than he was. His raised fist was about to pummel Obadiah's face.

"Tennyson Carter!" Emily used the voice of authority she had developed after three decades on the police force; it was deeper and more resonant than her normal voice. "Step away from him. Now."

Carter cranked his neck, surprised. With a grunt, he banged Obadiah's head against the wall, then let go. The bell master's limp body slid to the floor. Carter pivoted to face Emily, his glower deepening.

"I told you to stay out of this," he hissed.

"And I'm telling you that you don't want to end up arrested for assault and battery." She walked over to the man on the floor, crouched and felt for a pulse. He was unconscious, but alive. She stood and faced the still fuming Tennyson Carter. "The police are on their way."

Carter cocked his head as if listening for sirens, trying to figure out if she was yanking him around or telling the truth. "Bah!" he waved his hand as if dismissing the man on the floor. "That man's an idiot. The guy I'm after is Judge Calderwood," he snarled.

"Let the police handle Calderwood," Emily said, rising to her feet again. "It will do you no good if you end up in prison."

"If I have anything to say about it, he'll end up in hell! I don't much care where I end up." He shoved past Emily, throwing her off balance, and stomped down the stairs.

"That's your car!"

Philip squealed to a stop behind the Volkswagen and they jumped out of the SUV. Before they could get to the VW, the door swung open and Wynter stepped out.

"Dad? Grandpa?"

"What are you doing here?" Philip asked.

"Grandma went in to get some stuff for Rhea." She pointed at the church.

"How long have you been here?" Stan asked.

"I don't know, ten minutes maybe. She wanted to talk to that bell guy again."

The two men looked at each other, alarmed.

"Honey, did you see anyone else go in?"

Wynter shook her head. "It's closed. I was surprised Grandma got in."

"Philip, you stay with her." Stan walked around and opened the trunk of the car. "I'll go find her. See what's happening."

"Are you sure?" Philip asked nervously as Stan flipped open the lid of the wheel well and reached in. A gun. His eyes went wide. "Shit, Stan. Is that necessary?"

"I hope not."

He loaded a clip into the chamber, checked the safety, then tucked the gun into his belt, tugging his shirt out and over it.

"I'm going in with you!" Philip was adamant.

"No. You stay with Wynter."

"Stan, I can't let you go in there alone." He motioned to his daughter. "You get back in the car and lock the door."

"But, Dad!"

"Go!" he barked, just as a streak of lightning slashed the sky, followed by the clap of thunder.

Wynter scurried back into the car and slammed the door behind her. Sucking in a deep breath, Stan strode up to the church, feeling the first splashes of rain on his balding head.

Ignoring the "Closed" sign, the two men cautiously stepped into the building. The cold metal of the gun chafed against the slight roll of belly fat Stan kept meaning to exercise away. He grimaced. He had never shot at a living thing before—his forte was tin cans, stacked in a pyramid atop an old beat up saw horse—and he hoped like hell he wouldn't have to shoot at anybody today. *I'm over-reacting. Emily probably has everything under control already.* He pictured Tennyson and the Judge sitting side-by-side with their backs to the wall, Emily towering over them, giving them hell. He allowed a grim smile, but only for a moment.

In a blink the image of his wife was replaced by that of Roger's body swinging from the bell casing. A wave of nausea washed over him as he scanned the gloomy foyer, his eye landing on the door to the bell tower. *Is that where she is?* He took a deep breath to pull himself together while Philip peered through the crack between the double doors to the sanctuary. They both froze at the sound of footsteps—loud, clomping footsteps—echoed from the stairwell. Someone much heavier than Emily.

Before Stan could react, the door swung open and Tennyson Carter barreled through, slamming into him and knocking him off his feet.

"What the—?" Carter growled, balling his fists. "What the hell are you doing here?"

Stan reached up to clasp the hand Philip offered. He stood clumsily, brushing the dust from his pants. "I was about to ask you the same thing."

"Stan?" Emily appeared in the door behind Carter.

"Emily, are you all right? What's going on here?"

Before she could answer, Carter yelled, "That lying shit scammed my mother then killed her!"

"Who?" Stan asked, even though he had a pretty good hunch.

Just then the front door of the church burst open and Wynter walked in, wet, white-faced and shaking. Judge Duncan Calderwood, also soaked with rain, had a tight grip on the girl's upper arm. With his other hand he held a gun to her head.

"Wynter!"

Stan's stomach lurched at the sight of his granddaughter

and the fear in her face.

Philip took a step toward her, but stopped when Calderwood jerked the gun closer to her head.

"I'm sorry, Daddy," Wynter whimpered.

"Let my daughter go," he demanded.

"Close that door. Lock it," the judge said to Philip, shoving Wynter farther into the foyer.

Philip's hands shook as he threw the dead bolt. "Don't hurt her. Please." Lightning and thunder punctuated his fear.

"Judge Calderwood." Emily had to work to keep the fear from her own voice. "What are you doing?"

"There is something here I need. And if you—each of you—will simply cooperate, I can get it and nobody needs to get hurt."

"You! You're the one! You killed my mother!" Tennyson Carter shouted. He lunged at the judge, but Calderwood pointed the gun at him, causing him to shrink back.

"I did no such thing. I don't even know who your mother is. Or who you are."

"My mother was Belle Carter."

Calderwood drew himself up into a self-righteous position. "Belle—? You would accuse me of such a horrendous act? Belle was someone I cared about."

Carter balled his fist. "Cared about? You used her, you maggot! You lured her into an affair with you, treated her like shit, then killed her."

"My dear man, you are obviously overwrought. Her death was unfortunate; however, she was alive and well when I left her that night."

"And what about Roger Hollinger?" Stan asked. "Was he alive when you left him, too?"

"You think I killed him? I have no idea what happened to that man."

"I think you know exactly how he died," Stan said. "I

think that extra rope mark around his neck was not from a bell rope, but from whatever you used to strangle him."

Emily looked at Stan in surprise. She had noticed the extra abrasion also, but she didn't realize her husband had spotted it. He had never said anything. In fact, he'd been very reluctant to say anything except the bare essentials to the investigating officers.

"He was a stupid man!" Calderwood's voice rose. "He would have destroyed everything I worked for."

"Destroy it how?" Emily asked.

"I am a sitting judge. I have stature in this community. It wasn't for him to decide what should happen to my property."

"What the hell property are you talking about?" Tennyson snarled.

"Roger Hollinger did not write that suicide note, did he?" Emily asked, ignoring the man's outburst. "You wrote it."

"Don't be preposterous," the judge said.

"Just as you forged Longfellow's signature in that book of poetry. The one I gave Stan."

"Now you're talking nonsense."

Carter glowered. "What the hell are you people talking about?"

More pieces of the puzzle clicked into place for Emily. "You buy your cigars from Churchill's Lounge."

The judge glared at her like she was crazy.

"Belle saw the receipt you used as a bookmark in Stan's Longfellow book, so she knew that book had once belonged to you."

"You have no proof," the judge blustered.

Emily pressed him further. "Roger discovered that one of the documents he sold for you was a forgery. Two people figured out your little secret. And they are both dead."

"He was trying to extort me!" Calderwood bellowed, tightening his grip on Wynter.

"Daddy!" she whimpered again.

"He and that fool of a woman. They were in collusion! They were having an affair. Hollinger's note said so."

"My mother was doing no such thing!" Spit was spewing from Carter's mouth now, and he shook his fist.

Emily felt the situation spiraling out of control. Lightning and thunder shook the building in ever increasing intervals. Rain beat a tattoo on the roof and windows adding to the tension in the room. *The first rule in a hostage situation is to keep everyone calm.*

"Tennyson." She lowered her voice and spoke slowly. "I need you to take a step back. Take a deep breath. Can you do that for me?"

Tennyson grunted and scowled, but took one step back.

The second rule is to keep the hostage-taker talking.

"Judge Calderwood. You're in an untenable position here. Let's talk. How can we help you?"

"Help him!" Carter bellowed. "I'll help him straight to hell!"

Without warning, he pushed Emily out of the way and charged the judge. Calderwood fired. Wide-eyed, Tennyson grabbed at his stomach and stared at the blood seeping between his fingers.

CHAPTER 29

BLAM!

The blast of the gun made everyone recoil. Wynter screamed. Philip and Stan both lunged for the girl, but Calderwood pointed the gun at her head again and the two men froze.

Emily watched Tennyson, a confused expression on his face, sag to the floor. Rushing to him, she searched for something to press against his wound. Philip offered his handkerchief.

Calderwood nodded toward the sanctuary. "You can help me by going through those doors."

The final rule in a hostage situation: don't let them move you to another spot. "I should stay with him," Emily said, still kneeling next to the bleeding man.

"I think not." The judge tapped the gun against Wynter's head.

So much for that rule. Reluctantly Emily followed her husband and son-in-law into the church, dark now because of the storm clouds.

"Keep going," Calderwood ordered, "that door up front, under the statue."

They shuffled down the center aisle. To the left of the

towering pulpit, the bust of George Washington danced in a flash of lightning from the arched, leaded windows.

"If any of you tries anything, the child's fate will be on your shoulders." Behind them, Calderwood's voice was eerily composed.

Once through the sacristy door, Calderwood barked, "Through there," indicating yet another entry.

Stan opened the door to reveal a set of stairs and, obviously reluctant, led the way down into the shadows. Philip followed, his sweaty hand pressed against the white-washed walls to steady himself. Behind them, Emily's mind spun as she tried to calculate a way out. The wooden steps curved down and around the corner, creaking and moaning under their feet.

The air in the crypt was damp but cooler than the church above. Calderwood signaled for Philip to flip a light switch. Stan caught Emily's eye and lifted his shirt slightly, briefly, just enough for her to catch the glint of metal. She blinked at him then nodded her understanding.

The group stumbled along the ancient brick tunnel taking them deeper into the crypt. One by one they ducked to avoid banging their heads against the low-hanging ductwork. Stan noted again, this time with dread, the tombs sunk into the walls.

Finally they came to a rough-hewn wooden door with a rounded top and brass hinges. Stan guessed it to be as old as anything in this centuries old building.

"Open it," Calderwood commanded.

Stan grasped the brass knob with both hands and yanked. The door creaked in complaint.

"In there," Calderwood said.

Stan didn't move at first, but when he caught sight of his frightened granddaughter's eyes, he did as he was told. Emily and Philip followed. Calderwood shoved Wynter in behind them, then slammed the door shut, enveloping them in tomblike blackness. The small dark room was dank and smelled of old timber and mouse droppings. Stan heard the sound of keys jangling, the dead bolt snapping into place.

Wynter whimpered. Stan could hear Philip calming her. He suspected his son-in-law had already found his daughter in the dark and had put his arms around her. At least he hoped so, since he himself didn't dare move for fear of crashing into someone or something in the absolute blackness.

A faint but eerie blue glow lit up the small area. Philip held his cell phone aloft. The clammy, foul smelling room was only about five or six feet wide and maybe ten feet deep. It was some sort of a storage area with boxes stacked in one corner, saw horses and assorted tools and implements scattered about. The light flickered out. He clicked it back on. A moment later it flickered out again.

"Shit." He tapped it again, but it went out a moment later.

A sudden sweat broke out on Stan's forehead even in the chill of this basement room. He could feel his heart pounding erratically. He took a breath and willed himself to calm down. But a sense of claustrophobia began to overtake him.

"Here, use this." Wynter's phone lit up with a bright steady beam from her flashlight app.

"Shine it on the door here," Emily instructed.

Wynter aimed the beam at the handle, revealing a simple locking mechanism that had been added to the door sometime in the last couple of decades.

"Stan, give me the gun. Wynter, I'll take the light. Cover your ears."

Stan instinctively moved with Philip to position their bodies between Wynter and the door. Hunching over, they, too, clenched their hands over their ears. But still he jumped at the force of the concussion. Emily rattled the handle and cursed under her breath.

"Again," was all she said, and he hovered protectively over Wynter.

She fired two shots this time, one right after the other. The wood around the lock splintered, but the door held fast.

"Let me try," Stan said. He took the light from his wife, shone it quickly around the pitch black room and spotted a thick metal rod lying near the wall. Wedging the rod into the splintered hole like a crow bar, he put his weight on it. Slowly the mechanism moved, then all at once it sprang loose, and Stan could open the door.

The family stumbled out into the corridor, blinking in the glare of the overhead bulbs.

"He's likely gone back upstairs," Emily said, peering around a bend in the hallway. "I'll check the crypt area just in case. Philip and Stan, you stay here with Wynter until I give the all clear."

"Grandma, be careful," Wynter pleaded.

"You're not facing that crazy man alone," Stan insisted.

"Stan can stay with Wynter," Philip said to Emily. "I'll go with you."

"No," Stan asserted himself. "You stay with your daughter."

"Look…don't do anything heroic. Okay?" Philip backed down and put his arm around Wynter.

"We'll be careful," Emily assured him. "Call 911."

"No bars," Philip said, peering at his phone.

"Keep trying."

Emily checked the chamber of the gun to confirm how many rounds she had left. She nodded at Stan and crept down the corridor toward the stairs, listening for the sound of footsteps overhead. But there were none.

Tiptoeing to minimize the creaking and groaning of the wooden steps, they made their way back up into the darkened sanctuary. Emily did a quick survey of the space to make sure there were no surprises. The only sound was the rain and the thunder. The strobe of the lightning caused shadows to dance, but she detected no human movement.

In the foyer she beckoned Stan to check on Tennyson Carter, who was lying in a growing pool of blood. The man was slumped against the wall, eyes shut, face white, Philip's ineffective, bloodied handkerchief clenched in his equally bloodied hand.

"He's breathing," Stan reported, his voice barely a whisper.

Carter opened his eyes; it was obvious he was having trouble focusing.

"Shh…" Stan held a finger to his lips.

"Upstairs," Carter whispered weakly.

"We'll be back," Stan mouthed.

Carter nodded and closed his eyes, his energy centered on breathing.

Stan pointed up and Emily nodded. The air in the stairwell was close and oppressive. At the first landing, Emily held the gun in front of her as she cautiously surveyed the archive room. She was puzzled to find it empty. Where was Obadiah Garde? She wondered if he had somehow gone down the stairs. Could he have possibly gotten past Calderwood? Then she heard his voice coming from above.

"I don't know where it is." He faltered. "M-maybe he h-hid it in the l-lantern room."

A scrabbling sound was followed by a low, angry murmur from the judge saying something unintelligible.

"What are you d-doing?" Garde again. "Have you g-gone m-mad?"

"You stay here," Emily mouthed to Stan as she started up the stairs. Immediately she felt his presence behind her, his breathing labored, and she wanted to throttle him. Without a sound, she inched around the corner and scanned the ringing room. The dim overhead bulb was over-powered by lightning flashing in the round casement windows; the accompanying thunder shook the rafters.

"Don't be an imbecile!" the judge barked.

Garde cringed. In one explosive move the judge backhanded him with his gun. The injured man staggered and slumped against the wall, one hand steadying himself, the other protecting his bleeding face.

The creak of Stan's foot on the step behind Emily caused Calderwood to swivel; he fired once in their direction. Emily ducked on instinct, pushing Stan against the railing. Luckily, the bullet went high and wide, splintering the wood of the door frame above her. Breath held, she checked to make sure Stan was okay. He had stumbled back down a few steps.

When Emily looked up again, Calderwood was already through the door at the top of the staircase on the far side of the room. She dashed up after him. The judge was surprisingly lithe and swift as he climbed higher and higher into the steeple.

Emily tripped over an uneven board but quickly regained her balance and kept going. She felt the barely perceptible change in the air first, like a delicate whoosh then, suddenly, a great clanging filled the tower. Gripping her gun awkwardly, she pressed her hands tight against her ears. She took a moment to regain her equilibrium before continuing the climb.

Reaching the landing she hesitated, hands still over her ears. The deep, uneven tolling of the bells reverberated against her, her entire body vibrating as she hugged the wall for support. The great bronze bells in front of her swung madly on their flywheels, upending to and fro in counterpoint.

A furtive movement at the bottom of the next staircase caught her eye. Calderwood was hunched over, his hands pushed against his ears. To her surprise he straightened, reached up and began to climb the ladder-like stairs.

"Calderwood!" she called out instinctively, but her voice was swallowed up in the clamor of the bells and the roar of the thunder.

At the top, he pushed against the trap door. But his foot

slipped and he tottered clumsily losing his balance. Emily held her breath as the man searched for a handhold, flailing about wildly. A streak of lightning connected with the weathervane atop the steeple, blinding Emily, the crash of thunder slamming against her. Blinking to regain her vision, she saw Calderwood flail one last time. Helplessly she watched him topple backward, falling through the air and onto the platform next to the gyrating bells.

After carefully checking to make sure the unconscious man was still alive, Emily edged back down the weathered stairs. In the ringing chamber a flash of lightning illuminated the silhouette of Stan engaged in a frantic dance, lunging from one rope to the next, reaching and tugging, reaching and tugging in an adrenalin-fueled fury.

She put a hand on his forearm. He jumped in surprise, the ropes sliding out of his hands, and he looked at her with wide, frightened eyes.

"It's over," she said. "You can stop now." He stood numbly for a moment then wrapped shaking arms around her.

Obadiah Garde, slumped against the wall, stared at them as the bells slowed their clanging.

By the time they'd helped Garde down into the foyer where Philip and Wynter waited with Tennyson Carter, the storm was receding and police sirens announced the arrival of help. The first squad drove up, its swirling red and blue lights bouncing off the rain-soaked street as they stepped out into the sultry evening air. The thunder was a distant rumble now. And Emily was glad for once to see Detective Ellison step out of the car.

CHAPTER 30

"WHAT are you girls doing up there?" Emily yelled.

She was frantic at the sight of the two nine-year olds running across the top of the RV doing…what? And why were they up there again?

"Come down here! Now!"

Watching the girls scramble down the back ladder, she took several deep breaths and willed her nerves to settle. She realized that the tension from the past couple of days—starting with the horrific encounter with the crazed judge in the church tower—was making her overreact.

"I don't want you up there anymore," she chastised, meeting them at the base of the ladder. "What were you thinking?"

"Sorry, Grandma." Allyn looked up at her with big, innocent eyes that Emily knew was an act. "Isn't it time for Tae kwon do?"

"We need to go get our belts!" Annabel tugged her sister's arm.

Emily frowned as they scampered into the RV, colliding with Stan coming out with a bag of garbage in hand.

"What was all the clattering on the roof?" he asked.

She was about to answer when a call from the road

257

distracted her. A half dozen women and a couple of men jogged onto the campsite, all wearing shorts and tank tops. Chatting and laughing, they positioned themselves under Emily's awning. She sighed. Her heart just wasn't in it this morning, but she took her place in front of the group and forced a smile. The twins charged out of the RV and pushed their way into the group.

"Taekwon," Emily said, bowing.

"Taekwon." The enthusiastic acolytes bowed back.

"Let's get started."

A few moments later, Megan emerged from the pop-up tent, her arm around Wynter. The teenager appeared tired and hollow-eyed.

Megan joined in as the Tae kwon do students began their warm up. Taking her usual place on the chaise lounge, Wynter pulled her knees up to her chin, wrapping her arms tightly around her legs. Emily could guess what her granddaughter was feeling—afraid that if she let go she'd tumble away.

"Allyn, Annabel can you lead the warm-up stances for me?" she asked.

The girls, beaming, eagerly took her place. "Taekwon," they mimicked and bowed.

Emily sat next to her eldest granddaughter. She studied the girl's face as Wynter watched the martial arts students, avoiding her grandmother's eyes.

"I had a hard time sleeping the last couple of nights," Emily said after a moment. "How about you?"

The girl shrugged.

"The world is filled with bad people," Emily said gently. "I'm sorry about what happened."

"I'm okay, Grandma."

"I don't know about you, but it makes me feel frightened and vulnerable. And I expect to feel that way for a long time."

Wynter's eyes widened in surprise.

"But then I remember the world is filled with more good people than bad. And they are the ones that will support and protect me."

Now the girl gave her grandmother a piercing look. "You protected me that night in the church, but you can't protect me forever. You'll be gone in a couple of days."

Emily thought about that for a moment. What the child said was true, and it wrenched her heart.

"At some point everyone has to learn to protect themselves. Especially we women. We have to work at being strong." She nodded toward the crowd under the awning.

Wynter wrinkled her nose. "Kicking and yelling like that will make me strong?"

"It's one way. The thing is, we can choose to live in fear, or we can choose to tell the world that we know how to take care of ourselves. It's not easy. It's never easy. But it starts by taking the first step."

Emily stood and offered her hand to her granddaughter. The girl expression was wary, but finally she let go of her knees. She reached up to take her grandmother's hand.

When the session was over, Stan and Philip emerged from the RV with a platterful of pancakes announcing it was time for breakfast. As the family sat down to eat, Annabel proudly held up a small digital camera.

"Whatchya got there?" Stan asked.

"Evidence."

"Proof that the witch stole our stuff," Allyn explained.

Megan furrowed her brow. "Girls, we've been through this. You are being unkind and unfair."

"But now we have proof!" Allyn insisted.

"Tell me about this proof," Emily said. She loaded a stack of pancakes onto her plate.

"We set a trap on the picnic table last night! We put out Grandpa's baseball cap."

"And it's gone!" Annabel chimed in.

"You left my Red Sox cap out for someone to steal?"

"Calm down." Emily patted his arm. "Tell me more," she said to the girls.

"So…we set up Daddy's' camera where no one would notice it. Up there." Allyn pointed to the top of the motorcoach.

"On the RV?" Stan asked.

"In the dark?" Philip added.

"It wasn't dark. Annabel had a flashlight."

"Dumbnuts," Wynter chastised, reaching for the maple syrup.

"We had to be sure she wouldn't see it. We've got the whole thing recorded."

The four adults exchanged skeptical looks.

"I suppose we could check it out. Just to see what's been going on," Stan said as a dark sedan parked in front of the RV.

Detective Ellison closed the car door behind her. "Good morning," she greeted them.

"Are you here to arrest the witch?" Allyn asked as the woman approached.

"I don't know. Is there a witch here that needs arresting?"

"Allyn…" Megan warned.

"Sorry."

"Can I get you a cup of coffee?" Emily asked.

"That's exactly what I need. Just black." She accepted the lawn chair that Stan offered.

"Haven't you run out of things to ask?" Philip said. He hadn't been happy with all the interviews and debriefings they had had to undergo the past two days.

"No. No more questions. Just wanted to see how you all are doing. Particularly Wynter."

"Are you going to arrest the witch?"

"Don't be stupid," Wynter chided. "She told you she didn't take your things."

"They always say that," Annabel insisted.

"We've got evidence!" Allyn held up the camera.

Just then Vinie came huffing up to the picnic table in a panic. "Oh help me, please. Someone! Help me!"

"What's wrong?" Detective Ellison and Emily spoke at the same time.

"Luna's gone missing again. I've searched everywhere."

"Under the RV?" Stan asked.

"That was the first place I looked." She twisted strands of her frizzled red hair.

"Who's Luna?" the detective asked.

"Her cat," Allyn said.

"She goes missing a lot," Annabel added.

"How long has she been gone?" Emily asked.

"Since sometime last night. She often takes a midnight stroll, but she never came back. What should I do? I'm supposed to leave today. But I can't leave without my Luna!"

"Calm down. Take a breath. You're going to hyperventilate," Megan said.

"We'll help you find her." Wynter stood up.

"Just a minute." Emily sighted a line from the roof of their RV to Vinie's. "We were just about to watch what the girls discovered through their little, uh, video surveillance. Maybe they caught something that can help."

"Good idea," Stan said. "Let's all go inside."

The group crowded around the TV while Philip hooked up the video camera. On the screen appeared a dark, but viewable, image of the picnic table with the baseball cap perched in the middle.

Detective Ellison scrunched her face at the screen, trying to figure out what it was she was seeing.

"Allyn," Emily suggested, "why don't you take the remote and fast forward until we see something happening?"

"There! Stop!" Annabel shouted.

Allyn hit the stop button, then backed the video up a few seconds, then hit the forward button again. And there on the screen came the thief, crawling into view on all fours.

"Oh my gosh!" Annabel exclaimed.

"Well, I'll be damned." Philip said.

"A fox! Daddy, you swore," Allyn whispered as she pointed to a small, long-tailed animal creeping into view. Putting his front paws up on the picnic bench, the fox sniffed at the table then leapt up. He poked at the cap with one paw, finally grabbing it in his teeth.

"There's your witch!" Wynter said with a delighted cackle.

The fox padded to the end of the table, but before he could jump off, a large gray cat came into view.

"Luna!" Vinie squealed.

The cat hissed at the fox. Slinking to the opposite end of the table, the fox tried to avoid an encounter, but the cat was quicker, hackles rising on her back. Confronted again, the fox crouched, cap still in his mouth, then quickly leapt over the cat, dashing off into the underbrush. The gray cat chased after it.

"Oh, no!" Vinie moaned. "Where do you think they went?"

"I can find them," Annabel announced. And before any of the adults could stop them, she and Allyn chased out of the RV and off through the bushes where they'd seen the fox and the cat disappear.

"Annabel!" Megan called. "Allyn!"

"I'll get them," Wynter yelled, and she ran out after her sisters.

"Oh, cripes!" Philip said, crashing into Stan as they rushed to the door, followed by the four women.

Emily cursed at the bramble bushes as they jogged along the narrow wooded path. Coming to a small clearing, they found all three girls staring up into an old oak where a soft mewing alerted them to Luna sitting on a branch high above their heads.

"Luna!" Vinie cried. "Oh, my poor little Luna, what are you doing up there?"

"Hey, everybody! Look at this!" Wynter was peering into a shallow opening in the ground under a fallen tree trunk. Lying just outside the opening were Allyn's goggles.

"Wynter!" Emily warned. "Don't go any closer."

"What is it?" Megan asked.

"Likely the fox's den," Stan said. "I'm guessing he'd had enough of the cat and treed her."

"Oh, my baby!" Vinie lamented. "Come down. Please come down."

Allyn danced from foot to foot. "Daddy, lift me up."

"Oh, honey, no," Megan said. "That cat is frightened. She might scratch."

"She knows me," Annabel offered. "I can get her down."

Megan shook her head at Philip uncertainly, but he reached for his daughter, and lifted her up until she could grasp the branch and climb onto it.

"Annabel, be careful," Megan warned.

"It's okay, Luna," Annabel crooned softy. "You can trust me. I'll get you down." With one arm around the trunk of the tree to steady herself, she slowly reached up and plucked the still mewling cat from the branch then handed her down to the anxious Vinie.

"Oh, baby! Are you okay?" The plump woman cradled the cat in her arms. "Thank you! Thank you!" she said to Annabel as Philip helped the little girl back to safety.

"Brave girl," Detective Ellison said.

"Look!" Wynter pointed at the fox poking his nose through the brush. He crept toward the opening near the fallen tree, but at the sight of all the people he turned tail and slinked off.

Wynter picked up a long stick and poked it into the hole.

"Oh, honey, be careful," Megan admonished again.

Wynter yanked the stick out and hooked onto the end was Emily's sandal.

"Oh, my gosh!" Megan said. "That's where all the missing stuff is!"

"Is my Red Sox cap in there?" Stan asked, peering into the hole.

"Will you look at this?" Emily reached for a zip-lock bag lying near the opening.

"Is that Roger's daybook?" Megan asked.

"How—?"

"Oh!" Wynter slapped her forehead. "I was looking at it and left it out on the picnic table. Sorry."

"That's one mystery solved," Philip said. "We'd better alert the camp manager to that fox's little treasure trove. I bet a lot of other campers have been missing stuff, too."

"Allyn. Annabel. I think you owe Ms. Pendergast an apology," Megan said.

"This might be a good time for me to update you on what we've learned from Judge Calderwood," Detective Ellison said as the adults gathered at the picnic table.

Vinie had invited the twins over to her camper to enjoy juice and cookies with the cats. Wynter hovered near her mother, her arms wrapped tightly across her chest.

"How is he?" she asked.

"A concussion and a broken leg, but he'll survive. And he's been talking."

"Come sit with us, honey." Philip slid to create a space between himself and Megan, and Wynter wedged herself between her parents. Philip wrapped a protective arm around her.

"Did he confess to killing Roger?" Megan asked.

"That and more," the detective answered.

Philip asked, "He killed Belle Carter with the antibiotic, didn't he?"

"Yes, he slipped it into her drink at the park."

"But why?" Wynter asked.

"Because they both knew too much," Emily said. "He had forged some high priced manuscripts and was about to be exposed."

"Not just some. He had quite a second career going."

"Forging manuscripts?" Philip asked. "Why would a judge do that?"

"Judge Calderwood was apparently heir to a large fortune," Ellison said. "But with the downturn in the economy and a huge money-pit of a mansion, he seemed to have whittled it away over the years. He had a certain lifestyle he wanted to maintain and a gift for reproducing handwriting which he found to be lucrative."

Philip whistled. "That's some way to increase your income."

"But what about Roger's suicide note?" Megan asked.

"The judge wrote that," Emily said. "Because he had been working with Roger for several years, he was familiar with the man's handwriting."

"You knew that, didn't you?" Megan asked. "That's what had you so distracted up on Meditation Point. But how did you know?"

"The receipt from Churchill's Lounge," Stan declared.

"The one that was missing from your book after we talked to Ranger Carter!" Wynter said.

"You're as good a detective as your grandmother." Stan complimented then spoke to Emily. "That was the missing puzzle piece for you, wasn't it?" But his demeanor darkened as he addressed Ellison. "If it weren't for me, Belle Carter would still be alive, wouldn't she?"

"What do you mean?" Philip asked.

"She knew the signature in the book I showed her was a fake. And I'm guessing when she saw the cigar store receipt she knew instantly that the book had at one time belonged to the judge."

Ellison shrugged. "That may be, but he had decided long before that she and Roger were both getting too close to the truth. Roger had apparently confronted him about the forged Paul Revere stanza. He had sold a copy to a client in Italy."

"The Italian idiot!" Megan blurted out. "Oh, sorry. That's what Rhea said Roger called him." She suppressed a giggle then got serious. "So, Rhea *is* right. Roger and Belle were not romantically involved, were they? But, Mom, didn't you say that Evelyn said Belle was seeing a man?"

Ellison spoke up again. "Actually, she and the judge were having the affair. That's why they were together down at the Esplanade. He tried to deny it, but Whitman turned Belle's diaries over to us as evidence. And, the judge's wife, of all people, confirmed it. She's known about it for some time. She just assumed that was what men of a certain societal stature did, so she never complained."

"Poor Evelyn," Megan said. "She's another victim in all this."

"And Whitman and Tennyson," Stan said. "How are they doing, by the way?"

"Tennyson's out of the hospital. No vital organs were hit," Ellison answered. "Whitman asked if you'd call before you leave town."

"One last game of volleyball?" Stan issued the challenge, bouncing a bright pink beach ball from hand to hand.

Detective Ellison had left short while before. The girls were back from their visit with Alvina Pendergast. Megan and Wynter helped Philip fold down their camper and hook it up to the SUV.

"I have something for you," Emily said, approaching her daughter with two small boxes in her hands.

"Jigsaw puzzles?" Megan asked.

"For next winter. When you're stuck indoors."

"Okay. Thanks?"

Emily nodded and headed back to help Stan prep the RV for their own leave-taking. She was feeling the usual mixed emotions after spending time with Megan and the girls— sorrow at having to say goodbye yet again, and eagerness to sleep in her own bed. The plan was to start out after lunch for the first leg of their trip home.

The twins were restless and in the way as Emily and Megan shared meal preparation duties one last time. Thus the invitation to the volleyball game.

"I'm in!" Philip yelled kicking up the beach ball with his foot and knocking it with his forehead.

"Me, too!" Wynter grabbed the ball. "Girls against guys!"

The twins shrieked in delight, their laughter contagious as they batted the ball, trying to keep it aloft and away from the other team. Vinie came to her door to see what was going on.

"Go invite her over for lunch," Emily suggested.

Megan nodded and jogged over to the other camper. In a moment she was back, positioning a lawn chair so Vinie could watch the game.

"I got it! I got it!" Wynter yelled.

"Mine!"

"Over here! This way!"

"Oomph."

"No you don't…!"

"I got it!" Wynter called again, lunging for the ball. She backed up, her hands held high, ready to pop it back into the air.

"Wynter!" Megan yelled. "Watch where you're—"

But it was too late. Wynter had backed straight into Vinie's chair. The orange cat sitting in the woman's lap leapt off as Wynter stumbled backward. She and Vinie ended up in a heap on the ground.

Emily gasped in horror. The twins covered their mouths with their hands, eyes wide. Megan held her breath, frozen in place.

"Vinie!" Stan and Philip jumped into action, hurrying over to the lady lying on the ground.

"Are you okay?" Wynter asked. "Dad? Is she…?" She stared in horror at the still form.

Stan reached out to touch the woman's neck, when with a shout she flipped over.

"Aack!" Stan yelled, jumping back, startled.

"What?" Vinie asked. "Did you think I was…dead?"

The family stared at her in stunned silence.

"My dears," she cackled. "It will take more than a game of volleyball to kill off this old witch!"

ABOUT THE AUTHOR

The writing team of M. J. Williams is comprised of sisters-in-law Peggy Joque Williams and Mary Joy Johnson (nee Williams). Peggy is an elementary school teacher and freelance writer. Mary Joy is a retired college professor and professional quilter. Both writers live in Madison, Wisconsin.

On the Road to Where the Bells Toll is the second in their On the Road... mystery series. Please check out their first book, *On the Road to Death's Door.* You can learn more about M. J. Williams by visiting their Facebook page: www.facebook.com/M.J.Williams.author

Made in the USA
Columbia, SC
04 August 2017